Cowgirl Tough

Cowgirl Tough

A Raffertys of Last Stand Romance

Justine Davis

Cowgirl Tough
Copyright© 2022 Justine Davis
Tule Publishing First Printing, April 2022

The Tule Publishing, Inc.

ALL RIGHTS RESERVED

First Publication by Tule Publishing 2022

Cover design by Croco Designs

No part of this book may be used or reproduced in any manner whatsoever without written permission except in the case of brief quotations embodied in critical articles and reviews.

This is a work of fiction. Names, characters, places, and incidents are products of the author's imagination or are used fictitiously. Any resemblance to actual events, locales, organizations, or persons, living or dead, is entirely coincidental.

ISBN: 978-1-957748-01-6

Dedication

Thanks to the great Tule team, in particular Jane, Meghan, Sinclair and Nikki.

And thank you to all the readers who have joined me on this journey with the Raffertys!

Chapter One

CODY RAFFERTY WATCHED the computer monitor to his right intently. He had been focused on the center one, tweaking yet another setting he hoped would help in his seemingly never-ending quest, but then movement on the other screen had drawn his attention. And once he'd seen what—or rather who—it was, he'd shoved the rest aside.

The rider was still some distance from the hovering camera. But he didn't have to see her face, or even the long flow of near-black hair to know it was Britt Roth. He could tell simply by the easy, confident way she sat a horse. He'd grown up seeing her ride, and later compete, and it was always the same; they appeared an inseparable unit. Sometimes he couldn't even see the commands she gave, with either reins or legs, yet the horse did what she wanted, be it rounding up others of its kind or doing an insanely fast cloverleaf around barrels in a rodeo arena.

Yes, girl-next-door Brittany Roth was a consummate horsewoman.

She was also the biggest pain his ass had ever had.

Despite that, and the way his jaw usually tightened and

his brows lowered every time he saw her, this time there was also a bit of a smile. Or, if he was honest, probably more of a smirk. Because she was riding Ghost, her gray grullo mare with the black dun stripe along her back and the flashy black bands of coloration on the legs. The horse who was a controlled, top-of-the-game athlete in the arena, and an utterly crazy demon outside it. Her best barrel horse. The horse who had debuted three seasons ago with a bang, taking her to a top ranking on day one and keeping her there ever since.

The horse who wouldn't be here if not for him.

He admitted that always gave him a snarky sort of satisfaction. That she owed him, and his favorite toys that she hated with a passion, for this. Because if one of his drones hadn't overflown that pregnant mare of hers who'd been downed in a remote part of the Roth ranch during a storm, and if he hadn't seen the footage soon after and notified her parents—thankful he'd reached them so he didn't have to call her—Ghost likely wouldn't be here.

And now, six years later, she had a champion. Because of him. And nothing she said or did could change that. Not that it made her hate him any less, in fact it probably just exacerbated the feeling, but he could put an end to any tirade she launched at him simply by saying "How's Ghost?"

Just knowing he had that weapon made him more willing to egg her on than he had been before. Like the time in middle school when he'd just walked away after she'd gotten a bunch of girls together within earshot of his group of tech-interested friends—otherwise known as the nerd herd—and got them talking loudly about how pretty he was. They wanted brain power, not looks, they often said, and after Roth's stunt it had taken a prodigious effort on his part—and inventing a virtual reality game they all declared they loved before he told them it was his—to gain acceptance.

Then she'd nicknamed him Cody the Coder, and he'd lugged that around ever since. Even his family used it when they wanted to tease him about something. He'd tried hanging "Britt the Brat" on her in turn, but somehow it had never stuck. Maybe because she wasn't a brat to anyone but him.

Of course he'd done his share of stoking the fires. From the time he'd sent her on a wild goose chase saying he'd seen roadrunner tracks in some brush down by the creek—he'd even faked some of the bird's distinctive X-shaped tracks, knowing she loved the things and would watch and wait for hours to see one—to when at fourteen, he'd made sure she'd overheard him saying a boy in his chemistry class liked her, knowing she already had a crush on the guy, and also knowing the guy was all about the girly-girls and had no liking for cowgirls like her.

The resulting embarrassment for her gave him an odd combination of amusement and twinges of guilt; it was different, somehow, using someone else to get to her rather than doing it himself. Yes, she'd done it to him first, but he didn't like the feeling, and so stuck to the old tried and true ways after that. And interestingly, so did she, and he briefly—very briefly—wondered if she'd felt something similar after the nerd-herd tactic.

What it boiled down to in the end was simply that she was the girl next door and the girl he'd disliked on first sight, all rolled up into one. And the feeling had clearly been mutual; his first memory of her had been the scowl she always wore around him. Now that they were a decade beyond high school, nothing much had changed except they both seemed to have less time to think up things to aggravate each other.

Well, new things anyway. The old aggravations were always there.

You two are a perpetual Mexican standoff.

The sentence leapt into his mind. He'd been eight when his amused father had made that observation. He'd only been puzzled. And had to ask.

"What's that?"

"A situation where nobody wins."

His stubborn had risen then. "I'll win, someday."

His father had given him a wry shake of his head. "Ever heard of mutually assured destruction?"

"No. What's that mean?"

"Look it up, son."

He made himself focus on the screen, before his mind wandered down the useless path of wondering how life would have been different for him—for all of them—if his father had come home from that last deployment alive. Unlike his brothers, who had at least had Dad into their teens, he'd been only nine when the world had fallen in on them. He'd only had him a third of his life. His brothers—Rylan, Chance, and Keller—had all had him over half. Not that it made it any different and certainly not any better for them, it was just the way his mind worked, to automatically put things in the form he could best relate to.

Roth—and Ghost—were growing larger on the monitor. And he had a decision to make. Grab the controller and divert the drone, at least to the Rafferty side of the boundary, or stick to the planned route. That he had every right to be there—or rather, the drone did—wouldn't matter to her, not with that temper of hers.

That thought made him remember the days right after Dad's death, the arrival home of the flag-draped casket, and funeral. She'd actually attended, which he'd belatedly realized he should have expected, since her parents and his had long been friends. He remembered bracing himself when she'd approached him, already confident and assertive at nine. But she'd surprised him.

"Truce," she'd said. Just the one word.

He wondered if she'd been forced to do this, by her parents. Decided he didn't care. He'd countered with two words. "How long?"

She ended it with three. "'Til you start."

And in that half-dozen words a genuine truce had commenced. One that had lasted longer than he would have ever expected.

Of course, he hadn't had time to even think about breaking that truce for a very long time. Much of that time had been spent in trying to wrap his young mind around the idea of death really being forever. That it wasn't all a mistake, that Dad wouldn't be coming home, ever. Of watching his mother, his ever-strong, ever-resilient mother actually break, for the first and only time in his life.

Before he could get lost in those memories, something on the screen snapped him out of it. Not just that she was much closer, but she'd moved a certain way as Ghost loped along, just a tilt of her head. As if she'd seen or heard something. He reached for the controller in the same moment Roth also reached down for something, pulled something clear of her saddle.

Cody hit the control to veer the drone to the right.

Roth shot it out of the sky.

Chapter Two

BRITT WAS RELATIVELY pleased with how that had gone. Ghost—Roth's Gray Ghost officially, and never had a horse been better named, her being spooky as a ghost—had stayed calm enough at the discharge of the shotgun, thanks to the practice sessions at the other end of the ranch. And watching that pestilential gadget hit the ground in pieces was worth the small dance the mare had done, since she'd been prepared and in no danger of coming off.

Take that, Cody the Coder.

She sheathed the shotgun neatly in the scabbard she'd hung on her saddle this morning for this very reason, rode over to the debris, and dismounted. She ground-tied Ghost, although she'd be keeping a careful eye on her since the mare was very good at forgetting she was supposed to stay put when those reins came over her head and hit the ground. One of the things she was still working on, along with the ridiculous jumpiness she hoped to at least calm a little by exposing the horse to everything she could think of.

Britt stood looking at what was left of the little spy machine. She considered just tossing the pieces back over onto

Rafferty property, but some innocent critter might get hurt on one of the shards. Maybe she should go present it to him in person. That would be fun. Then again, if she just waited right here, he'd probably show up; she had little doubt he'd seen what had happened, techie snoop that he was.

Her best friend, roommate, and fellow barrel racer from college, Jennifer Sawyer, had asked her once if knowing that Cody Rafferty was sort of spying on her creeped her out. She'd laughed. "He just does it to irritate me. Then I do something to irritate him. It's all part of keeping the world in balance."

"You are both very weird, you know that?" Jen had said. "Pretty, but weird."

"My mom says it's because we were born on the same day, almost at the same time. But," she'd added, her tone sour, "I owe him and his danged toy. Darn it."

"You mean because of Ghost?" She'd nodded. "You ever tell him that?"

"Once." Her mouth had quirked. "That was all I could stomach."

Jen had laughed at that. "Only you, Britt. Any other girl would be drooling over the guy."

"I've never denied he's pretty," she'd said, the memory of a day in middle school when she'd started a discussion about it, audible to everyone around, especially the wary techies he was trying to join, making her smile.

"You know," Jen had said, "you two are quite striking

together, him so blond and your hair so dark, his green eyes and your blue."

"Together? Wash your mouth out, girl!" They'd laughed, because Jen had been teasing her and they both knew it.

She left the pieces of the dead drone where they were, and remounted Ghost. She'd brought her here at a pretty brisk pace, and it was warm this Texas pre-spring day, so the horse was a bit sweaty. She'd walk her around until she'd cooled out a little, and if the Coder showed up during that time fine. If he didn't, maybe she'd just bury the thing and head home.

She wondered rather idly what he'd do if she denied all knowledge. Without the pieces of his precious man-made mosquito, what could he prove? Of course, knowing him—one should always know the enemy—he probably had a recording of the feed from his flying beast.

The flying beast that saved Ghost.

Well, not this exact one. Cody discarded old tech as fast as new came along, so this was probably five or so versions newer than the one that had found Cleo, Ghost's dam, in trouble that nasty winter day. The heavily pregnant mare had been down and hurt, and it was entirely possible neither she nor her foal would have survived had they spent the frozen night out there.

Not wanting to linger on the unpleasant memory, she switched to wondering how he afforded all his toys. She knew he built custom computer systems for people, but did that really make that much money? She herself had a laptop, although she preferred her phone. Her father had only a phone, while her mother had a desktop she used to manage the ranch books. But the gadgets didn't run their lives. At least, not the way they ran Cody Rafferty's.

She waited, walking Ghost slowly as her mind ran once more through all the preparation she had yet to make before heading out for the rodeo season in a couple of weeks. She had her own plan and had spent a lot of the winter as she always did, working out her personal circuit. She loved it when she was able to time being in Ft. Worth near her aunt Naomi's birthday, and in Oklahoma City for Jen's.

Then came the two most personally important events to her. First, coming back to the Last Stand Fourth of July rodeo, where she'd gotten her real start by winning the town scholarship in high school, and later launched her pro career. Second, she always made sure she was in College Station for the annual All Aggie Alumni Rodeo in September. It was great to see old friends, and she wasn't too proud to admit that having them gush about her success was good for her ego. But she also knew better than to let it carry her away. And if she ever forgot, Ghost here wasn't afraid to remind her that better riders than she were tossable.

She was just about ready to give up the wait when the gray's head came up, swiveling to the right, ears pointed that way. She reined the antsy mare to a stop and looked. And a minute or so later a smooth-moving bay horse crested a hill on the Rafferty side. Trey. That made her smile. At the horse, not the rider.

The youngest Rafferty rode, bareback, with the ease of someone who had grown up doing it. But as his own mother said, sometimes he got distracted by what he was thinking instead of focusing on what he was doing. She knew Cody's brothers ragged a lot on him because the bay was so smart he kept Cody out of trouble. The clever animal had a way of looking at him that even Cody had learned meant he should probably think twice about what he was doing.

But right now, he seemed pretty darn focused on getting here in a hurry. A big hurry. Which pretty much answered the question of whether he'd seen or not. He had. A grin curved her mouth.

This should definitely be fun.

She thought about staying mounted on Ghost for the height and quick departure advantage but didn't want her adversary to think she was ready to run scared. So with the horse cooled out now she slid off, and just so she didn't have to think about it looped the reins over a piece of low scrub. That slight tug back should keep the sometimes—okay, often—skittish mare anchored better than a simple ground tie.

She crossed her arms and waited with a smug smile as the new arrivals approached the fence. The barrier was more of a formality between the two ranches. As good neighbors for three generations—her family were the newcomers, the

Raffertys had been here seemingly forever—the occasional trespass of livestock was expected. That contraption of his didn't get that exemption, not in her book.

Cody, on the other hand... She tried to be honest with herself, so she couldn't deny that if they were talking livestock, he'd be a prime specimen. Anyone who knew what he did but hadn't seen him would probably have certain expectations about how he would look. And they'd likely be wrong. He was tall, built, and obviously fit. He didn't look like the stereotypical computer nerd in any way, shape, or form. As Angie Roth had once quipped, Cody Rafferty could give nerds a good name. Which earned her a sour look from her daughter.

No, he looked, especially at this moment, like the Texas cowboy he'd grown up as. Even bareback, he sat the big bay easily. And he dismounted before Trey had even come to a full stop, with all the grace and coordination his big brother Keller, the calf roper, showed when heading for the critter he'd just caught.

But then the real Cody appeared. He spotted the wreckage of his flying pet, and headed toward it, completely forgetting to ground tie the big bay. Trey shook his head and snorted, loudly. Cody stopped mid-stride. Looked back. Grimaced, but walked back and pulled the reins over the horse's head and dropped them.

Britt was inwardly laughing, but outwardly shaking her head in an intentional show of exaggerated disgust as he turned again and headed back toward the pipe-rail fence that ran along this section. And toward her.

But then he put a hand on the upright post of the fence and vaulted it in one easy, powerful move. And as she barely managed not to gape, she abruptly remembered he'd also been a promising gymnast in high school, before he'd been bitten by the tech bug. He came to a halt in front of her, and as usual she hated that she had to look up at him.

He glared at her as he covered the last feet between them in long strides, his light green eyes narrowed. "What the hell, Roth?"

She didn't move. "Warned you," she pointed out.

"Alpha wasn't even close to you."

She blinked. "You *name* those pests?"

"Of course. Everything else is numbered, it would get too confusing." She'd forgotten the Rafferty habit of numbering things, be it animal names or the stalls they lived in. "And they're not pests, they're tools."

"The only tool I see here is you. I told you what would happen if you buzzed me with one of those again."

"And I just told you it wasn't even close!"

"Thanks," she said blithely.

He frowned. "Thanks?"

"For the compliment on my shooting."

He rolled his eyes. They were pretty eyes, to go with the pretty rest of him. Which was highly annoying.

"We'll see how you feel when you get the bill," he

ground out as he crouched down and gathered the pieces of his mechanical pet into a small pile.

"Ha! You were the one trespassing, even if it was by proxy."

He stood up, still frowning. "It's not trespassing if you have permission."

She laughed. "Permission? To spy? What, you think you're some government agent now or something?"

He stared at her. "No, just somebody doing what they were hired to do."

Her laugh faded away. "What are you talking about?"

She didn't like the way he was suddenly the one laughing. "You don't have a clue, do you?"

She bristled at the thought that he meant that in more ways than just about his silly drone. "You can just take that thing and—"

"You'd better go home and talk to your folks, sweetheart," he said, and there was nothing but sarcasm in the faux endearment. He was talking to her in that infuriating way tech people sometimes did to those who didn't get their world. Worse, he was talking to her as if she were a child and he the adult, despite the fact that they were the same age almost down to the minute.

And then he did the worst thing of all. He yanked off his shirt.

For an instant she could only stand and stare. Damn, he was built. And that was so unfair she felt like yelling "Foul!"

He didn't even look at her. He knelt back down, spread the shirt out on the ground and put the pieces of his precious machine on it. Then he gathered it up into a makeshift bag and stood up again. She found herself staring at him, at the way he moved, at the ripple of muscle, the size of his arms, the broadness of his chest and the flat belly. And the sleek skin over it all.

She yanked her gaze away before she could focus on the narrow band of hair that arrowed down to the waistband of his jeans.

Annoyingly, he turned and walked away without another word. The back view was just as amazing. Especially that backside of his, filling out those jeans in a way that made the pockets…tempting.

She told herself he was being rude and called after him, but he ignored her, annoying her even more.

But the most annoying thing of all, besides that he managed that dramatic vault again, even holding on to the shirt with the pieces of the broken drone, was that all she could think was that Cody the Coder was dazzling.

Chapter Three

THE ONLY TOOL I see here is you.

Dead drone still wrapped in his shirt—it rattled, she'd so thoroughly destroyed it—Cody mounted Trey and headed home. He filed that taunt away with all the other things she'd called him over the years. Considering how many times they'd been at each other's throats that file was about a terabyte by now.

"Just forget about it, Cody," his mother always advised when they had another squabble.

"Wait, aren't you the same person who keeps bragging my memory is prodigious?" was his standard response.

It had become a joke between them, but there were times—many times—when he wished his memory wasn't quite so good. Because it wasn't that he wanted to remember every time Roth had yelled at him, or every word of every angry thing she'd ever said to him, he just did. Like he did most things. It was just the way his brain worked.

The consolation was it came in handy much more often than not, like when he was writing a program or app, or when someone needed to know exactly when this, that or the other thing had actually happened. It had also helped him get through some classes in school that had required mainly remembering events and dates, with little effort.

Some people thought that made him brilliant. He knew better. Because one of those things he remembered vividly was his father explaining it to him, also on that last time home.

"It's a knack you've got, that memory for technical details, son. And it's a particularly useful one. But don't go thinking it makes you better than someone who doesn't have it, because they've probably got a different useful trait you don't. Like your brothers do."

"But all inherited from your father," his mother had added, with a look at Dad that had made Cody feel funny inside. Funny, but good. When he'd been older, he'd realized it had been the comfort of the unassailable knowledge that your parents loved each other completely.

And Mom had been right, Cody knew. Keller had Dad's sense of responsibility, which had helped save them all. Chance had his devotion to duty and country and had made them all as proud as they'd been worried. And Ry was every bit the artist their father had been, although it had taken Kaitlyn to get him to admit it.

And he himself had inherited this, his version of his father's logistical brilliance, the aptitude for something that happened to be the biggest thing on the planet right now. So their father had left them each something, something that made them who they were.

Something that didn't even come close to making up for losing him.

Trey let out a sharp snort, giving Cody a split second of warning before the horse danced sharply sideways, jarring him out of his reverie. It was just enough time for him to instinctively settle himself to stay aboard. He looked around for what had set the horse off and saw the tail end of a rattler slithering out of sight behind a rock he'd probably been sunning himself on, taking advantage of the warm almost-spring day.

"Thanks for the alert, buddy," he said, patting Trey's neck. "Extra apple for you when we get back."

Trey nickered in approval of that idea.

The horse's gait was a bit exaggerated for a few yards, as if he were on the lookout for the snake's brethren, but eventually he settled back down. And Cody smiled wryly at his mother's wisdom in assigning him the smart animal. She knew him well.

Maggie Rafferty knew all of them well. How they thought, what they wanted, and often what they needed even before they did.

Like she'd known almost immediately how Sydney would change things for Keller, and all of them. Had known Ariel would bring the healing Chance needed. And that Kaitlyn would reach Ry in a way none of them had ever been able to.

He suppressed a little shiver that seemed quite out of place on this warm March morning, even without his shirt on. Warm, but not hot. Nobody Texas born and raised could think seventy-six was hot. Still, he couldn't explain the shiver. Except for the feeling he tried to quash, that now that his brothers were settled, Mom was going to turn her sights on him. And he very much did not want to be the one she was focused on. She was too good at getting done what she wanted done.

His only advantage at the moment was that she was so busy with the upcoming Bluebonnet Festival that she didn't have much time to think about him being the only Rafferty son left footloose and fancy-free. Yet. But given time, it was inevitable. And he wasn't sure how long he could use being the youngest as a shield. He hoped it would at least buy him another couple of years, until he turned thirty. Maybe.

Thinking of the festival, he supposed he should be glad the pieces he was carrying weren't from his newest baby, the video drone. He was proud of that one, with the hi-res camera, his new stabilizing system, the long-distance remote control, and above all the edging closer to his holy grail, time and distance flown on a single battery charge. He'd put it together specifically at his mother's request; she wanted a long, uninterrupted flyover video of miles of Hill Country bluebonnets for the festival website.

Now he just needed the perfect combination of weather and blooms, and as soon as possible, so he could get it posted. Mom said after the winter they'd had, there probably wouldn't be any February or early March rush of blooms. So given they wanted the video up as soon as possible he wouldn't have much margin since the festival was the second weekend in April. But he already had it all planned out, mentally. Most importantly, he knew his spot. He wanted that sunrise effect, with the camera capturing how the blue of the early morning sky matched the blue of the flowers, then as the sun rose and flooded the hills the incredibleness of it all burst to life. If he could pull it off, it would be spectacular.

By the time he had Trey back in his stall, he was calmer. In no small part because Lucas, Sydney's young cousin Keller had taken in after his parents had been killed, was in the barn saddling up to go for a ride and chattered the entire time; it was good to see the kid happy.

But as he walked toward the house and saw his mother standing on the porch by the front door, wariness spiked. Something about her posture was all too familiar. Somebody was in trouble. It obviously wasn't Lucas, and he was the only other one home at the moment.

And she didn't wait to let him know. "I'd ask if you were raised in a barn, but you're usually more careful with the barn doors."

His brow furrowed as he thought back to the moments after he'd seen the blast that had wiped out the drone. He'd simply leapt to his feet and charged out to the barn, intent on getting over there as fast as he could. It was entirely possible he'd blasted through the front door and not bothered to see if it closed behind him.

"Never mind the bugs and possible critters, how about paying to air-condition half the Hill Country?"

Explanations and possible excuses tumbled around in his head, including that he hadn't been gone all that long even if he had left the front door open. But this was his mother, and he knew what the best course was.

"I'm sorry."

"In a hurry, were you?"

He nodded. "I yanked it on my way out, but it must not have caught."

"A little more care in the future, please. I'm overly fond of this door."

Cody felt a sudden rush of that feeling he'd remembered earlier, that funny but good feeling. Because he knew about that door, that solid oak, hand-hewn and fitted door. His father had made it, and installed it, while home on leave one late summer, before heading back on deployment the first week of November.

Exactly nine months before Cody was born. Something his brothers had ragged on him about for years, calling it Cody's door. Of course he hadn't understood why until much later, when he knew enough to do the math. And not until much, much later had the appreciation of what his parents had had outweighed his embarrassment at the connection.

"Me, too," he said softly.

She looked a little startled. But pleased. And he couldn't help himself—he pulled her into his arms and hugged her. "Love you, Mom."

"Love you back, Triple B."

He groaned, but then laughed at the childhood appellation she'd used on him until he was about eight. Her blond baby boy. He knew it had been because he was the only one of her sons who had gotten her own blond hair.

"So," she asked as they stepped inside, and he carefully closed the door behind them, "what's in the shirt, and what was the big rush?"

He grimaced, undid one edge of his makeshift bundle, and pulled out the biggest surviving piece of the drone. She looked at it, frowning. "It crashed?"

"It did not," he said, offended. "She shot it down. She freaking shot it down, with a shotgun."

His mother's eyes widened. She didn't ask who—he knew she didn't have to. Only one person wound him up like this. "Why?"

"Why? Because she hates them, and she hates them because she hates me. That's all the reason she needs."

Her mouth twitched, and he knew she was trying not to laugh. And right now he wasn't in the mood to be her source of amusement for the morning. "Well," she said in a thoughtful sort of tone he knew was put on, "she did get thrown because of one of them last spring."

"I can't help that. It wasn't in her air space." *That time.*

"Still, she's bound to be a little cranky about that."

"So she shoots down an expensive piece of equipment, which was doing a job for her family I might add, in retaliation for falling off a horse?" He couldn't believe his mother was standing up for her.

"Britt Roth doesn't get tossed off a horse often."

"I know. I should have posted the video online. 'Famous barrel racer takes a header.'" His mother went suddenly still. Her gaze sharpened. "I didn't do it," he reminded her, and he sounded a bit childish even to himself.

"You need to get over this whole enmity thing with her. That was a vindictive thing to even think of doing," she said sharply. "Something like that could do real damage."

He felt stung; his mother didn't usually get angry with him. At most she got exasperated now and then. "She wasn't really hurt," he protested. "Keller saw her in town soon after and she was fine except for a bruise. And like they say, there are only riders who have been thrown, and those who are going to be."

"I meant damage to her future plans."

"She still won the championship after that," he said, not sure what her point was. "And won a lot of money."

"Her business plans," his mother said, in that tone of patient explanation she took on when someone wasn't getting it.

"Business plans?" This time he sounded blank even to himself.

"Yes, to train and breed barrel horses."

"I…what?"

His mother went on as if he hadn't spoken.

"She's got Ghost, of course, and her dam, but she's shopping for a good stud. She's been saving almost all of her prize money for that and some other mares. And given her winnings the last couple of years with Ghost, she'll probably pull it all off."

Cody simply stood there, not knowing what to say. He'd had no idea. And his usually agile brain was having trouble wrapping around this one. Britt Roth, businesswoman? With a long-term dream and plans to make it come true? He wasn't sure he could adjust to that.

Wasn't sure that to him, she wouldn't forever and always be Britt Roth, irritating, bothersome, and occasionally infuriating brat-next-door.

Chapter Four

"**D**AD!" Her yell echoed around the house. Made it sound empty, as she guessed it was at the moment. Her mother was over in Fredericksburg visiting a friend, which might be just as well. She and her mother were very close, but Dad would appreciate this more.

She wasn't sure what her father had on tap for today. Work was always a safe bet—the man never stopped—but specifically what she didn't know. But obviously, and expectedly, whatever it was wasn't here inside the house. So she resorted to her new locating method.

She stepped out the front door and whistled as loudly as she could. In less than half a minute a German shepherd appeared at a run, coming around the side of the large barn. The big dog loped toward her, head and tail up, looking amazingly normal, given everything.

"Answers that question," she said aloud, with a grin as the dog, tail wagging now, trotted up to her. "Hey, Dodger," she said, bending to pet the dog and then scratch his ears.

They'd gotten the dog from Cody's brother's military

dog rehab months ago. Chance had done a wonderful job with the initially traumatized dog, who had turned out to indeed be a shepherd, and wonderful at moving herds. They'd borrowed him as a test last year, and the dog had done so well and bonded with her father so strongly they'd decided to keep him. And after observing them together for a few days, Chance had agreed and signed off.

Britt and her parents had been delighted. Britt had always thought what Chance was doing was a wonderful thing, and when she'd started finishing high in the money since starting to run Ghost, she'd made donations to his nonprofit.

With Dodger, she had even written what Chance called the update, short statements on what had happened and how the dogs once given up for lost had found new lives. The updates were then posted on the website and sent back to the processing center for the dogs coming home. No doubt in the hopes it would encourage them to give Chance a shot before they wrote off any animal as unsafe or unsalvageable, dooming them.

Doing that statement, she remembered with a grimace, had been when she'd found out Cody had both designed and maintained the *They Also Serve* website, because she'd had to send the statement to him. She'd stewed over that for a while. In the end she'd figured if he saw an email from her, he'd just junk it, so she'd used her father's address instead. She'd gotten no answer to the email, but the statement had been posted later that same day. Probably because he'd assumed it had been her father who had written it, not her.

Dodger backed up a couple of feet, tail still wagging slightly as he stood looking up at her expectantly.

"He's in the shop?" The dog whuffed softly. "Okay, Dodger my boy, let's go find him."

The dog trotted back the way he'd come, clearly understanding at least the "find him" part. She followed, trotting herself to keep up. The dog rounded the corner of the barn and darted quickly through the open door of the smaller building on the far side, which her father had set up years ago as a workshop for his various skills.

He was at his workbench, working on repairing what looked like a large gate hinge. He looked up when she and the dog came in.

"Figured that was your whistle."

She smiled and patted the dog once more before the animal trotted over to his chosen master, who gave him a scratch behind the ears that made the dog look blissful. And a million miles from the battlefield he'd survived.

"Just got back," she said. "Is that from the main corral gate? Want me to help you put it back on when you're done?"

"That'd be nice. You want to explain that shotgun round I heard go off a while ago?"

She should have known. "Target acquired and taken out," she said with a grin. "All that practice paid off."

"You bring back a carcass?"

"No, it went home wrapped in a shirt."

Her father stopped, put down his small hammer and turned around to face her. His eyes, so like her own dark blue, narrowed. "What?"

"With Cody the Coder," she said with a laugh. "Took that stupid drone of his out with one shot."

He stared at her. "You shot down one of his drones?"

"Anybody else around here fly the darned things? You should have seen his face."

"Oh, I'm sure I will," her father said, and his tone was sour. "And I hope you've got enough money to pay him for it."

She blinked. "What?"

"I swear, girl, you two are worse than oil and water, you're fire and tinder. But now you've really done it."

"Dad—"

"That drone was doing a job. For me," he ended pointedly. She opened her mouth, found herself speechless, and shut it again. "Cody was checking the fence lines for me. I haven't had time to do a full circuit since winter, and he said he could do it in half an hour. He does it for a lot of ranchers."

She gaped at him, and said rather blankly, "He does?"

"He does. For miles around. Not just Last Stand but over in Whiskey River, up to Round Mountain and all the way out to Kerrville."

"With those drones?" she said, knowing she was sounding stupid but seemingly unable to help it.

Her father nodded. "He's got them programmed somehow to register if there's a break in what should be an intact fence line. And there's an app that goes with it, that gets the mapping data and gives you an exact location if there's a problem."

That sounded so useful she was having a little trouble processing it. And connecting it to the nuisance next door. "I...that's handy."

"Almost as handy as your mother's record-keeping software."

She blinked. "The one she's teaching me, for when I start my own business? Yeah, that's great, the way it's tailored to ranch..." Her voice trailed off as the obvious hit her. "He did that, too?"

"He did. He designed it for them, but let us have a copy after Maggie showed it to your mom and she was amazed. Oh, and that weather system that warned us that thunderstorm had changed course last summer, and let us get your horses into the barn? That's his, too."

She was gaping again. Her mind was tumbling chaotically, but her father kept going.

"And his drones also keep an eye out for smoke in brush fire season, so we have a chance to stop them before they get out of hand. The Ranchers Association pays him for that."

"How did I not know any of this?" she demanded.

"Honey, if there's anything we all know, it's not to bring

up Cody Rafferty around you."

She was starting to feel…she wasn't sure what. Sheepish, maybe. And something else, a memory, suddenly came back to her. Of talking to Slater Highwater that day she'd stopped into the Last Stand Saloon for one of his genius peach lemonades. Luke had been there, the young man Slater had hired a few years ago, taking a chance on him when few would. Luke had trouble interacting with people in person, but he was a dedicated and thorough worker who had, Slater had told her, paid him back a hundredfold for the risk.

And that day Slater had mentioned how Luke had blossomed online, making connections he could never make in person, through his new computer and software. Designed, built, and paid for by Slater's brother Sean…and Cody Rafferty. A project that had led to them partnering for more of the same kind of thing, custom designed for particular issues people might have.

She hadn't known that until Slater had told her.

She hadn't known any of this.

Because apparently nobody would ever dare even mention Cody Rafferty's name to her.

And for the first time in her life—a life shared almost from the moment of birth with that unmentionable name—she questioned exactly why he irritated her so much. Why it was he, of all the Raffertys, who rubbed her so wrong. She liked and respected Keller, and the way he'd stepped in for his family after their father's awful death. She admired

Chance tremendously, both for his service and what he was doing now, for the dogs who had also served. And she was a bit in awe of Rylan's artistic talent and felt honored to actually own one of his beautifully carved leather belts.

But Cody? Cody was that pesky kid who was always getting on her nerves, who had tormented and teased her all through school. Although to be fair she'd done as much right back at him...except for the truce she'd declared after his father had been killed in action when they were both nine.

She had her mother to thank for that. She'd been stunned herself, having thought Kyle Rafferty a kind and wise man almost as nice as her own father. And she had only to think how she would feel if he had died to get an inkling of how all the Raffertys had felt. But she hadn't known what to do about it. It had been her mother who had suggested she announce a truce; no antagonistic actions while they were grieving.

Of course, at the time her mother hadn't explained that the grieving would never really end. But the truce had ended, although she'd stuck to the agreement that he would have to be the one to end it. Which he had, almost a year later, sending her old buckskin gelding home with a painted red target on his butt.

She'd been almost relieved. They'd continued the fray, until she'd headed off to College Station and Texas A & M, while he—of course—had headed for archrival UT in Austin.

Longhorns vs. Aggies, forever.

Her parents had thought the realigning of the athletic conferences might change sentiments between the two schools. She'd known better.

Once off to college she'd had four and a half years of relative peace, running into him only twice on simultaneous weekends home. But then they'd both graduated and returned to Last Stand, and the old enmity had arisen anew as if it had never paused.

And she had made a lot of assumptions, at least some of which were apparently untrue. He didn't just play with those gadgets she'd always thought a childish thing he'd never outgrown. It seemed he turned them into actually useful devices. And helpful ones.

How she was supposed to reconcile that with Cody Rafferty, lifetime enemy, she didn't know.

Chapter Five

"CODY, CAN YOU come here, please?"

His mother's cheery voice, calling out from the main part of the house, held a note of...something. He wasn't sure what, but it was enough to pull his attention away from that blip that had developed in the new app he was trying to get moving.

If it had been anyone else, he probably would have answered, "In a minute," and then gotten lost again until the request was repeated, or until the requester arrived at his door. But this was his mother, and judging by that tone of voice, something was going on. Maybe with a capital S.

At least she didn't sound mad, he thought as he got to his feet, smothering a yawn. He stretched wearily. He'd been working on this darned blip since the early hours when a possible—but in the end futile—solution had occurred to him. He rubbed a hand over his face as he started down the long hallway to the main house. Stubble roughened his jaw, and his eyes were a bit bleary, so he rubbed at them, too. The hems of the jeans he'd yanked on hurriedly in the wee hours brushed against the floor around his bare feet.

"What's up, Mom?" he asked when he reached the main house and spotted her pouring a cup of coffee that suddenly smelled irresistible. He'd started that way before she gestured toward the living room.

"You have company," she said, in that same cheery tone as before.

A tone that should have been a warning. Crap. As he started to turn, he was trying to remember if he had a client meeting he'd forgotten. If so it was going to be embarrassing, given he hadn't bothered to put on a shirt and his jeans weren't even zipped all the way. He was—

Double crap.

It was Roth.

Instantly his guard went up. "Bring that scattergun with you?" he snapped.

"Good morning to you, too," she retorted.

"It might have been," he said, so pointedly she couldn't miss the inference it was her presence that—despite the fact that most guys would probably think she looked pretty sweet in those snug jeans and soft sweater over curves that even he had to admit would be interesting on anybody else—had removed that possibility.

"If you two are going to be your usual sweet selves, I'll just take myself off to my committee meeting," his mother said. "Try to leave the house standing, all right? Quinta," she added to her loyal dog, "come with me. I love you too much to leave you with these two adolescent adversaries."

Cody watched his mother go, scowling.

"Not that she has an opinion or anything," Roth muttered, also watching his mother go.

Cody spun back. For him to scowl was one thing, Roth something else altogether. "Show some respect or shut up," he snapped.

To his surprise, she looked chagrinned. "You're right. She deserves respect. I *like* your mother."

"It's me you've got the problem with, so keep it there." He gave her a sour grimace. "Or you could just leave. That'd fix everything."

She opened her mouth as if to snap back at him, as usual, but then she stopped. He saw her take a deep breath. "I am here about fixing something."

"If you mean a certain expensive piece of equipment, there's no fixing it. You did what you intended, destroyed it."

She winced, somewhat to his surprise. He'd expected her to be pleased. Given the distance, it had been a good shot. "Just how expensive?"

"Ask your dad. I'll send him the bill." He wouldn't—on Keller's wise advice he'd insured everything when he'd started the service, and this was hardly her father's fault—but she didn't need to know that.

"No. Don't." She sounded actually anxious, and his brow furrowed. "Look," she went on, "I didn't know it was…that you were doing a job for him. I thought you were just…"

"Just what?"

"Trying to tick me off," she said bluntly.

"Because it's always all about you, huh?"

That got her; he saw faint color tinge her cheeks. "Just tell me how much it cost." She pulled out her phone. "I'll do a transfer right here and now. Or if you want, I'll write you a check. Either way, I'll pay for it."

"What if I tell you it's got a comma in it?"

She winced, but repeated determinedly, "I'll pay for it."

She's been saving almost all of her prize money.

His mother's words came back to him, along with the part about Britt Roth's dreams for the future. And the urge to get back at her faded a little.

"How do you know I won't double the real amount or something?"

She met his gaze then, steadily. "Because you're a Rafferty. You wouldn't do something that would shame your father's memory. Not even to get back at me."

That she used the exact words he'd just thought delayed his reaction to the rest of what she said for a moment. And then he couldn't speak himself, because his throat was crazy tight. He tried to swallow. It almost hurt.

He coughed. That was better.

"Please, I need to do this," she said almost urgently when he didn't speak. Please. A word he'd rarely if ever heard from her. "Like I said, I didn't know you had a legitimate reason for that thing being there. I had no idea my father had hired it. You. Whatever. If I had, I never would have done it."

"So, this is because your father got mad when he found out?"

"No." A strangely soft note came into her voice. "It's because he didn't."

In a crazy way that made sense to him. He let out a breath, trying to let go of some of the seemingly natural tension she set off in him as he did. "I'll get the original invoice," he said. He started to turn, to head back to his lair, as Mom called it. Then he looked back. "And there's no comma. The basic ones are cheaper these days."

He thought he saw relief flash in her eyes. No need to mention his modifications, which had probably doubled the value of the thing. As he walked back the way he had come, he had to toss that into the pot of new data on his oldest enemy. And he had no idea what kind of stew that was going to produce.

BRITT TRIED TO stop herself from pacing the floor, but the moment she stopped thinking about stopping, she was doing again. She wanted this over with. She wanted to pay this debt. She wanted to be able to tell her dad she'd made it right. She wanted to get back to working with Ghost.

She wanted Cody to put on a damned shirt. And zip up.

She'd spent more time than she cared to admit trying to put that image of him yanking off his shirt to gather up the drone out of her mind. It hadn't worked, so she'd told herself she'd only imagined how good he'd looked.

He'd just blasted that thought out of the air as thoroughly as she'd blasted his precious drone.

It would have been impossible, with her friends pointing it out all the time, to deny he was a hunk. And if they'd seen him as she had yesterday, or as he'd been just now, with that bare, broad, muscled chest and obvious six-pack, that arrow of sandy hair heading from his navel downward, they'd never shut up about it.

The fact that he was also a computer nerd, as she'd often derisively called him when they were younger, seemed to fascinate them even more. She'd only wondered how he stayed in such shape when he seemed to spend most of his time in a chair in front of screens. But Mom said he worked on the ranch like the rest of the family, so she'd figured he must do enough.

Her friends didn't understand why she disliked him so intensely. To which her standard answer was "You didn't grow up next door to him." An answer that didn't account for the simple fact that both their ranches were big enough they probably could have avoided encountering each other anywhere but school without a lot of effort.

Effort neither of them seemed inclined to expend.

She was pacing again. She stopped in her tracks. Sighed.

He'd only been gone a minute, maybe two, and she was already winding up as if for a second clash.

You will not argue with him. You will pay what you owe and go home. That simple.

She turned her head slightly, looking at the big painting on the wall. She'd seen it before. She'd actually been here many times, although she tried to time it when Cody was somewhere else. She truly had liked, although been in a bit of awe of his father, she genuinely did like his mother, and his brothers. And now their ladies as well. Sydney had such fascinating stories to tell, and Ariel was so kind and understanding. She'd only met Ry's Kaitlyn twice since they'd connected a couple of months ago, but the quiet woman had the air of someone who saw much others overlooked, and she wanted to know her better.

Soon, she thought as she looked at the glorious explosion of color Cody's father had captured so vividly. Soon her beloved Hill Country would look just like this, the luxurious swaths of bluebonnets softening the rough edges of the escarpment, looking like some kind of carpet unrolled by God.

She found her eyes stinging a little as she looked at the painting. He'd been such a nice, good man, but also as tough as he'd needed to be in the one-of-a-kind job of standing for them all in brutal places around the world.

Every Rafferty had one of his paintings, each with an aspect that related particularly to them, except Cody. Maggie had explained that to her once, and she'd seen genuine pain in the woman's eyes as she spoke of how it hurt Cody, a lot, to be the only one without that one-of-a-kind gift, from a one-of-a-kind man. Their father had always waited, Maggie said, until he had a good idea of who his sons were, and what they would value, before setting out to do their painting. For Keller, it had been when he was ten, because his love for this place and his family's history had been clear early on. Chance had also been pretty clear who he was by ten. Rylan had been trickier, Maggie had said, probably because of the talent Ry shared with him, and he'd been twelve.

But Cody never got his. Because Kyle Rafferty had been killed in action before he could do that last one.

Britt looked away, annoyed that she was tearing up even more at the thought. Why on earth would she care if Cody's feelings were hurt? No, that couldn't be it. It was his father she was feeling sorry about. Because she'd liked him.

And he'd been amused by the constant contretemps between her and his youngest son.

You two are like members of a tribe that have been at war for centuries and don't even remember what started it anymore.

I like you, Mr. R, and everybody else. I just don't like him.

He'd grinned then, and it had made her laugh. *It's good for him. Keeps him on his toes. He's too pretty for his own good anyway.*

She hadn't fully understood what he'd meant, she'd only been eight at the time. But later, when hormones started stirring among her friends, she realized all too well what he'd been talking about.

She remembered his mother saying he was the one who got the most obvious parts of both his parents, her hair and his father's spring-green eyes. And she'd had her own opinion on their constant sniping at each other. *He'll find enough things easy in life, looking like that. A few bumps in the road won't hurt him.*

"Here."

She spun around, startled. She hadn't heard him. But then, he was still barefoot. He had, however, put on a shirt and zipped his jeans. Thankfully. She took the paper he was holding out. It was from a company in Dallas, and the amount at the bottom did not, as he'd promised, have a comma. It was close enough, though, that she was going to grit her teeth when she paid it.

"You want to do this by app, or—"

"A check is fine."

It had taken her an extra moment this morning to find the checkbook she rarely used anymore. She walked over to the coatrack where his mother had hung her jacket, pulled it out of the pocket and walked over to the kitchen counter. She wrote the check quickly, made a note in the space to remind her—as if she'd need it—and tore it off the pad. She thought about handing it to him, but a vision of him, muscled and shirtless, flashed through her mind and made her leave it on the counter. If he hadn't been so obviously oblivious, she would have thought his appearance in that state had been intentional. And it was all too easy to imagine the reaction he would have gotten from practically any woman on the planet.

Except her.

She pulled on her jacket, then turned to face him. And said the words she'd rehearsed all the way over here. Two words shouldn't have taken that much practice, but to be spoken to this one person, they did. She kept wanting to add more, but it all sounded like excuses to her, so she didn't. And after a deep breath, she got them out.

"I'm sorry."

He raised a brow at her. "No 'It won't ever happen again'?"

"I don't make promises I might not be able to keep."

To her surprise, one corner of his mouth twitched, as if he were trying not to smile. "Probably wise."

And for some reason that little quirk of his mouth got stuck in her head all the way back home.

Chapter Six

CODY SAT IN his big gaming chair, tapping the paper check against his business desk. Trying to decide what to do about it. He leaned back, staring up at the ceiling.

Some people were boggled at the size of his space here. His bedroom off to the right was normal sized but seemed like a closet compared to this room, the room that would have been a big living room for anyone else. It was for him, too, if by living room you meant where you spent the most time.

Anyone who was allowed in here—he wasn't as protective of the space as, say, Ry was about his studio, but he was cautious—was usually more boggled by his four-desk setup, one on each wall. To him it made perfect sense. He'd started with his gaming gear, on the wall opposite the door. Then when he'd started creating things, writing software and apps and building specialized systems for people, he'd needed a different kind of setup. When he started using the drones for more than just trying to accomplish that life goal he harbored, he'd needed a monitoring station; that was number three.

And then, when he'd finally gotten it through his head that he could be making a living, and more importantly contributing to the family upkeep, he'd needed what he called the business center, where he tracked all the necessary things. That was number four, which he hated because it was bookkeeping, not making or building anything, but also enjoyed because it did let him see the income stream, which felt good.

He kept staring at the check in his hand, wondering what had possessed him to ask for it instead of just doing an app payment. Maybe he'd just wanted to make her do it by hand. Pound home the lesson, as it were.

Geeze, he was talking like Mom. She was all about life lessons. Like the discussion they'd had when Sydney had first arrived, and he'd decided he hated everything about her. It had been Mom who had made him see it was the change coming that had colored his thinking. She had—

His phone notification went off. It was Sean's ring, so he picked it up. The middle Highwater was a couple of years older, but they'd bonded in the tech club at Creekbend High School and had stayed close friends. And now they were business partners of a sort, working together on the specialized computer systems they built.

"What's up?" he asked.

"Two things," Sean replied, sounding so cheerful Cody suspected his wife Elena must be close by. "Shane says to tell you the new camera system you put in is working great. And

Marcos wants to make sure we're on for game night. He—" Sean broke off for a moment as someone spoke to him. Cody could almost see his friend grinning when he went on. "You'd better come. Elena's making enchiladas."

"That," Cody said, "I wouldn't miss for anything." Elena managed Valencia's, which was the best Tex-Mex restaurant in town, and she was a big part of why.

After they'd hung up, he sat and pondered the huge changes in his friend's life. Christmas the year before had been a turning point for him, as it had been this year for Chance. It was enough to get you believing in Christmas miracles. He grimaced to the empty room; maybe he should start making sure he was nowhere around that time of year. That ought to buy him a year or two. Although seeing Sean and Elena together...

He'd once been intimidated by Elena, but he'd gotten to know her now, and knew that among other things she had a surprisingly wicked sense of humor. Something he never would have guessed at, going by her mother, the stern, imposing Mrs. Valencia, whose reputation as the toughest teacher at Creekbend still stood several years after she'd retired to help Elena care for her son Marcos. Marcos, who was so like his stepfather Sean and he himself that they called themselves Nerds Anonymous, a joking nickname Marcos had coined.

Sean had done wonders for the boy, and vice versa. And it left Cody sometimes feeling a bit...left behind. The odd one out again, as he'd felt back in school. Except, he didn't want what Sean had. Oh, the woman to be crazy about and who was crazy about you, sure, that'd be nice. Maybe. Or maybe he'd had enough of that, with all his brothers crashing like felled oak trees.

Yeah, he should probably avoid that. Especially after he'd been practically smitten with the gorgeous blonde who had arrived back in January to do a feature story on Ry for an art magazine, and she'd turned out to be the worst kind of…witch. Obviously, his judgment left something to be desired. So, it was just as well there was no one in the picture, or even on the horizon. Now if Mom would just back off…

You're next, bro.

Never happen.

I know. That's why I'm safe.

The joking exchange he and Ry had had—before Kaitlyn had dropped into his life—had seemed probable at the time. It would take a special woman to accept Ry's life and lifestyle. He'd never expected it to happen soon, let alone so fast. But it had, and Ry was so obviously happy and Kaitlyn so nice, he couldn't begrudge him.

Even if that left him as the last single Rafferty.

He opened the drawer to his right and dropped the check into it. It landed atop a large, printed photograph. He resisted the urge at first, but finally pulled it out. He stared at it, thinking of all the times he'd thought about framing it and hanging it up in here. But he always turned coward and put it away in the drawer again. He didn't think he could take seeing this image of his tall, strong, impossibly brave father holding the eight-year-old he'd been every day. In the picture he was grinning up at the man in uniform with pure delight; Dad was home, and all had been right with his world. And Dad was grinning back at him, the love practically pouring out of his green eyes. Eyes he'd passed down to that boy in his arms.

With a deep sigh he moved to slide the photograph back in the drawer. But he spotted the other picture that had lain beneath it and stopped. This one was smaller, and newer, printed off by a friend's new pocket printer bought just for the purpose of printing photos from his phone. It had made the guy a hot property at that convention in Dallas five years ago; for all that it was a tech con and digital was everything, there was still something about a print copy you could hold in your hands or give to the friends the shots were taken of.

He lifted the second picture out of the drawer and looked, not at himself—he didn't need any reminders of how dorky that particular spiky haircut had been—but at the girl beside him. The girl he'd spent four days—and nights—almost nonstop with. The girl he'd bonded with unlike anyone else he'd met. So petite she seemed almost tiny, Gwen had had a brain the size of Texas. She had been quick, clever, witty, and a genius with just about any kind of tech there on the convention floor.

She'd also been dying.

He dropped the smaller photo back in the drawer. Put the bigger one on top of it. Pulled the check Roth had written back out. And slammed the drawer shut with a bang.

I really am going to start calling that the death drawer.

He gave a sharp shake of his head and got up abruptly, sending the chair rolling halfway across the room. He ignored it. He reached out and grabbed a pushpin from the corkboard where he pinned temporary reminders and stuck the check up there. That he wouldn't mind looking at every day. Remembering her face as she'd grimly written the thing out. He could use the laughs.

Then he headed over to the kitchen alcove. His was a bit better equipped than Ry's in the barn—although he had a feeling that might change now that Ry wasn't alone over there—but not much bigger. He put on a pot of coffee that he knew wouldn't taste as good as Mom's in the main house. They all agreed on that, although none of them could figure out why. But it would be caffeine-laced, and that was all that mattered at this point.

Then he turned and walked into his bedroom. Which was, he noted, a mess. It was a big enough room to withstand a bit of clutter, but this was insane. Tech diagrams here, his big tablet there, e-reader on the nightstand, next to a couple of books he hadn't been able to get in that form— that all would have been fine. But when you added clothes and shoes tossed everywhere, forgotten as soon as he shucked them off, wrappers from his caramel habit, and the overflowing wastebasket, it was a bit of a disaster even to his eyes.

His mouth twisted wryly. Sometimes he was so focused on some problem in his head he really did look past what was right in front of him.

With a sigh he started picking up the clothes at least. He was down to his last pair of jeans and a couple of T-shirts, so he was going to be forced to do laundry soon. Remembering his earlier thoughts about him being next on her target list, he made a mental note to be sure and do it on a day when Mom had a committee meeting for the Bluebonnet Festival.

Assuming the darn flowers ever showed up.

He grimaced. He was just worried about getting that video Mom wanted as soon as possible. He knew the signature Texas flowers would bloom, they always did, and for a few weeks every bit of open, unpaved ground would be covered with them. It was like a rite of passage every year.

The image from that photo in the drawer shot through his mind again, along with a memory of that first spring without Dad. The emerging flowers had been one of the biggest steps on his path of grief, when he'd realized that Dad, who had loved them and painted them so beautifully, would never, ever see them again.

Mom had found him out in the south pasture, where a big swath of the flowers always erupted. He'd been there a while, tearing the bluebonnets out of the ground as fast as he could move. She'd understood immediately. As she always seemed to. She'd pulled him into her arms, and he'd gone from angry to broken so fast it had made him almost dizzy.

"It's all right, Cody. I understand. Sometimes I want to rip the world apart because it took him from us."

"'s silly," he'd mumbled, gulping the words out between sobs. "Just flowers."

"And they're back again and he never will be. It's not fair."

He remembered clinging to her, taking comfort not in the words stating the cruel reality, but in the realization that he wasn't alone in this consuming, horrible feeling. And that Mom knew, as she always seemed to, what not to say. Not to give him any platitudes or phony reassurances that everything would be all right. No, she'd acknowledged and made clear she shared his pain and anger. And that had somehow lightened it, just enough that he could go on.

Until the next time. And the next.

He closed his eyes for a moment, then opened them and went back to picking up dirty clothes. And thinking maybe he wouldn't wait until his mother was gone to do laundry, after all.

In fact, maybe he'd make sure she was there.

Chapter Seven

WHEN SHE RAN into Chance and Ariel in town, Britt found herself smiling before she realized it. Seeing Chance out and about in itself was beyond rare. Elena, Sean Highwater's wife, was walking them out of Valencia's restaurant near where Britt had parked. They were all chatting in a lighthearted way that Britt would never have expected from Chance a mere three months ago. He deserved that kind of happy, and so did Ariel. And Elena, for that matter, who had surprisingly found it with Cody the Coder's best friend, Sean Highwater. The elegant woman and the quirky detective—funny how Sean was quirky, but Cody was just annoying—had made an unusual but obviously very successful match.

It hit her then that these three had something deep and painful to bond over—they had all lost someone in the military; Chance his father, Ariel and Elena a husband—and yet they were all smiling. Had found happiness again. Quite a tribute to the human spirit, she supposed. And she stifled the odd sort of longing she'd been struck with on occasion recently.

Stop. You've been lucky. You've never lost anyone you're really close to.

"He's doing great," Ariel was saying to Elena as Britt approached to say hello.

Chance nodded. "I was worried about that dog. Thought he might be the first failure. He wasn't adjusting to amputee status well at all. Not like Tri." Britt knew Tri was their own dog, a huge part of their amazing story.

"Those geniuses are most helpful sometimes," Elena said with a broad smile.

Chance grinned back at the woman. Britt realized that since he'd come home for good, she'd never seen the man grin like that. "They do have their moments."

And then, as if he'd known all along she was there, Chance looked past Elena to her. They all turned to greet her warmly.

"Was that about the Doberman you had for a while? The one who'd lost a foot?" she asked when the hellos had been said all around.

"Yep," Chance said. "He couldn't handle the standard prosthetic, kept gnawing it off. But Cody came up with a new kind and he really took to it."

Britt frowned. Cody? She'd thought Elena had been talking about Sean. "I didn't realize he was...that involved."

Prosthetics for amputee military K9 heroes? One more thing to add to the list of good things she hadn't known he did. She had been blinder than she ever realized.

"I've learned," Ariel said with her sweet smile, "that if you have a problem, asking Cody if he has any ideas usually ends up with your problem solved."

"Unless it's a people problem," Chance said, grinning again. "Don't ask him about those. Although I have to admit, he's scarily good at the perfect payback."

"I know," Britt said, unable to stop herself. "Like the one where he arranged for my term paper to get waterlogged after I waterlogged his phone."

The women laughed, while Chance nodded. "Like I said, perfect payback."

"It was…fitting." Despite the fact that the years-ago memory still irritated her, she smiled. Not for anything would she inject her problems with Chance Rafferty's brother into this pleasant encounter.

She was still smiling as they said their goodbyes, at least until Elena, turning to go back into the restaurant, said gaily, "See you at the party!"

The party. Maggie Rafferty's birthday party.

To which her family was, as always, invited. Would attend. And would expect her to attend.

She sighed. She would attend. Not only for Maggie, but also out of respect and liking for all the Raffertys and their recent significant others. All but one, anyway. And while her respect for Cody might have undergone a bit of a tweak now that she knew about some of the things he was doing, her dislike hadn't changed a bit. He was still an insufferable pain.

Determinedly she shoved her annoying neighbor out of her mind as she drove back to the ranch. She carried the bags of groceries she'd picked up into the kitchen, where her mother was already working away on tonight's meal, her delicious meat loaf. Since she herself was, except for some basics her mother had forced her to learn, hopeless in the kitchen, this had been good news, and she'd quickly invited herself to dinner.

And the sight of the meat loaf always made her smile, not only because she knew it would be a great dinner, but because it reminded her of the day as a teenager when she'd awkwardly asked her mother if she'd teach her how to make it.

"You actually want to learn how to cook?" her mother had asked in astonishment.

"No, I just want to know how to make that," she'd said, with a nod at the minuscule remainder of what had been a platter almost full of the beef concoction.

"I'm not sure," her mother said thoughtfully. "Seems it might be a guarantee that you'll always come home."

That had caught her off guard. "I'm not going anywhere until college," she pointed out.

Her mother had let out a sigh and given her a look she couldn't quite describe. "Yes. And that's only a couple of years from now."

To her sixteen-year-old mind, a couple of years seemed like an eternity. And all her father's warnings, that there would come a time when two years would seem like a blink, made sense intellectually, but nowhere else. So she filed it away in that "worry about it when you're older" part of her brain that contained things like buying a car, choosing a college major, and planning a future. And settled her focus on more urgent things to her at sixteen, like cutting a second off her barrel time, finishing a term paper, and thinking up the next prank to play on Cody Rafferty.

"Now that's a dangerous combination."

Cody glanced in the direction Sean Highwater was looking, and smothered a wince. Not because of Sean's sister, Sage. He genuinely liked her, probably because thanks to Sean she understood his love of tech, even appreciated it for how it made ranch life—her life—easier.

No, his wince was because the woman she was sitting at the small table with was Roth.

The two women hadn't noticed them—they were so deep in conversation over whatever frilly drink they'd come in here for. They probably had a lot to talk about, since both of them were cowgirls to the bone. Or maybe they were talking about other things. The possibilities there made him nervous. Cody wondered if it was too late to turn around and bail out of the coffee shop.

Should have just gone to the bakery and had done with it.

We could be deep into a game with Marcos by now.

"Thinking of running, buddy?" Sean asked. Cody glanced at him, and grimaced when he saw his friend was grinning.

"Yeah, yeah," he muttered.

He'd told Sean what she'd done, and he'd been appropriately outraged on Cody's behalf.

"Want me to arrest her?" Sean had joked.

Cody had felt the jolt he sometimes did when he was reminded that Sean was a police detective, and one with a reputation for solving tough cases that had spread statewide and beyond.

"No," he'd answered, then added, "Much as I'd enjoy seeing it, no. This is between her and me."

They'd made it to the counter and gave their order—five words or less, they always joked, just enough to say coffee with cream and sugar—and neither of the women had noticed them. Cody was starting to hope they'd escape unscathed. But in the moment after he was handed his cup, he heard Sage's voice behind them.

"Congratulations, Rafferty."

He braced himself and turned around, determined to not even look at Roth.

She wasn't there. It was only Sage. His gaze flicked around the room to be sure, but she definitely wasn't there.

"Congratulations for what?" he asked, looking back at Sean's little sister.

"You're the only guy I know who could make someone as tough as Britt dodge you."

Dodge? Was that what had happened? "Is that what you were talking about? Did she tell you what she did?"

"If you mean take out one of your flying monkeys, yes, she did."

He heard Sean sputter, and choke down a swallow of coffee. "Flying monkeys," he said at Cody's glance. "That's pretty funny, sis."

"Ha-ha," Cody muttered.

"She also feels guilty about it. So cut her some slack, huh?"

"He did," Sean said with a grin. "He said no when I offered to arrest her."

Sage glared at her brother, looking like she'd like to follow it up with a punch. "Very funny." But Cody thought he saw the slightest twitch at the corners of her mouth as she turned to exit the shop.

After the required stop at Kolaches—Marcos was a big fan of their version of yoyos, a traditional Mexican pastry made of soft cookies glued together with strawberry jam and then rolled in coconut—they'd headed to the Highwater ranch and Sean's quarters, which had expanded since Elena and Marcos had come to live there. Marcos, Sean told him, had taken to ranch life beautifully, and Elena was…well, Elena.

"She'll be heading off with her mother tonight, so we'll

have the place to ourselves, just us guys."

"Excellent," Cody said. He really did like Elena, all the more because she made sure her son and Sean had plenty of guy time.

She was, however, still there when they arrived. To Cody's surprise, she gave him a hug when he came in.

"I...thank you?" he said, hesitantly.

Elena laughed, and as he remembered how many times her killer wit had skewered someone who richly deserved it, he relaxed a little. "That was for your computer-building skills. I never thought I'd see my mother spending hours chatting with friends all over the country, and even the world. And loving it, I might add."

Cody smiled at that. "I just helped Sean a bit."

"You wrote the software that was intuitive, that fit the way her mind works."

"Her mind," Cody said, wearing his most serious expression, "is terrifyingly brilliant."

"And unique," Sean put in, after greeting his wife with a kiss that stopped just short of being passionate enough to be embarrassing. It still managed to invoke a strange sort of feeling in Cody, however. He knew Sean had never, ever expected to find a woman who "got" him, and that it had turned out to be the woman he'd adored from afar for years only made it more amazing.

He was too happy for Sean to be envious. But he felt...something. A wistfulness, maybe. Like he felt about his brothers.

He shook it off, smiled as she gave Sean careful instructions on how to warm up the enchiladas, gave her son a hug and a kiss as he barreled into the room to greet Cody with a grin and the highest five he could manage, then left them to it with a cheery wave and a promise to see him at his mother's birthday party.

Cody watched Marcos—the kid had grown a few inches, although not as far or fast as Lucas had, yet anyway—happily dart over to the gaming setup he and Sean had put together and begin to get out the controllers.

He looked back at his old friend. "You struck gold, you know," he said quietly.

Sean met his gaze steadily. "Believe me, I know."

And there it was again, that same wistful feeling. He was really starting to feel the odd one out, even here. But then Marcos had the game they'd had to stop last time just before a breakthrough booted up.

"Let the game begin!" Cody boomed out in his best announcer voice. Marcos laughed, Sean grinned, and the weird feeling receded.

Relieved, he sat down, took up one of the controllers, and the game began.

Chapter Eight

BRITT WASN'T CERTAIN what had brought on this urge, whether it was the discussion with Sage or her mother's request, but she'd already spent more time getting ready for this party than she had spent on anything else in recent memory, except training Ghost.

She'd blame them both, she decided. Sage for throwing it out there as a challenge, which one of them could glam up the most, and her mother for asking in that long-suffering tone that she show up in something other than a slightly less worn pair of jeans and boots. And repeating it every day including this morning, when the Tuesday of the party had finally dawned.

It had been a while since she'd bothered with anything more than the basics, so she was a bit out of practice. But after a couple of false starts resulting in washing her face and starting over, the makeup thing started to come back to her.

Then came the harder part. She walked over to her closet and pulled open the door. Frowned at the pile of clothes in the corner; she'd meant to do laundry the other night, but had been so distracted all week long, after The Incident, as she'd taken to calling the encounter with the drone, she'd forgotten about it.

But her everyday clothes were not the issue here. No, what she needed was in the back, rarely visited section of her closet. Here were the fancier duds, as her father called them. Not just the suit she wore when she needed to impress a potential sponsor with her seriousness, but the dresses. The one she'd worn to the Highwater weddings. The one she'd worn to the Christmas ball last year. Even the one she'd worn for her college graduation. She pushed them all aside and went for the one that had been tickling the back of her mind all afternoon.

The bright, royal-blue, deep V-necked dress, made out of a soft, slippery sort of fabric that stopped just above her knees, still had the tag on. She'd bought it on a shopping trip with Sage before her wedding last year, only because Sage had practically demanded it.

"It matches your eyes, it shows just enough cleavage, and enough leg with that flippy skirt, and besides, it's sexy as hell on you."

"You're supposed to be shopping for you," Britt had pointed out.

"I am. I can multitask," she'd said blithely.

But then, Sage had been blithe ever since Scott had come home and they'd patched things up. No, more than that, they'd rebuilt from the ground up, and were now rock solid.

Britt smothered a sigh as she looked at the blue dress.

She didn't begrudge Sage, she was delighted for her; she'd been in love with Scott Parrish since they were teenagers. In love in a way Britt doubted she herself would ever find. But then, Sage had doubted too, and now there she was, hog-tied and happy as she always said. They'd be there tonight, of course. Half the town would be there over the course of the evening, such was the standing of Maggie Rafferty in Last Stand. Throw in having the Last Stand Saloon to themselves with food catered by Valencia's, she'd be surprised if the whole town didn't drop in.

She grabbed the blue dress before she could change her mind.

CODY CAME INTO the living room with Lucas, who looked uncomfortable in the more formal wear, just as Mom finished fussing with Chance's string tie. For a moment taking another step was beyond him. It wasn't that Chance was going—he always honored their mother in that way—it was that he was smiling about it.

Before he would have been stone-faced.

Before, it would have been a task he had to do.

Before Ariel.

"Chance is going," Lucas whispered, sounding as happy about it as Cody felt.

Cody—who had neatly tied his own string tie, because to

him the process was as clear as a geometry problem—walked right past his mother and elder brother to the tall, elegant redhead who stood watching, a similar smile on her face. He gave her a rather fierce hug. She let him, but there was a question in her blue eyes. A light blue, compared to Roth's darker blue. He nearly frowned at the intrusion of that particular set of eyes into his mind.

"That," he said quietly, "is for the smile on my brother's face."

She smiled back then, and he felt an odd sort of tug inside at the love reflected in those eyes.

"You look rather…spiffy," she said after a moment, eyeing the suit he'd donned for the occasion.

He rolled his eyes, but he was smiling. "Mom's orders."

And Mom's choice. It was western cut, with black piping that gleamed just enough to be seen against the matte black of the cloth. Or so his mother said; he just knew he got compliments when he wore it.

"And today of all days those must be followed." Ry said it with a grin as he and Kaitlyn came in the front door in time to hear the exchange.

"Is there ever a day when they're not?" Keller mused out loud from the kitchen, where he and Sydney stood, also looking at Chance with ill-concealed happiness.

"Point taken," Chance said. And as Mom reached up to cup his cheek, he put his hand over hers and smiled down at her.

Cody felt a wave of…something rise up and nearly swamp him. Something about this moment, about seeing his brothers here like this, together, gathering to honor the woman who had held them all together long enough to find the women who now stood beside them, and Lucas, as much a part of this family as if they'd all been born to it, made him feel…he wasn't sure what. Love, certainly. Gratitude. Appreciation. A fierce sense of belonging.

All of that, leavened with the ever-present wish that the one man missing could be here, or at least somehow know how much they all loved the woman he had wisely chosen as the foundation of the Raffertys.

He swallowed hard, but it didn't quite clear the odd tightness in his throat. He couldn't speak for a moment, so instead he walked over to his mother. As the only unattached Rafferty here, it seemed the right thing to do. Very formally—Gwen had taught him that, at a costume ball at that convention—he bent slightly and offered her his arm.

"Madam, if you will allow me to escort you?"

She looked startled at first, but then she smiled, a warm, delighted smile that made him feel like he had as a kid the first time he'd put real thought into her birthday present, buying her something he knew she would like, not something the kid he'd been would have. She slipped her arm into the crook of his, and the celebration officially began.

That strange feeling lingered as they arrived at the saloon, which had been closed for the private party tonight. Of course in this case, private meant locals, so the place was already crowded with people wanting to pay their respects. His mother stretched up to give him a kiss on the cheek, in thanks for accomplishing his duties.

"You go have some fun now, Triple B."

He glanced around quickly, hoping there was no one close enough to hear who he might have to explain that nickname to. No one, thankfully.

He knew almost everyone here. The Highwaters of course, including Slater who, although he'd no doubt be keeping an eye on things, had turned the actual function of the saloon over to his assistant manager for the evening and was greeting Mom now.

Cody picked up one of the glasses of champagne from the table, snagged a chip and scooped up some of the luscious guacamole Elena had just put out, and relaxed. Finishing the chip, he grabbed one of the taquitos on the platter beside the chips, took a sip from the glass and started to walk around the room. His duties, and that of his brothers, hadn't ended when they got here; thanking everyone for coming was going to be an all-night task.

As he wandered, greeting friends, neighbors, and some people he barely knew, remembering the time when he'd felt enough the odd one out to be very uncomfortable at such gatherings—a feeling he and Sean had also bonded over—he had a different sort of feeling. That feeling of belonging to this family he loved expanded, to this town that was also part of him, all of it interwoven together. And at this moment, there was no place he would rather be.

Cody's gaze snagged on a woman across the room, her back to him as she looked at the pool table in the alcove at the back of the saloon, where Gary Klausen from the hardware store and another guy who looked vaguely familiar had started a game. Long, dark hair tumbled down her back in silken waves. She was wearing a short, bright blue dress that bared a nice length of long, slender legs above a pair of flashy cowboy boots that he thought had to be from Kelly Boots over in Whiskey River, black trimmed with a blue that matched the silky, slinky dress. The dress that practically caressed a trim, taut backside that had him looking a bit longer than he should have.

"Now that," his brother Keller said with a nod toward the woman in blue as he passed Cody, on his way to no doubt make sure Lucas wasn't tempted by the champagne, "is what some guys call a wowgirl."

"Wow, indeed," he muttered, familiar with the play on cowgirl, for a particularly attractive or sexy woman. Which definitely applied here, even if all he'd seen was her back.

Keller chuckled and kept going. A moment later, an amused-looking Slater Highwater paused beside him. "Careful there, Cody."

"What?" Cody asked.

"Last time someone looked at a woman at that pool table the way you're looking at her, they ended up married." He was grinning now. "And he's never been able to see that table the same way since."

Cody laughed, knowing Slater was referring to himself and Joey, but sensing there was also a private joke beneath the words. He wondered exactly what the pool table had to do with connecting the saloonkeeper with the town librarian. He told himself he was just glad everyone was in such a good mood.

Lucas came up beside him, holding a napkin with a couple of small spheres that looked fried. "These are really good," he said. "Sean's wife said they're called papas re...re something."

"*Papas rellenas*," Cody said, as he glanced back at the woman again, seemingly unable to stop himself. "Means stuffed potatoes."

"Yeah, well, they're stuffed with good stuff," Lucas said with a grin. Then, seeing where Cody was looking, he added, "She looks really nice tonight, huh?"

That was enough to pull his gaze away from the vision in blue. Odd. Lucas had said that as if he knew the woman.

"Too bad you hate her," the boy added.

He blinked. "I what?"

"Hate her," the boy repeated patiently. Then he looked at his now-empty napkin. "But I love these. I think I'll go get some more."

Cody kept his gaze on the boy who was going to legally be his nephew as soon as the formalities were done. He kept it on Lucas because if he didn't, he was going to look at that woman again.

Lucas was wrong. He had to be wrong. There was no way in hell he'd been staring at, admiring, practically lusting after the only woman in the world he hated.

There was no way in hell that vision in blue, with the gorgeous legs and the more gorgeous backside was…Britt Roth.

But he had to know. He wasn't even sure why, just that he did. His pulse had kicked up, and he was certain it was because he'd had a narrow escape, because given another moment he probably would have walked over there and said something…stupid. To her back.

He tried to imagine how he'd have felt if he'd done that, she turned around, and it really was her.

He couldn't.

He gave Lucas a silent thank you and started to move. Not toward the pool table but toward the bar, where he'd just spotted Luke, who shyly smiled at him. He'd been much more approachable since he and Sean had built that computer for him. No one would be surprised to see them talking.

And it was just a side benefit that when he got there, he'd be able to take a sideways glance at the woman at the pool table and see her face.

"How's the machine running, Luke One?"

They'd made up the teasingly affectionate nickname for him after Lucas had come along. It was part of the Rafferty number thing, he'd told the young man. Which had come down from Dad, accounting for everything from Mom's horse Seven and her dog Quinta, to the descendant of Dad's prized stallion they called Two, to his own horse Trey. And the numbered stalls that accounted for the rest of the convoluted system.

And when he'd explained Lucas was just Lucas because it already had two syllables, it had made perfect sense to Luke. And he'd decided he liked it, and liked being Luke One, like it was some honored title.

"Computer's great," Luke said.

They talked a little longer, Luke excitedly relating his progress on a new game he'd tackled, before he dutifully excused himself saying it was exactly time to make another round for used glasses. Only then did Cody risk taking that look, half hoping she'd be gone, that vision in blue.

She wasn't.

She was standing there, laughing as the two players put their best braggadocio on display. In fact, egging them on. They, on the other hand, were not too subtly admiring the cleavage shown by that damn dress. Soft, luscious curves that would make any man breathing stop that breathing for a moment.

And he could see her face now. She looked different, more dramatic, more striking, but there was no denying who she was.

Britt Roth, wowgirl.

He'd never denied she was pretty enough, and he'd heard enough from friends to know other guys—guys who hadn't grown up with the pest next door—found her attractive. Very attractive.

But he'd never, ever, been attracted to her himself. Not like that.

Determined not to even glance that way again, he headed for the food table. Although he suddenly seemed to have lost his appetite.

Chapter Nine

"WE NEED A framed copy of that for the history wall," Joey Highwater was saying to Maggie as Britt approached. They both looked and smiled at her, so she decided she wasn't an unwelcome interruption.

"I love your history wall," she said, thinking of the section of the library where Slater's wife had begun putting various objects directly connected to Last Stand's fabled history, to go along with the various books and documents she'd already collected there. Then Britt asked, "Copy of what?"

"The letter, from the Rafferty at the last stand."

Maggie nodded. "It's a wonderful idea, and we'd be proud to be there."

Britt looked at Maggie. "I've heard about that. My mom said the first time she saw it, it made her cry."

"It has the same effect on me," Maggie said.

"Me, too," Joey said. "That incredibly brave woman, writing that note to her children, even knowing that if she was right and she died in the battle, it would burn along with her body. She knew what had happened to the defenders of the Alamo."

"And then picking up her dead husband's weapon and rejoining the fight," Maggie said, and the pride that rang in her voice was unmistakable.

"Exactly as you did, in a different way," Britt said quietly.

Maggie looked startled, then pleased. "I'd like to think I have a little of her grit."

"Mom," said Keller as he came up behind her and put his hands on her shoulders, "you have all of it. Raffertys chose true. Happy birthday."

Maggie leaned back against her eldest son, smiling up at him. Britt's eyes stung a little. She was such a petite woman, yet she'd borne four big, Texas-strong sons. And every darn one of them was as beautiful as she was, in their own way.

Even the Coder.

She'd seen him, a bit ago, over talking to Luke. He was dressed up as she'd never seen him before, in a western-cut suit with piping, a crisp white shirt and a perfectly tied string tie. In fact, she'd spent a split second admiring the way the suit emphasized broad shoulders and trim waist before she'd belatedly realized who was wearing the thing.

"—have your copy?"

She belatedly tuned back into the conversation she was supposedly part of, mentally chastising herself for letting that pest distract her.

Keller was pulling out his wallet, and she watched as he

fished out a folded piece of paper.

"You carry a copy with you?" she asked, smiling in appreciation of the idea.

"We all do," Keller said, giving her a look with those green eyes that were a shade darker than Cody's. And even as she—unwillingly—thought that, he added, "It was Cody's idea to scan the original, so we could all have copies to keep with us."

She managed to stop her habitual grimace at the mention of his name. Even managed to get out what she would have said easily had it been anyone else. "Wonderful idea."

Keller grinned at her as if he'd somehow known what an effort that was for her. But when the unfolded page made it to her, she could think of nothing more than the words, written in an old-fashioned but amazingly steady hand.

My little loves,

Things are looking bad here. Your father is down, and I fear he is gone. This may well be our last stand, but we fight on. We are outnumbered, outgunned, the only hope we have now is that this Texas stone will hold. But if it does not, know that we loved you with all our hearts.

You are Texas born and bred, so I know you will survive even if we do not. Never forget that you are proud sons of this land we love. Make your own stand here, and never run. That is all that is required of a Texian.

They are circling back now, and we must be ready. If this is goodbye, my beloved boys, then so it must be. Know that you are ever and always loved.

Your mother

A Texian. Those who had been here when Texas had belonged to Mexico, and who had fought to free the land they loved. Britt's eyes stung a little as tears gathered. She herself felt like a Texan to the bone, but this…this was different. This was history, with living descendants of it standing before her.

"I'll have Cody email you a clean copy," Maggie said to Joey.

To divert her thoughts from darting down that unwanted path, Britt said the first thing that popped into her head. "You should have Ry do a leather frame for it."

Joey's brows rose. "What a brilliant idea!" Then, hesitantly, she added, "Not sure the library can afford him, though."

"He'll do it for nothing, or he'll answer to me," Maggie said firmly.

They all laughed at what Britt figured was the very idea one of her sons would dispute her seriously on anything.

"Well now, that has to be a first," Keller drawled. "Britt Roth and Cody Rafferty collaborating on an idea."

Britt gaped at him.

"Well," Maggie said thoughtfully, "they have been in the same room for a couple of hours and haven't come to blows."

"That's a collaboration in itself, isn't it?" Joey said, her tone a hair too bright.

They were teasing her. All of them. As if they found the antagonism between her and Cody a source of great amusement. And she found she didn't like that idea. But she tried for a thoughtful tone, like Maggie's, when she said, "I think for a collaboration both parties have to be aware, don't they?"

Maggie gave her a look then that she couldn't interpret at all. "You two are very aware. Of most things, anyway."

Britt had no idea what that was supposed to mean.

"Yes, strictly element and composition wise, it would be very dramatic," Kaitlyn was saying as Cody walked up to them. Leave it to those two to carry on some esoteric artistic conversation at a party. But he was smiling, because Kaitlyn had come such a long way in a short time, from the shy, almost beaten-down woman she'd been to this, a welcomed and confident member of the Raffertys. And because Ry was obviously so darned happy it fairly radiated from him.

Ry nodded at her assessment. "It would be Dorado and Flyer."

"What would?" Cody asked, wondering what Ry's own gleaming black horse and Chance's flashy palomino had to do with anything.

They both turned to look at him. "You," Kaitlyn said. He blinked.

"And Britt," Ry added, as blithely as if discussing some perfectly natural idea. Which this assuredly was not.

"Wash your mouth out," Cody said ungraciously.

"We were speaking visually, of course," Kaitlyn said. "About color contrast."

He grimaced at them both. "I don't know which of you to worry about most—you trying to get us to pose for a photo, or you doing a painting."

Kaitlyn was a brilliant photographer who could probably even make a couple as impossible as he and Roth look like they belonged. Ry could probably make them look inevitable, and he wouldn't need them to pose to do it, because he had inherited that from their father as well, that amazing memory for detail that he was able to replicate on canvas.

And you are going insane.

If this was anything other than his mother's birthday party, he'd have bailed a while ago. Like right after he'd realized the woman he'd been about to approach was Roth.

"Oh, I'd never try to get you two to pose together," Kaitlyn said. "My equipment is too expensive to replace."

"Exactly," Ry agreed. "That would be like throwing a pair of cranky pit bulls into the proverbial pit."

Cody wasn't sure how he should feel about that assessment. "How's Nick?" he asked abruptly, not caring if the subject change was obvious.

Kaitlyn smiled warmly, as she always did when the subject of her father-by-choice came up. "Great. That pacemaker has made all the difference in the world."

"I'm glad. I liked him," he said honestly.

"He's going to be after you to build him a computer," she warned, but with a smile.

He grinned at her. "We already talked about it."

She looked surprised but pleased. Then, as something across the room caught his eye, Ry leaned in a little.

"You notice Shane and Lily?" he whispered conspiratorially.

Cody's brow furrowed. "I saw them, yeah, but only to say hello and thanks for coming. Why?"

"They're joined at the hip tonight."

"Aren't they usually?" Cody said it wryly, but he had a healthy respect that he considered well earned, for Last Stand's police chief.

"Not like this," Kaitlyn said. She and Ry exchanged a glance. Damn, they were already communicating in that wordless way really together couples had, like Keller and Sydney, Chance and Ariel.

"We think they're pregnant," Kaitlyn said, in practically a whisper.

"Whoa." He blinked, scanned the room until he saw them, Shane tall, strong, and impressive, and indeed still glued to his wife's side. And even he, usually oblivious to such subtleties, had to admit there was something different there.

"Now we're trying to figure who'll be next," Ry was saying. "Slater and Joey, maybe."

"Now that'd be a brilliant kid," Cody said, turning back.

"Or," Kaitlyn said, a little too breezily, "maybe Keller and Sydney." Cody and Ry both gaped at her. "Oh, please don't tell me you haven't even thought about that possibility?"

"I…have," Ry said slowly. "But I figured they'd want to give Lucas a bit more time to get used to all the changes."

"How about giving us all time for that?" Cody said protestingly, not wanting to admit how much the idea, further proof that time was marching on, rattled him. A sudden vision of new nieces and nephews popping out all over had him wishing once again this was anything except Mom's birthday.

Because his lair had never seemed more appealing, more the place he'd rather be, than right now.

Chapter Ten

CODY WOKE UP in a rush, just as the dream hit peak hotness. He swore into the darkness and sat up.

It had taken him a long time to get to sleep last night. He'd hoped the alcohol he'd consumed would do it, since he didn't drink that much very often, but he'd still found himself pacing the floor well after midnight. A couple of rounds of the current video game in progress had only hyped him up more, and he'd ended up putting the controller down in disgust after an hour.

And he knew he wasn't going back to sleep now. Not after that too-vivid, too-haunting, and too damned arousing dream. Starring that gorgeous, compelling temptress in the blue dress.

The word that burst from him then was a bit cruder. Aimed at himself, for actually thinking the word *temptress* in conjunction with Britt Roth.

"You have freaking lost your mind, Rafferty," he muttered as he rolled out of bed. A glance at his phone on the nightstand told him it was a little after five a.m. It wouldn't even start to get light for nearly an hour and a half.

Shower and shave could kill half an hour, if he took his time. Then he could get to work on...something. Anything. Anything to get his recalcitrant brain out of this unexpected and unwanted canyon he'd taken a nosedive into.

But trying to lose himself in that game, or anything on a screen didn't feel like it would be enough. He needed something physical, to work off this edge he'd suddenly developed. He was caught up on his ranch chores, but he knew Keller could come up with something that needed doing if he asked. But if he asked, his too-wise brother was going to guess something was up, and he didn't want to have to deal with that. No, this was his problem, and he'd deal. Even if it was before the crack of dawn.

And where the heck had that phrase come from, anyway? It wasn't like the sun made a noise as it cleared the horizon. Normally he'd track that down, answer his question by diving into the internet, but he'd already decided that wasn't going to do it today. Even if he did want to know who had come up with the idea of dawn cracking.

Dawn.

That was it. In fact, he was stupid not to have thought of it before. Or tired. Or distracted. But it was perfect, because he could claim this was his plan all along, to do a test flight for the bluebonnet run. Not that it made sense to plan a dawn excursion the morning after Mom's birthday party, but hey, they couldn't prove he hadn't. And since it was for Mom in the first place, they couldn't argue with him needing to do it.

His mind was racing ahead as he jumped into his plan. He already knew the route and knew he wouldn't run into any airspace problems since a large part of the flight would be over Rafferty land, and the rest was either open space or somewhere he could check the app he'd helped write, which would get him permission in the two necessary spots. The closest airport was Devil's Rock over in Whiskey River, and he'd stay clear of any traffic from there, both distance and altitude wise.

And he'd stop thinking about that damned dream.

BRITT YAWNED. AGAIN. As she had been doing all morning. And moving slow. Too slow, because before she got out and going, her mother knocked on the door.

Britt sighed. She'd renovated and moved into the onetime bunkhouse because she needed to stay on the ranch, but she'd wanted her own quarters. And she paid rent for it, after some research on what the same-sized place in town would cost her. Her parents had protested, saying it wasn't necessary, this was her home, but she'd been determined, especially once she'd started making some decent prize money on the circuit. She'd wanted to up the amount when she'd broken three-quarters of a million last year—although a big chunk of it had been eaten up with expenses, which included the large portion earmarked for her future plans—but they'd adamantly refused.

But if she'd been after total privacy she hadn't gotten it. Telling herself it was their ranch, they could do what they wanted—and besides, she spent more time under their roof than they did under hers—she ran her fingers through her hair trying to untangle it a bit, knowing it spoke of her sleepless night. Then she went to the door and took back all her thoughts about her mother's intrusion. Because she was holding out a steaming mug of her specialty honey latte, hopefully with a big shot of espresso, made with the machine Dad had bought last year.

"Bless you," she said, taking it gratefully.

"It was a late night," her mother said. "Your father had three cups of that black sludge he drinks before he even left the house."

She wanted to both gulp the warm brew and go slowly and savor it, so compromised with long but slow sips, letting the flavor flow over her tongue.

"It was a lovely party," her mother went on.

"Yes," Britt agreed between sips. "And Maggie seemed to enjoy it."

Her mother smiled. "She's an amazing woman." Her tone shifted just slightly as she added, "Those Rafferty boys certainly clean up nicely."

And that easily the image that had caused her restless night was back. Not cowboy strong Keller, or Chance with his ramrod straight, chiseled features, or even Ry, notorious among the women of Last Stand for his wild good looks. No, what haunted her was her lifelong nemesis, who had absolutely no right to look as good as he had last night. It wasn't that she hadn't seen him dressed up before, she had at various functions, and even the Christmas ball. But somehow last night seemed…different. As if she'd never seen him, really seen him before.

Maybe it was the way he'd avoided her. Or the way she'd caught him glancing at her even as he did so. He usually just ignored her, as she did him, whenever they were required to be in the same place at the same time and other people were around. By tacit consent neither of them wanted to prod the all too efficient Last Stand grapevine by giving it something juicy to feed on.

But last night he'd been hard to ignore. The contrast of that incredibly well-fitting black suit with his blond looks was beyond striking. She was honest enough to admit that. She was even willing to admit that half the reason it looked so good was the body underneath it. After all, she'd seen him half-dressed twice lately.

And she'd had crazy dreams after those encounters, too.

"Britt?"

"What?" She refocused abruptly. "Oh. Yes, they do clean up nice."

"The bane of your existence looked especially nice."

"Mmm." She was not going to get lured into that discussion.

"I loved his suit. And I asked him how he got his string tie tied so perfectly. He said it was mostly a geometry problem."

"Well, that figures," she muttered.

Her mother laughed. "I swear, you two are enough to make me believe in predestination. You came into the world at practically the same moment, in the same hospital. The minute you saw each other in the hospital lobby, the squabble started. And you haven't been able to stand each other ever since."

Britt nearly gaped at her mother. Her parents had always told her she hated Cody at first sight, but she'd never realized they'd meant it literally.

"We met as babies in the hospital?"

Her mother's brow furrowed. "Of course. You know that. We've talked about it often enough, how Maggie and I both left the hospital at the same time."

"But you never told me it started right there in the lobby, before we even came home."

Her mother studied her for a silent moment, long enough to make Britt a little nervous. Then she said quietly, "I have. At least twice I specifically remember, when you were a child. But you have a habit of ignoring anything having to do with Cody. Obviously that started early, too."

Britt thought, searched her memory, and came up empty. "Apparently I didn't just ignore it, I erased it," she said with a grimace directed at herself. She didn't like the idea that her mother had told her this story of her birth more than once and she couldn't find a trace of it in her brain. It had been bad enough when her father had told her they purposely never mentioned him. This was worse.

And as her mother left her to ponder that—reminding her that mug had best be clean when it came back—Britt couldn't help wondering what else she'd scrubbed out of her memory.

Chapter Eleven

CONSIDERING HE'D HAD two nights of very little sleep, it went fairly well.

Which today only means I didn't crash.

Cody yawned, widely, then shook his head. Or rather, snapped it side to side to try and shake off the lingering tiredness. It worked for a few minutes.

"Up to you, Trey," he muttered to the horse. "Get us home."

The big bay snorted and shook his head almost as sharply as Cody had. But he clearly knew what the word *home* meant, because he turned that way. Cody concentrated on hanging on to the expensive device he was holding. The drone was only about seven pounds on its own, but the camera, gimbal, and other gear made the case it was now back in fairly heavy, and too big to fit into a saddlebag.

It would have been easier to do this if he could have driven, but the last half of the trek was impassable by vehicle unless he wanted to mow down exactly what he'd be trying to capture on video when those bluebonnets finally showed up.

He could have chosen an easier route for the drone, but he had it set in his mind what he wanted, especially the ending. He wanted it to make that last turn around the stone outcropping, where it would go from a long trail of the vivid blooms to a vast, impossible explosion of them in every direction, as far as the eye—and camera—could see. The trick would be timing, to catch the sunrise at the exact moment when the blue of the flowers was almost exactly the same color as the gradually lightening sky. He'd come out and time that a day ahead. Then he would keep recording until the sun cleared the horizon or he ran out of flowers—like that would happen in the Hill Country in bluebonnet season—or battery.

He grimaced at the thought as Trey picked his way down the slope, occasionally sending a pebble rolling. That had been the holy grail for him for so long, to come up with a longer flight time, allowing longer distances on battery. Silent running, as it were. Some called it his obsession. Maybe it had been. But he'd turned a corner after that con in Dallas, when Gwen had wisely said to him that he needed to give up on the possibility it would happen tomorrow. That it should be a life goal, not a next week goal.

Or if he wouldn't listen to her, she'd added with an impish grin, he should listen to Bruce Lee—they had just seen a tribute to the martial arts star at the con—who'd once said a goal wasn't always meant to be reached, that it often served simply as something to aim at.

He'd often wondered if the fact that Gwen was already staring death in the face at an age where most were planning their futures was what had made her so wise. She'd told him the only reason she'd allowed him into her heart and mind was because he knew. Knew about death and forever. Understood that one weekend was all they would ever have, because she would not allow them any more, wouldn't let him fall in love and lose again, or herself to have one more person to leave behind.

So, he'd lost the rock of his life, and a big might-have-been. And even today, two decades after his father's death, and nearly five years since Gwen's, he occasionally felt the bitterness try to rise, that the man who had been one of the pillars of his life, and the girl who could have become another, had both been taken from him. And only something else she had said, about how bitterness only hurt the person who felt it, kept him from sinking into a morass full of it.

He was lost in thought—as he so often was—when Trey nickered. Cody came back to his surroundings and realized with a little jolt that they'd crested the last rise and he could see the ranch house in the distance.

Rolling his eyes at himself, he leaned down to pat the big bay's neck. "I'd be dead by now without you, buddy."

The jovial horse gave a snort then, a sound Cody could only interpret as agreement. The animal picked up the pace a little from the leisurely stroll, although since he'd been given no command he remained at a walk, just a little more energetic one now that home was in sight. For both of them, since now that they'd gone down the rise far enough, the barn was in sight as well.

Home sweet home.

Some people raised an eyebrow at him when they learned he still lived if not in, then connected to his mother's home. He dismissed them easily; clearly they hadn't grown up on a family ranch. He was a Rafferty, and this was the Rafferty place. To him it was self-explanatory. Even at college, when people had been discussing where they were going to live and start their future, it had never occurred to him that he might live somewhere else. He had always intended to go home. Most of his classmates thought he was weird for that. Or as one particularly snobby one had said, provincial. He hadn't cared, but he'd gotten tired enough of the reaction to point out that he'd done his homework, that he'd researched how much it would cost him to live elsewhere with the same amount of space and the same benefits, and it made no financial sense to leave.

Of course, as soon as he started making enough money to pay for a different place he was even more settled here. With his side gigs and the setup in his lair, he'd be crazy to leave. Not to mention trying to duplicate it all somewhere else. So instead he put what he would be paying, plus a little more for food and incidentals he sometimes "borrowed," into the ranch kitty, just as his brothers did. Well, except for

Keller, who simply didn't take a salary for the incredible amount of work he put in. Given the current rates for ranch managers, he was probably contributing the most of any of them.

It worked for all of them. And they had the added benefit of being all together, but not on top of each other. He loved his brothers, but they were all so different it would be tough trying to live under the same roof. So they lived on the same land, and it worked.

They were down on the flat now, and he headed the horse toward the house. He'd get the drone put away, and the footage downloaded later. Right now he was thankful enough for Trey's intelligence and calmness that he decided a treat was in order, and there was nothing the big bay loved more than a bath.

He rode over to the house first to get the case with the drone back inside. He tossed the reins over the hitching rail near the front door, knowing Trey would then consider himself anchored. The itch to at least take a look at the video was there, but he knew if he started he'd get sucked in and Trey was his priority at the moment.

He toed off his boots and grabbed the rubber ones they all had for just this purpose. He also shucked his shirt, since half the reason the horse loved baths was that he loved to splash the water back at him. If it had been a little warmer he would have just gone for swimming trunks and be done with it. But it was rather chilly—by Texas standards—today, as winter and spring carried on their annual give and take.

When he came back outside Trey's head came up. "Come on, buddy, let's get that ol' saddle off and then a bath, hmm?"

He'd swear the horse's eyes lit up. And he was sure that bob of his head was a nod. He laughed, and the world seemed a little brighter.

He got Trey unsaddled and traded the bridle for a halter and lead rope. Then he led the bay over to the wash rack, thinking that for all the ragging he got about he and Chance's Dorado being a better match, it was a good thing his mother had had the wisdom to put the kibosh on that. Dorado might match his hair, but the strong-willed palomino needed a steadfast, always alert, ready-for-anything hand, and that was Chance, not him.

No, Trey was the perfect horse for him, and he deserved a little pampering now and then. So he'd make it a nice long bath.

Even knowing he'd end up as wet as the horse.

TECHNICALLY, BRITT THOUGHT, she was trespassing. Not that it had ever been an issue between the Roths and the Raffertys. They were, as her parents often said, the best kind of neighbors, the kind that were welcoming, and always there if you needed help, but never tried to mind your business for you. And they didn't hold it against the Roths that they had been on this land for less than a century, while the Raffertys had been here nearly two.

Nugget sidestepped carefully to close the gate, the one in the main fence line between the two ranches. She'd ridden the gelding, her primary barrel horse before Ghost had turned out to be such a treasure, just in case Cody was playing with one of his toys. Nugget had done well enough, but the better-natured gelding didn't have the aggressive edge Ghost did in competition, and seemed just as happy, if not happier, doing ranch chores. She'd prefer to ride Ghost, but she couldn't risk the horse reacting crazily to one of the flying pests and getting hurt this close to the start of her rodeo season. Besides, Ghost would never do what Nugget was doing, allowing her to simply reach down and refasten the gate without having to dismount.

A phone call or text, of course, would have been easier, but she knew Cody would never answer her. She had the feeling he had her blocked, or at least muted. No surprise, since she'd muted him long ago, despite her mother pointing out what an unneighborly thing that was to do, in the sense that neighbors might one day need help or vice versa.

She could have called his mom, but that seemed like cheating. Besides, she remembered Maggie's words to her beloved Aussie as she'd left them last week.

I love you too much to leave you with these two adolescent adversaries.

Adolescent? That had grated. Because deep down she had the niggling feeling there was a little truth to it.

Okay, maybe more than a little.

She sighed, trying to shake off those thoughts as she rode. She should be focused on the upcoming season, which for her would start right after the Bluebonnet Festival, just over three weeks away. Last year they'd won in Abilene, San Angelo, and San Antonio, taken second a half-dozen other places, and turned in their best time ever at the National Finals Rodeo. Despite the fact that she wasn't manic about hitting every possible competition within reach, she had nearly doubled her yearly winnings since she'd started with Ghost—the horse was that good. She wanted at least ten more years of competing on her career history. If this kept up, the mare was going to put down some great numbers on that résumé.

Which, she figured, was worth the slightly deranged skittishness outside the arena.

For a moment she let herself think about that future she was working toward. Breeding and raising barrel horses, training them for herself and others, and maybe even someday running a school of sorts, teaching kids the sport she loved. All the possibilities in this world she so loved spun out in her mind, seemingly endless, and she felt a pang of sympathy for all the people who were stuck in jobs they hated or work that had grown boring.

It seemed so bright in that moment that she didn't even

mind what she was doing right now, going to talk to the one person in that world she always tried to avoid. Even Cody Rafferty couldn't rattle her now.

She was approaching the big barn, which sat next to the smaller one where she knew Ry now had his studio. She heard a horse whinny, a happy sound, and wondered if somebody had just gotten fed.

She rounded the corner and realized it wasn't food but a bath that had the horse so pleased. Some horses were like that, and this one was so obviously enjoying the water it made her smile.

Belatedly, she recognized the big bay. And as the animal moved its head, with the clear intent of splashing the man holding the hose, she could see that man.

He was laughing, in a way that lit up his face, and she'd swear she could see those bright green eyes alight from here. And he was holding the hose in a way that actually made it easier for the delighted horse to deflect water right at him.

He was soaking wet already.

And shirtless. Again.

She stared at him, at the way the water made every taut muscle stand out, the way those shoulders, those abs rippled as he moved. He glistened in the pre-spring sunshine, and she suddenly envied those lucky drops of water.

She hated her own reaction. It shouldn't be happening. She hated the guy. But she couldn't deny the beauty of the sight before her.

Nugget tossed his head in protest, and she realized she'd unconsciously tightened the reins.

Had she really just thought Cody Rafferty couldn't rattle her?

Chapter Twelve

WHAT THE HELL was she doing here again?

Cody lowered the hose, frowning as the woman on the palomino horse approached. With a wide white blaze and four white stockings that came all the way up to the knees, it was a pretty horse. Not as flashy as Dorado, a more muted gold, but very eye-catching. Nothing to do with the rider, he assured himself.

Trey had turned his head to look at the duo as well, otherwise he'd likely be protesting the end of the fun. The actual cleaning part of the bath had been done a few minutes ago; they'd only been playing now. The part the big horse liked best. And if he was honest, the part he liked best as well. It made him smile to see the horse who looked out for him so well having so much fun.

For a moment he considered just keeping the water turned on. In case he needed a weapon of sorts. He settled for leaving it on but letting the pistol-style nozzle cut off the flow. He watched warily as the pair came to a halt just a couple of feet away. At least she wasn't riding the crazy grullo. But he barely noticed that. Her hair was in a thick, long, loose braid that came down in front of her left shoulder. She was wearing her usual jeans, and today a long-sleeved T-shirt in a bright blue that nearly matched her eyes.

And matched that dress. That damned dress.

Britt Roth, wowgirl.

She didn't dismount. He should be relieved, since it likely meant she wasn't going to be here for long. Instead he felt even more wary. Especially given the way she was staring at him, as if she wasn't quite sure what species he was.

"If you shot down another one, it wasn't mine," he said when time spun out and she didn't speak.

To his surprise he thought he saw a touch of color in her cheeks. "I didn't. But that's what I came about."

"What?"

"You going to cash that check, or what?"

Ah. Now he had a reason, and his wariness eased a bit. She wasn't here on some stealth mission to make his life miserable. Well, no more than usual, anyway. Although his answer was likely to set her off.

"Nope," he said.

She frowned. "What?"

"You asked, I answered," he said in his most reasonable tone.

"You're not going to cash it?"

"Nope," he said again, barely managing not to smile, knowing it was getting to her. But it was difficult. He felt so relieved that they were back into their usual parrying, fencing with words and attitude, it was almost as if the party had never happened.

Or at least, it hadn't changed anything.

Of course, the nights he'd spent fighting off dreams about that blue dress slipping off of her had certainly changed his sleeping habits. To nonexistent, mostly.

"What'd you do? Lose it?"

See, it's fine, we're back to insults. "Nope," he said a third time, and she rolled her eyes. Deciding that was mission accomplished, he elaborated. "It's pinned on my corkboard."

She blinked. Finally, her brow furrowed again, she asked, "Why?"

This oughta do it. "Because I like seeing it. I think I'm going to frame it and hang it on my wall permanently."

Her dark, arched brows shot upward. "Frame it?"

"Yep."

Her expression cleared. Not to a friendly one, but to one of understanding. "So you just like the reminder that I had to write it."

"Yep."

"That check is for almost a thousand dollars."

He grinned at her; her tone had gotten edgy. This was the Britt he was used to. "Yep." There, that canceled out the three nopes.

She shifted in the saddle. He was just deciding he didn't really like looking up at her like this. Just as he didn't like the way she'd looked him up and down when she'd ridden up here; he knew he probably looked ridiculous, soaking wet head to toe from playing with a horse who liked to splash.

"So I'm supposed to just ignore the fact that you have a big check from me that you could decide to cash at any moment and put me in a bind?"

He barely managed to stifle a frown of his own. He hadn't actually thought about that aspect. He'd been too busy enjoying looking at the thing and remembering her expression when she'd had to write it. He felt a twinge, an echo of that feeling he'd gotten way back when he'd used someone else to get back at her for whatever thing she'd done to him. Like he'd crossed some invisible line he shouldn't have.

He supposed he could tell her he'd never cash it. It would be worth it to him. He was enjoying having that thing in view, knowing she'd had to pay for at least one of her crazy harassment episodes. And he didn't really need the money.

Which made him wonder, if she'd been winning so much money on the circuit, why a check under a grand would put her in a bind.

"I thought you were rolling in it, Roth, now that you're racing the crazy Ghost."

"That money is invested, for the future. And she's not crazy, she's just...spirited." He snorted out a laugh. "She's not," she said, her voice sharp now as she defended her horse. "What makes her difficult outside the arena is what makes her nearly unbeatable in it. She knows what her job is, and she's the best at it, so she's allowed a little…eccentricity in her off time."

"Eccentricity? Is that what you call it?"

Suddenly her tone was sweet. Too sweet. "What do you call a horse that likes you to take a bath with him?"

"Friendly," he shot back.

She gave him a thoughtful look he knew was pure mockery. "Well, at least one of you is. Cash the damn check, Rafferty."

She reined the palomino around and left without another word. And Cody stood there, hose in hand, wishing he'd unleashed a spray of water at her.

Except then an image of what she'd look like with that T-shirt as wet as he was formed in his mind, along with thoughts of who else he'd like to take a bath with.

He turned the hose on himself instead, certain he was flat flipping losing his mind.

Later, when he had Trey as dry as he could manage and back in his stall, with a bit of apple to top off the day, he headed inside. He was still soaking wet and had picked up enough dirt with the bottom of his jeans that he was probably trailing mud. That wouldn't go over well. He probably should have headed around and used his own back door rather than trek through the main house. Mom wouldn't appreciate muddy streaks all over her clean floor.

But he was already committed, so instead he stopped inside the front door and peeled off the wet jeans. Maybe he'd just throw them in the washing machine as he passed. He could—

"Is this where I'm glad you don't go commando?"

He spun around, startled. Mom had gotten home from her latest meeting. She was grinning at him, but still he instinctively held the wet jeans in front of himself because his knit boxers weren't much drier. Yes, she was his mother, had seen all there was to see over the years, but it was still embarrassing.

"I...sorry, didn't know you were home."

"Obviously."

"I didn't want to get dirt on the floor."

"Points for that," she said. The teasing grin became a warm smile. "And watching you and Trey having so much fun would be worth a little dirt."

"He's the best," he said with a smile. "I did a test run for the video this morning. I think it'll work."

"Like you planned, a continuous shot?"

He nodded, feeling a spark of the familiar excitement. "When I get it downloaded and set up, you want to come see what you think? You'll have to picture what it will look like with the flowers, but it'll give you an idea."

"I'd love to," she said, with an even wider smile.

He headed back to his lair. When he'd changed into dry clothes, he settled in to download the video he'd taken. He called it up and ran it on his biggest monitor; when Mom got here, he'd mirror it to the big screen on the far wall.

As he watched he occasionally made a time marker to note where he wanted to slightly adjust the course, but overall it was almost exactly what he wanted. And right now he was satisfied that the retractable landing gear had worked flawlessly, as had the remote control and the obstacle-avoidance system. With a video resolution of a little over 5K, he thought it was going to be amazing.

The only thing missing was the freaking flowers. And that was totally out of his control.

Some things only happen when they happen, son. You can't force them or hurry them.

He and Dad had been talking about his impatience waiting for a mare to foal. The baby would be an offspring of his father's beloved buckskin, Buckshot. She would later have a foal of her own, who would in turn have another, and finally result in the rangy, athletic colt even now out in one of the big corrals who was the spitting image of his great-grandsire down to the white blaze that ran crookedly over his nose.

He was sure Dad would have said the same thing about the blessed bluebonnets. They happen when they happen. In fact, now that the connection formed in his mind, he thought maybe he had heard him say it. It was hard for him to tell sometimes.

Sometimes memories got tangled up with wishes and he wasn't certain which was which.

Chapter Thirteen

GHOST ROUNDED THE third barrel at what seemed like an impossible angle, then blasted out the other side and sprinted for the arena gate. It felt good, it felt fast. When her friend Jen let out a whoop from where she sat on the fence with a stopwatch, Britt knew she was right.

The grullo danced sideways the moment they were clear of the gate. The horse clearly knew, in that twisted little brain of hers, that she'd done well. She also knew the minute she was through that gate her work was done, at least for the moment. It was as if she could count and knew that Britt had said, "Just three runs today, girl. Just to keep in form."

She wanted the horse fit, but also a bit pent up, so that when official competition began she'd be explosive. So, it was lots of riding the ranch for the exercise, but not a lot of time in the arena. Which made it harder on her, because the minute they were out of the arena, Ghost reverted to her tap-dancing, spooking-at-gnats self. Just as she did right now.

But Britt was ready for her. The only question was which way the mare would skitter. In this case it was to the right, toward Jen.

"Sixteen-seven," Jen called. "Not bad for a practice run on a standard course."

"And I wasn't really pushing her," Britt said happily as she reined Ghost in beside the fence.

"I could see that. She's amazing, Britt."

"I know."

"Of course, she's also bat-shit crazy," Jen added with a grin.

"Yeah, well. There's always a price." Britt's mouth quirked wryly.

Now that they'd taken the edge off, she and Jen had planned a ride around the ranch. Jen hadn't been here in a while, and while she was here for the weekend, she'd told Britt she wanted to take advantage of the wide-open spaces she didn't have at her smaller place out near Waco.

She waited while Jen saddled up Nugget. Once mounted, Jen looked over at her. "Need to ride fence?"

Britt grimaced. "No."

Jen's brows rose. "What was that look for?"

Because it was Jen and she never lied to her, she sighed and told her the sorry tale of the downed drone. And because it was Jen, she told it all. Jen burst out laughing before she'd even finished.

"So how is Ghost's godfather?"

Britt grimaced again. Jen had coined the joking term long ago and insisted on continuing to use it. Britt saw the point, could even admit that in a certain sense it was true, but that didn't mean she liked it.

"As big a pain as ever," she said.

But suddenly an image from her visit to the Rafferty place two days ago shot through her mind yet again. Cody, soaking wet and glistening in the pre-spring Texas sun, grinning as he played—there was no other word for it—with the equally wet horse. It wasn't just that he was quite a sight for feminine eyes, because he certainly was that. But there was something about that grin, the pure happiness in it…she couldn't doubt he genuinely loved that horse.

And that had surprised her. She'd always thought he was so into his tech crap he didn't have much left for the ranch life she loved.

She'd also found herself thinking as she'd watched the playful pair, she'd never seen him look so…light. Carefree. As if the rest of the time he wasn't like that. As if the rest of the time he was shadowed somehow, despite the light green of his eyes and the blond of his hair.

They all carry the weight of losing Kyle, honey.

The words her mother had spoken long ago, just a couple of years after the dreaded news had come, when the child she'd been had asked why the Raffertys were never happy anymore, came back to her suddenly.

She'd had a hard time understanding, back then. She still had no idea what it was really like; imagining the tragedy of losing either of her parents even now was horrible, thinking what it would have been like at age nine was beyond her. Or at Lucas's age, when he'd lost both parents at once in a car crash. She couldn't even picture that much awfulness.

When Cody had broken the truce with that painted target on old Champ's butt, she'd been a child, young enough and foolish enough to think that meant he was done with the grieving.

Now she knew better. Knew it was never done.

Geeze, I'm feeling sorry for him.

She gave herself a sharp inward shake. This had to stop. It was throwing her whole world off-kilter, all these crazy thoughts about her lifetime enemy. But then, there were all the new things, things she hadn't known about him before, things no one had dared tell her for fear of setting her off. And that bothered her in a different way.

She smothered a sigh. Maybe she should have planned to start her season on the circuit a little earlier. If she hadn't promised Mom to stay home through the Bluebonnet Festival…

Running now, Roth? From Cody the Coder, of all people?

Exasperation, aimed at herself, flooded through her. With more effort—much more—than it should have taken, she shoved him out of her mind, and turned back to what she should be paying attention to, her best friend's visit.

Cody the Coder would, annoyingly, be there later.

SUNDAY EVENING, AS they were all gathered for dinner

around the Rafferty table, Mom looked at him over her last cup of coffee. "I saw Shane in town today, and he said that spot on their place erupted last Thursday."

Cody felt a release of tension. They all knew that one spot on the Highwater ranch was the harbinger of the season, although nobody quite knew why. But if the bluebonnets were popping there, they'd be out in force everywhere a few days later. Which meant right about now.

"I noticed a few at the far end of the dogs' enclosure a couple of days ago," Ariel said with a smile.

"Then they're definitely arriving," Keller said. "I'll ride out and take a look along your course in the morning. I need to head out that way anyway, see if I can track down that surly old cow and her calf."

"Take Quinta," Mom said, reaching down to pet her beloved Aussie. "If those two are to be found, she'll do it."

"I'll do that," Keller agreed, then looked back at Cody. "And I'll let you know how it looks."

"Excellent," Cody said. "I've got a fence run to do over in Whiskey River tomorrow, at the Kelly ranch, so I'll watch for them there, too."

"Kelly as in Kelly Boots?" Chance asked as he set down his now-empty mug.

"And champion quarter horses." Cody grinned. "I'm moving up in the world."

"Indeed," Keller said with a smile Cody would have sworn was proud. Which made him feel...he wasn't sure what. Maybe a bit of what he felt when he thought of what Keller had done, what he'd given up to come home and help Mom hold this family together. It took him a moment to go on.

"If they pop and the weather holds, I'll do the video run Tuesday morning."

Mom nodded. "If it's all right—and I vow I'll stay out of your way—I'd love to come along and see how you do it. So I can talk it up better to the committee. Although I'd do that anyway, I'm so proud of my boy."

It practically rang in her voice, the truth of her words. When he'd been a kid his response would have been something like, "Yeah, yeah, stop, you're embarrassing me." But that was before. Now, his reaction was different.

"Love you, too, Mom." Then he grinned at her. "Sure, come along. You can help carry gear."

She laughed, and yet again he counted himself, and all his brothers, as lucky their father had chosen her to be the mother of his children.

Late Monday morning, as he watched the video on the remote control and saw the profusion of brand-new blooms on and around the sprawling Kelly ranch, he knew it was definitely time. Tomorrow morning. Luckily, not much of a moon left. He'd have to check the weather, hoping for clear. Then the exact time of sunrise for the location, by latitude and longitude. He wanted to be there before astronomical twilight so he could gauge when to actually start, to get the combined effect of the matching blue of the flowers and the sky, and then the sun clearing the horizon and flooding hill and valley, lighting up the covering of the flowers that meant Texas.

When he passed on the good news of no fence issues on the Kelly place, he turned to the next task. A quick search told him he was looking at 6:17 a.m. for the start of twilight, with true sunrise at 7:37.

He wondered if Mom would be up for a pre-dawn ride, or would decide she didn't want to. He nearly laughed at his own thought. If he knew her, she'd be up and ready before he was. He headed back into the house to let her know what time they were talking about. When he got to the kitchen Kaitlyn was also there, over at the coffee machine. When she saw him, she smiled. They'd gotten along wonderfully from the first time they'd met.

"Hi," she said as she gestured toward him with the coffeepot in query.

"Yes, thanks," he said.

Kaitlyn got a mug, filled it and held it out to him. He took it and walked over to his mother.

"You sure you want to do this?" he asked. "It's going to have to be early. And it'll be tricky."

"Before sunrise, you said?" she asked.

"Yes. I mean, the tricky part isn't sunrise, that'll be when it'll be, obviously. The tricky part is going to be getting the exact timing I want. When the sky is just the right shade of blue, that night-heading-for-morning shade that matches the blue of the flowers."

His mother lifted a brow at him. Ry did, too. "That was quite a description, my tech-headed bro." He shot his teasing brother a mock-nasty look. "Developing an artistic sensibility?" Ry asked, undaunted.

"No."

"Then why so picky about—"

"Because," Kaitlyn interrupted him, but her voice was soft, "he wants to capture that amazing effect." As she said it, she nodded toward the large painting that hung on the wall in the big room.

Ry's eyes widened, then he smiled at Kaitlyn, with a warmth that seemed to fill the room. Mom just kept looking at Cody, but now with understanding, and that gentle, unfailing, ever-present love in her bright eyes.

Cody had known the minute Kaitlyn had said the words that she, with her photographer's eye, had been right. It hadn't been a conscious thing, he hadn't looked at the painting and decided that was his goal, it had simply been there in his brain all along, that this was the way the video should look.

He lowered his gaze to the plan outlined on his phone, not knowing what to say and doubtful he could speak anyway.

Then Mom shattered the mood, either unintentionally or on purpose. "You'd better let the Roths know. Particularly

Britt, in case she's out early with Ghost."

His head came up instantly. "We won't be on their property."

"But we'll be close enough that silly horse could take a notion," Mom said. And somehow hearing her disparage Britt's precious Ghost lightened his mood.

"I'll call them," he promised her, since it did seem only neighborly.

But not Britt. He wasn't about to end up having to actually speak to her; that had happened too much recently. So, he'd send a text warning.

And if she didn't see it, so be it.

Chapter Fourteen

"You're not heading out to the east side this morning, right?"

Britt covered a yawn before answering her father; it was still pitch-black out, so she assumed he meant later. Then again, the man was up well before dawn most days, so who knew?

"Wasn't planning on it," she said.

"Good. Glad to see you're resisting temptation."

It was way too early in the morning to figure out one of her dad's subtleties. "I don't find anything tempting this hour of the morning."

She wouldn't be up at all if her sleep hadn't gone all haywire for the last week. But since she was up, she was going to go over her planning for both this rodeo season, and her list of people she wanted to touch base with on the circuit. People who might be able to help her on her way to her goal, either with potential breeding stock or simply information. She loved what she did, and the thrill of a good run was unmatched in her view, but she had to look ahead, too. There weren't a lot of fifty-year-old barrel racers out there still competing.

Then, through the sleepy fog, she finally thought to ask, "Resisting what temptation?"

"The temptation to go out and harass Cody while he's working," her mother said as she came into the kitchen and headed for the coffeepot.

She blinked. "What?"

"Didn't you get his message? He said he'd texted."

She pulled her phone out of her pocket and looked at it blearily. She had to open the app and hunt down his name, but didn't say anything about that, not really wanting her parents to know she'd muted him. He was still on the contact list in case of emergency anyway. She hated the guy, but not enough to risk the ranch or her horses. She knew if something happened close by, like a fire or flooding, he likely would be the one to let the neighbors know about it. And her parents weren't always here, after all.

With a reluctant sigh, she unmuted him as she called up the contact, then looked at the conversation list. There wasn't much to go through under his name, obviously, so she quickly found the short, blunt message.

Video flyover near NW boundary Tuesday morning starting before sunrise. Stay away.

Well, that was tactful. Not.

"Nice of him to let us know, wasn't it?" her father said.

Britt thought he was asking her so grabbed a swallow of coffee so she couldn't answer. But then her mother was answering blithely as she sat down at the kitchen table, "So good to have good neighbors. And he's such a sweet boy."

Britt almost choked on her swallow of coffee. *Sweet?*

Sweet.

Cody Rafferty.

She escaped with her coffee before she said something stupid. Like that Cody Rafferty was anything but a boy. He was one hundred percent man, and a Texas man at that.

And she had the bare-chested images infecting her brain to prove it.

CODY HEARD HIS mother take in a breath as she watched the screen on the drone remote. He smiled; it was working even better than he'd envisioned so far. He'd started a little farther out than he'd initially planned because they'd found a spot that had sprouted more flowers than usual, and happened to be where the slowly brightening sky sent the faintest bit of light through a couple of outcroppings, given just a hint of what was to come as the camera flew by. If he didn't like how it turned out, he could edit it to start when he'd originally planned.

He guided the agile little craft he called Vid—for obvious reasons—around an outcropping, careful not to go too fast so that, as his mother had pointed out, they didn't make motion-sensitive people airsick by proxy.

"Let me know if you see anything to worry about."

"Like?" Mom asked.

"Like a hawk deciding to take on the invader," he said, his mouth twisting at one corner.

"All right." There was a moment of silence before she said, "Not worried about the champion next door?"

Champion.

He bit back a retort because it would have been something about smug arrogance, and even he knew that didn't apply when you could back it up. And Roth could. She had come home a national champion two years in a row, and she'd finished respectably every year before that since she'd started professionally.

"She'll be a world champion before she's through," his mother predicted.

"Mmm," he muttered noncommittally.

His mother just smiled at him, but stayed quiet now, as she'd promised she would once it got close.

He kept his gaze fastened on the remote screen. The sky was getting slowly lighter, that moment he wanted to capture nearer. Timing. It was all timing… He looked at the timer he'd clipped onto the remote, counting down the seconds before his best calculations told him the sun would be close enough to rising that those colors would match.

He remembered Kaitlyn's quick, knowledgeable assessment of what he was trying for, and why. Ry had gotten lucky there. But then, so had Chance, and then some. And, he admitted, Keller. Despite his own efforts. He'd disliked

Sydney the moment she'd shown up. And he'd let it show, hoping she'd give up and go back to her life on the road.

She hadn't.

He knew now how grossly he'd underestimated the woman who'd fallen for his oldest brother. It had taken their mother to gently explain to him why he'd reacted that way, that Sydney represented change, for all of them. Cleverly, she'd put it in the terms of an operating system on one of his computers, saying change was going to happen whether he liked it or not, and if he resisted, he'd just get left behind.

Not all change is bad, bro.

Keller's own wise words echoed in his mind. He couldn't deny them, especially now that he saw responsible Keller as happy as he deserved to be, haunted Chance stepping back into the light, and wildfire Rylan channeled and steady.

The warning chime went off on the timer, snapping him out of the uncharacteristic reverie. Not that he didn't get lost in his thoughts—he did that all the time. It's just that they weren't usually about personal things.

He double-checked where the drone was, gauged the sky, and decided he needed one more second before he made the big turn. He'd worked that into his plan if necessary and sent the drone on a small loop toward the oak that grew just before the outcropping; there were enough blooms to make it reasonable, and in fact, now that he thought about it, it might be more impactful to see the smaller patch before…he zeroed in, concentrating fully now, counting down in his head as the timer ticked. Not too fast, he chanted to himself. Nice, slow sweep.

Three…two…one…now!

He nudged the control, starting the arc. Counted the seconds as the scene in his hands segued from near black to the deep blue that blended the distant, flower-covered hills with the horizon. Then the seconds as the sky got lighter, hinting at what was to come.

And then it happened. The rim of the sun appeared. It poured golden light over the horizon. And in that moment, it seemed as if there had been a true eruption, with massive rivers of blue blossoms pouring over the hills, pools of them gathering in the hollows between. It looked endless, unfathomable.

He flew the drone on and on, careful to be at the exact place he'd chosen before sending it on another slow, arcing turn. This time it was to the right, and when the course was set and straight, the buildings of Last Stand were visible in the distance. Making sure the bluebonnets were on screen all the way, he sent the drone along the road—that had been the permission required part—until it reached the city limits marker, the big stone with the name Last Stand carved into it. And then he sent the drone upward for its final bow, an in place, three-sixty-degree turn that showed the fields of blue stretching out around the entire town.

He gave it as long as he could and leave it enough juice to get at least back on Rafferty land. That extra loop, and the extended hover had eaten it down to the bone. The bane of his existence, the limitations of distance while maintaining silence. But the sound of a fueled motor would have been more work to remove from the result than it was worth.

"Mom? Looks like there's just enough to get over the line. I'll have to land it out in the west quadrant. Could you text Chance—no, Ariel, since she's more likely to have her phone on her—and let them know it's incoming?"

"Of course. And bless Ariel for that," she added as she pulled out her own phone.

He brought it down gently, marked the coordinates, and took his first full, deep breath since he'd started. He made sure the video was saved properly, already thinking ahead to the download and big-screen viewing. He was almost positive he had it, just like Mom had wanted. And that had him smiling.

And he was still smiling when Trey snorted and gave a head shake that rattled his bridle. Cody spun around, wondering if some dangerous creature had snuck up on them while he was so engrossed.

One had.

Roth.

Chapter Fifteen

BRITT HESITATED, BUT Maggie Rafferty waved her over. Cody was still gaping at her as if she'd risen up out of the earth. Just to be safe, and perhaps head off an attack from him, she slid off Nugget a good twenty yards away, ground-tying the cooperative gelding.

She wasn't even sure why she was here. Wasn't sure why, when the sun was well and truly risen, she'd gotten this wild hair to ride over and see how it had gone. She'd told herself she was merely curious. But she'd find out when the final promo for the festival went live. She'd told herself it was to make sure it was done and one of those infernal devices wouldn't be buzzing the boundary the rest of the day. But she could have accomplished that with a phone call to Maggie.

Maggie. Maybe that was it. That at least made sense. Yes, it had to be because Maggie was going to be there. The Bluebonnet Festival was her baby; she was deeply involved. And Britt liked and respected Maggie, a lot. Even if she had birthed her nemesis.

She walked up the rise toward where they were standing.

Cody had turned away, the control for his infernal device still in his hands. He didn't quite turn his back on her, but close.

"—nice of her to be so careful, don't you think?" Maggie was saying cheerfully as she approached. Cody grunted something typically male and utterly noncommittal.

Maggie turned to look at her, giving her a big smile. "I think it's going to be wonderful," she said. "Just perfect."

"It's a beautiful spot for it," Britt said.

She'd had a feeling, since his text had narrowed it to the northwest boundary, that this particular spot would be where they were. This spot that was preserved in full, brilliant color on their living room wall.

"Cody had it planned out perfectly," Maggie said. "He timed it exactly to hit this spot with the sunrise, and with the blue of the sky and the flowers…well, I can't describe the result, but it's magnificent."

Britt couldn't help but notice that, even though he didn't look over, appearing fixated on the device in his hands, Cody smiled at that. So, he was pleased with the results. Or his mother's praise. Or both.

"So your promo video for the festival will be set?" she asked Maggie.

"Yes. And if it's as wonderful as I think it is, we'll be using it every year for a long time."

"Hey," Cody said with a sideways look at his mother, "if you're going to use it every year, the price is going up."

He charged his mother?

Even as she thought it, Maggie laughed. "Okay, two weeks of me fixing you dinner, then."

Cody grinned suddenly. His strikingly light green eyes seemed to flash in the morning sunlight that gilded his blond hair. The effect was devastating. That was so not fair.

Britt shook off her reaction and focused on the simple fact that there was no denying every one of the Rafferty boys adored this petite, blond woman with the pixie haircut.

If you want to know how a man will treat his wife, watch how he treats his mother.

The old saw rang in her mind before she could stop it. She had no idea why. Because how Cody Rafferty might someday treat the woman crazy enough to marry him was no concern of hers.

Maggie turned back to Britt. "You should come over for the unveiling, as it were. Your folks are coming, come with them."

She heard a strangely strangled sound from Cody. "I doubt the video maker would want me there," she said dryly.

"But I'm paying the bill for that video, so I can invite who I wish," Maggie said airily.

"Dinner for two weeks?" Britt asked, the corner of her mouth twitching.

"If you'd ever eaten his cooking," Maggie said in a quite audible stage whisper, "you'd know it's a worthy price. Barely edible. You can't imagine."

"I'm afraid I probably can," Britt admitted with a rueful laugh. "Because I'm awful in the kitchen."

Cody gave her a quick glance, as if she'd surprised him by admitting to anything in common with him. Understandable, she supposed. But it was the truth; she sucked at cooking. She could fix, like grill a steak or make a great salad, but actually cook? Except for Mom's meat loaf, not happening.

Besides, she wasn't about to get into one of their usual spitting matches in front of his mother.

"Then you should come for dinner as well," Maggie said.

"You don't have to do that. I only rode over now to see if you were done, and the UFOs would all be on the ground."

Cody gave her a longer look that time. "They're not unidentified."

"The U stands for unsightly, in this case," she said sweetly. "Or just plain ugly."

"You two," Maggie said with a shake of her head, and Britt wasn't sure if she was only pretending exasperation or seriously feeling it. She went on briskly enough that Britt decided she'd been putting it on. Mostly. "Cody says it will only take a day or two to put it all together now that he has the aerial video, so we're going test run it on the big screen Friday evening. The whole family will be there, so you might as well come."

Britt smiled at the obviousness of her pointing out there would be plenty of…insulation around in the form of family members. Which Britt knew to Maggie included Sydney, Ariel, and Kaitlyn. And of course, Lucas.

"Unless you have plans, of course," Maggie added, one brow raised. "Friday night and all."

Friday night. Date night. Right. As if. Who had time—or the patience—for that? Her dating life had ended with that short connection with Wayne Matthews, which had ended amicably enough when he'd walked away, saying he felt like the abandoned party in that Garth Brooks song about rodeo. She hadn't been angry or even hurt much, which she supposed was a sign; Wayne was a good guy, but her first love was indeed her career. And that had been…

Her brain did the math but couldn't accept the result. A year and four months? Had it really been that long? She worked it out again. Same result. That was a bit much, even for her. She might have to be a bit more open to possibilities this year on the circuit. But truth be told, those usually ended up a quick hookup, and that wasn't her. She didn't mind going in knowing it wouldn't be serious, but it would be nice if it at least lasted the season. She wanted the stability.

Or you just don't want to have to search for company, because it takes time away from the plan.

Some part of her mind realized she should be paying attention, perhaps at Maggie's mention of a specific time.

"—about six o'clock for dinner, then we'll have the viewing," Maggie was saying, then she laughed. "Sounds like we're unveiling a newly discovered Rembrandt or something, doesn't it?"

I'm sure the creator thinks it's on par.

She didn't say it, and as she remounted Nugget to head home, she congratulated herself on staying civil for the whole—well, almost—conversation. Maggie's presence, obviously. Because Cody hadn't taken a single swipe at her, really. She couldn't remember the last time that had happened.

Maybe that's the answer—never deal with him without his mother around.

Three days later, she wasn't smiling at all. She was yanking on a jacket in aggravation, wishing she'd never told Maggie she'd come. Wishing she'd never told her parents she would, making it doubly impossible to cancel.

And on top of all that wishing it hadn't started raining. She'd planned on riding over, so she could leave on her own at some point. But the rain had started late this afternoon, her mother wouldn't hear of it, and now she was stuck in the car with her parents because she couldn't insist on driving separately without them tumbling to her plan for an early escape.

At least there would be others there. It wouldn't just be her and the Coder.

Maybe they could actually get through an evening under the same roof without drawing blood.

Chapter Sixteen

CODY WATCHED IN satisfaction as the video on the screen unrolled exactly as he'd envisioned it. Behind the graphics promoting the Last Stand Bluebonnet Festival, it flowed as if the viewer was in free flight. The camera began at the start of a narrow path bordered with the blue flowers, their brilliant color muted slightly in the pre-dawn light. It followed the path until the blossoms spilled into a wider field, looking like a stream flowing into a pond, except the pond kept going. On and on until the rocky outcropping appeared in the distance. It grew larger as the image got closer, the flowers becoming a single unbroken mass, and he guessed people were half expecting to see the lapping of ripples against the rock.

And finally the scene turned as he'd directed the drone alongside the big rock, positioning it so the rock was always on the upper edge of the image, the masses of flowers up against it. And just when it seemed the rock would never end, the camera made the last turn around the edge of the outcropping and the world opened up.

There were several seconds where you couldn't tell where

the deep blue of the dawn sky ended, and the flowers began. And then the rim of the sun cleared the horizon, light poured back toward the camera and the image exploded into the seemingly endless expanse of brilliant blue, flower-covered rolling hills. He heard more than one exclamation and several quick intakes of breath in the room, and satisfaction filled him.

When the group gathered—which included most of the Highwater clan, in particular Sean because he'd helped with the graphics promoting the festival and Kane because he'd contributed the beautiful, soaring music that accompanied it—broke into applause at the end he couldn't help grinning.

Nor could he seem to help slipping a glance sideways, denying even to himself he was scanning for Britt. He spotted her tall, long-legged form standing beside where her parents were sitting on the couch in the living room, across from the big flat screen he'd cast the finished product to. She was wearing a pair of black jeans that hugged every lean curve, a bright blue sweater with black trim, and a pair of black boots Chance would call spit-shined. For Britt Roth, this was downright dressed up. And he'd looked just in time to see her clapping along with everyone. She was even smiling as she watched the final image fade away.

He felt as if he'd been hit by a brick. A smile like that, at something he'd done? A smile that lit up her blue eyes until they practically glowed brighter than that sweater that clung to her in all the right places…

He gave himself an inward shake and focused on the triumph of the moment. Britt Roth, clapping and smiling, at *his* work. This wasn't just a red-letter day, it was a day that needed to be blocked out entirely in red. He'd have to figure out how to do that on his calendar.

And then she startled him. She looked over at the painting on the wall, his father's painting, the work that he'd finally, thanks to Kaitlyn, realized had inspired his own. As if she'd recognized it, as if she knew.

He hadn't, would never have expected that.

"Well," his mother said with obvious delight, "I'd say that's a go." She leaned over and put an arm around Cody which—thankfully—drew his attention away from Britt just as she turned her head and would have seen him watching her. *No, admit it Rafferty, staring at her. Gaping like a landed catfish.*

That extra helping of Mom's cheesy potatoes seemed to have settled into a heavy glob in his gut. He wanted more than anything to bail and retreat to his lair, just for a breather. But when his mother announced, her pleasure with the finished video still in her voice, that it was time for dessert, he knew he couldn't. But for the first time in his life the thought of her amazing apple pie didn't set off a growl in his stomach.

Coward.

Run from Britt Roth? *No way in hell, Rafferty.*

So he stayed. There were nearly a dozen people here, he

should be able to keep a few between him and her the rest of the evening. And he managed it, most of the time. Even managed to stop thinking about her as he and Ry and Kane got into a discussion about the piece of music Cody had put together for his artist brother, with a virtual orchestra playing a hammering version of Verdi's *Requiem*.

"I just reinterpreted something that already existed," he said, looking at Kane. "You're the one who came up with that incredible music that captured the feeling I wanted exactly."

"And someday soon," Ry said with a grin, "we're going to be using the fact that we have original music by superstar Kane promoting our little festival."

Kane looked down almost shyly, as if still unused to not just the acclaim, but the acceptance of his family and their friends. Cody couldn't imagine the hell the guy had gone through in the years he'd been on the run. But now, with his beloved Lark by his side, he was coming into his own.

Cody felt a sudden wash of that feeling he'd had before. All the Highwaters, settled and happy. All his brothers the same. If it wasn't for Lucas, he'd be the only solo act around. And Lucas was only fourteen.

But he liked his life the way it was. Had no desire to change it. He was sure of that. Wasn't he? An image of an old man holed up in a room full of lit screens, virtual relationships the only ones he had, shot through his mind and he mentally recoiled. People like he and Sean, tech fans, got ragged on about that all the time, being so in love with their machines they lost touch with real, live people. And maybe to some extent it was true. But Sean and Elena put the lie to the stereotype, in a big way.

He shoved the wonderings back into the cage where they belonged. Time spent thinking about such things was better spent elsewhere, he was certain. Anywhere else.

In fact, a second small slice of that pie he hadn't been sure he wanted at all was in order. After all, Mom had made three of them just to be sure there'd be enough—he knew because he and Kaitlyn had peeled the darned apples—so it'd be a shame to let all that work go to waste.

"Nice to see you and Britt in the same room but not at each other's throats."

The deep drawl came from behind him just as he was about to take a bite of pie. Behind and above, he corrected as he turned around to face six-foot-two Shane Highwater. The Last Stand police chief was a towering presence in more ways than one.

"Give us time," he muttered.

"You know," Shane said, with a trace of a smile, "time was Lily and I were the same way."

Cody blinked. What the hell was that supposed to mean? He couldn't be implying what it seemed like. But Shane only chuckled and walked off, no doubt to find the wife he'd just mentioned. The wife who was now officially pregnant with their first child.

What was it about all these guys who'd gotten hog-tied anyway? Could they just not stand to see a guy still footloose? First Mom, then his brothers, and now Chief Highwater? But that wasn't the crazy part, the crazy part was the barest idea that he and Roth—

He broke off the thought fiercely. That was the most ridiculous idea ever. He'd rather spend his life playing the futile game of tic-tac-toe. Against himself. With a pencil.

BRITT WAS TRYING to focus on her task list for tomorrow—Saturday was just another workday for her—when her mother said, "Well that was a lovely evening." They were making the short drive out of the Rafferty gate and back through their own just down the road. "We should do that more often," her mother went on. "We'll have to have them all over soon."

Warn me so I can be gone.

Britt sucked in a breath and managed to say nothing aloud from the back seat.

"And I'm proud of you," Mom added with a glance back at her. "You managed to act like an adult all evening, even with Cody being in the spotlight."

Britt's brow furrowed. "You think I'm jealous of him? What am I, a little kid?"

"Around him, you act it," her father pointed out.

"Oh, for—" She broke off what she'd been going to say, afraid it might prove their point. "I can be civil. And fair. That video turned out great."

That did as she'd hoped and got them off talking about the reason for the gathering. And besides, it was true. She couldn't deny that. The combination of the video—from one of those dratted drones—and Sean's graphics that framed it, and Kane's incredible music, was amazing.

Which reminded her of the conversation she'd overheard, about the music Cody had created for Ry, a custom reinterpretation of an old masterpiece that Ry said was his working music, both inspiring and energy-producing.

She'd never denied Cody was good at what he did, she'd only said he was obsessed. And she still thought she was right about that.

Just as you are, about your chosen path.

Her father had said that after hearing about her first encounter with one of the Coder's flying beasts, when she'd been so furious she'd come looking for something to do to work it off.

She hadn't liked the comparison. Horses were living, breathing things, beautiful, and worth obsession. More than a concoction of metal, plastic, and batteries, anyway. But one of those concoctions had produced that beautiful piece she'd just seen. That beautiful portrayal of this country she loved.

That beautiful recreation of the painting Kyle Rafferty had done.

In his own way, Cody had honored his father just as his brothers had. It was one of the kindest thoughts she'd ever had about the guy, and she wasn't at all sure she liked it.

She kept her mouth shut the rest of the way home.

Chapter Seventeen

"NEVER LET A computer know you're in a hurry," Cody muttered as he watched the little icon spin.

He tapped a finger on the desk, waiting for the seemingly endless upload to finish. It was high-quality video and sound, and the city server's upload speed left a lot to be desired for that kind of thing. He should have just done it from home, but the mayor had wanted to see it before it went public. And since the guy had been willing to come into city hall on a Saturday morning, Cody could hardly complain.

As it had turned out, the mayor had brought friends, and when they all reacted much as the group at the house had last night upon seeing the video, the man had had little choice but to simply give Cody the go-ahead.

The spinning finally stopped. He leaned forward and made a couple of tweaks. Then he exited the program and loaded the city's festival website. And grinned as the video started and ran perfectly. He grabbed his phone and sent a text to his mother, who was standing by at home ready to run a test from her end. A couple of minutes later he got back a hugely smiling emoji. He then tried it on his phone, because sometimes those settings needed adjusting. But it also ran perfectly, sized down for the smaller screen yet everything still readable.

He was grinning as he exited the website, removed his drive from the city machine, and got up. It was only 9:18 a.m., and he was done with the big chore for the day. Heck, for the month. He walked away with a spring in his step, looking forward to a day free to dig into the work that meant the most to him.

There was already traffic on Main Street as he pulled out of the city hall lot. Bluebonnet season was officially here. Tourists galore in Last Stand for the next month. Then they'd have a bit of a breather until Independence Day and the rodeo.

He arrived home focused on his plan for the rest of the day. He didn't hold out a lot of hope that the tweaks he'd made to the Fox—named after his father's platoon—would do what was needed, but it was worth a try. It had veered off course with the previous sensor adjustment. Only the built-in obstacle-avoidance system had kept it from crashing. He'd obviously gone too far, so today he was going to back it off a bit and still hope the stabilization system could compensate for the extra weight of the bigger battery.

He made the adjustments, set up the drone for takeoff, then went to the main system in his lair. He watched the video from the adjusted drone on one monitor, scanning the readouts from the various systems on another. He was well used to this remote piloting—it was second nature to him now, something he barely had to think about.

When it had first lifted off, he thought he saw a wobble. But it didn't occur again, so he decided it must have been a gust of the wind that had kicked up on his way home from town. He would only have time for a short flight today, since there was weather heading in, but it might be enough to see if the changes worked. Eventually the little flyer was going to have to be stable enough to take on inclement weather, but until he got this new combination of settings sorted out he'd be avoiding storms.

He heard a string of barks coming through the headphones. He smiled; obviously Tri had spotted the drone. Or knowing the hyper-alert former MWD, he might have heard that faint whoosh of the propellers chewing the air. He turned the drone that way, and saw Chance and Ariel, out in the smaller pen with one of the newer arrivals, a wire-strung yellow Labrador who could single-handedly destroy the breed's reputation for being easygoing.

They looked up at Tri's barks, and Cody saw his brother searching the sky. As he'd expected he spotted the drone quickly and waved. Cody dipped the drone in answer, then sent it off in another direction so as not to rattle the newcomer. The dog was no doubt used to drones—they were in such common usage now—but Cody knew Chance tried to give them a break from any reminders when they first got here. And Cody wasn't about to argue with his brother's success rate with the animals the military had written off as unsalvageable.

He veered the drone to the west, toward the wall of limestone they called the ridge even though it was barely taller than he was. The rain had begun up there, but he thought he had time to finish the run.

He let out a weary breath, as if all the changes in the last year had worn him out. Mom, on the other hand, was delighted. She was the one who kept track of all those things that tended to slide right past him. Including Roth and her future goals and plans. While he'd been half convinced her main goal in life was to make his miserable.

The rain was getting heavier. He frowned. The front had picked up speed. He decided this would be the last loop before bringing it home. Better early than sorry.

He grabbed one of Mom's famous butter pecan cookies that he'd snagged and hidden here last night during the screening, knowing how fast they always disappeared. An image of their pain-in-the-backside neighbor, watching and cheering his video just like everyone else, formed in his mind. She hadn't let the lifetime of friction between them get in the way. He felt a little jab; he wasn't sure he would be able to be as fair-minded.

He slid into more tangled thoughts. Could she do it? Could Brittany Roth make her big dreams come true? He knew, sometimes to his dismay, that once she seized on an idea she rarely gave up. If she applied the same kind of determination and ingenuity to her business plans as she did to driving him crazy, she'd probably get it done. Which would mean she really would be the girl next door for the foreseeable future, no relief for him, no hopes that she'd strike out on her own somewhere else? Why would she, when she had the perfect setup for it already?

Just like you do, here. She's no more going to leave than you would. This place was paid for with the blood of your ancestors. It's in your soul, Rafferty, and you're not going anywhere.

And neither was she. His mouth twisted as he realized the truth of that. The Roths might not have been rooted in this Hill Country soil as long as the Raffertys, but they were solidly here just the same. And she—

An abrupt acceleration of the image on the main screen snapped him out of his unexpected and unwanted reverie.

The sky had opened up and rain had begun to pour up at the ridgeline, but he barely noticed as he stared at the camera image from the drone.

Sideways. The image was sliding sideways.

He shifted the controller to adjust.

The video image kept sliding. Toward that solid wall of pitted stone.

He tried another adjustment.

It kept sliding.

He went for up, just wanting it higher for more space to maneuver.

Sideways.

"Shit." He knew what was coming. He could feel it. He had no control. The momentum had outpaced his ability to pull it back. He heard a loud scrape. Then a shattering loud enough to make him yank his headphones off.

The monitor flashed white for a split second.

Then dark.

Blank.

Dead.

He dropped the headphones on the table as he let out a fouler, louder oath. Then repeated it.

He'd have to go get the pieces. And hope something was salvageable, for parts at least. Problem was, he'd had his head in the clouds so long he wasn't sure exactly how far along the wall it had been when it crashed.

If you'd pulled your head out sooner, maybe it wouldn't have crashed at all.

He'd been going down rabbit holes in his head, which wasn't that unusual. He and Sean often joked about it. But going down the one named Britt Roth was. He checked the weather radar. Swore again, harsher this time. The heart of the cell was right there at the ridge. It would be here to the house soon. He wouldn't be going anywhere for a while.

"Welcome to spring," he muttered under his breath.

"Cody? Do you have a flyer out? I think you need to bring it back now, if you do. I was just in town and that storm's moving fast."

He turned back to the door and saw his mother standing there. "I did," he said in exasperation. "It crashed. Up near the ridge. Where the storm has already hit, and hard."

"Ouch. Not the new one you did the bluebonnets video with?"

"No, not that one." He decided not to mention it was the one inspired by Dad. "I was going to go get it, but..." He gestured back toward the radar on the screen.

"Good call," his mother said.

"Maybe it'll clear soon. The storm cell looks small."

She nodded. "It'll be fast. One of those March things that are portents of bigger ones to come. Sorry about your drone. That makes two this month."

He grimaced. "Yeah." *Can't blame this one on Roth, either. This was fully designer/operator error.*

He decided to spend the time he was trapped here going over the settings, analyzing the tweaks he'd made to see what had gone wrong. He'd have to check and see if the stabilization system had sent any odd readings, or if the obstacle-avoidance system had malfunctioned.

A half an hour later, two things happened almost simultaneously. The pouring rain he'd seen at the ridge started at the house—no thunder and lightning yet, but a healthy downpour—and his mother yelled his name.

Yelled. Not called, but yelled, with a touch of urgency.

He immediately got up and quickly headed down the long hall to the main house. When he got there, he saw

Keller was already putting on a slicker and his black cowboy hat. Lucas was beside him, pulling on his own rain slicker. Before Cody could even speak Ry was belting in the door, already wearing his own black hat, and carrying a waterproof jacket.

Crap. This was something bad.

His mother put the phone she was holding into the pocket of her own jacket. "Chance will take Tri out, in case he can help."

She turned then and gave Cody the look that he knew brooked no dispute, no protest. "Angie just called. Ghost came home five minutes ago, without Britt."

Chapter Eighteen

CODY'S GUT WAS churning. The gut that had leapt to a conclusion he wanted to deny.

That damned spooky horse had come home empty five minutes ago.

It was a half-hour ride from the limestone ridge, both to here and the Roth place, just different directions.

Probably a few minutes longer for a horse finding his way on his own.

His drone had crashed exactly thirty-six minutes ago.

"Do they know where she was going to be?" Ry asked.

"No," Mom said. "So there's a lot of ground to cover. The Roths and some hands are dividing up the south section. I told her we'll take the north."

"What about one of Cody's drones?" Lucas asked.

"I believe the fleet is down by two," she said. "And unless I'm mistaken, the one that's left isn't designed for this."

"I could adapt it," he managed to say, "but it would take time."

"Then we're back to old-school," Keller said, and it was in the tone of the man who ran this place with cool efficiency. The storm didn't matter now, they'd do what they had to do. That's what Raffertys did. "I'll take the far boundary." He looked at his soon-to-be son. "Lucas, everything between their house and the road." The boy nodded, eyes wide, but with a touch of pride in Keller's trust.

"Chance said he and Ariel and Tri will cover the flats," Mom said.

Ry chimed in, "I'll take the west hills."

"I'd go with you," Kaitlyn said, "but I'm afraid I'd do more harm than good since I'm so new at riding, so I'll stay here by the phone." Ry hugged her. Mom nodded her approval and smiled at the woman she'd taken to immediately.

"Quinta and I will take the stream, east to west," she said. "Cody, get that flyer adapted as fast as you can."

"No."

His mother blinked. They all went quiet, staring at him. And he couldn't find the words that would explain what he was feeling without it sounding crazy. When he didn't speak, that "No" to their mother hung in the air.

"That," Keller said, his tone icy and his gaze the same, "is taking this silly hostility between you and Britt too far. Way too far."

Cody gave a sharp shake of his head, stung by his usually slow to rile brother's reaction. "It's not that. It'll take too long. Changing the drone, I mean. And I think I—" He cut himself off. He didn't want to say what he thought, what he suspected, in case his gut was wrong. So he said instead, "I'll cover the ridgeline. She rides up that way a lot. I've seen her before."

"Steep climb," Ry said. "On uneven ground."

"I can understand her doing that, it's good balance conditioning for a horse," Mom said, seeming to have forgiven him for his abrupt refusal. Or at least not making an issue of it now. "All right. First aid kits, everyone."

"And make sure you've all got a weapon and ammo in case she's in a bad cell spot," Keller said as they turned to go. "Two quick shots if you find her. Three if it's a mistake."

"Why two or three?" Lucas asked as they headed for the door.

"In case you have to take out a snake or coyote with one." Leave it to Keller to think of that. Cody ran back to his lair to switch to his boots and grab his own slicker. At least his brother was thinking; he couldn't seem to.

He couldn't think of anything beyond what his gut was screaming at him. Because what he'd said was nothing less than the truth. Britt did ride the ridgeline. Regularly. And it was a half-hour ride, give or take a minute. And his drone had crashed a little over that half hour ago.

And his gut was screaming that yes, he'd been in the ozone long enough that the out-of-control drone could have slid across the boundary into Roth airspace.

Maybe he was wrong. Maybe it hadn't. Or maybe she hadn't been there at all today. Maybe something else had spooked the easily spookable Ghost.

Maybe.

Too bad he couldn't convince his roiling gut.

Her getting tossed and ending up with a bruise was one thing.

Her getting tossed and ending up being unable to control her horse—Britt Roth, the toughest rider he knew after Keller and probably his mother—was something else altogether. She would never, ever let her precious Ghost loose like that if she could stop her.

Which meant she couldn't.

Which meant she was in trouble. Bad trouble.

Trey looked at him as if he were crazy when he mounted up and headed out into the rain. He gave the horse a pat. "Yes, I mean it," he muttered. Trey snorted, shook his head, but stepped out of the barn as ordered.

He wasn't a cowboy hat kind of guy, but he'd borrowed an old one of Keller's at Mom's insistence, and as the rain was directed down the back of the slicker he'd put on instead of the back of his neck, he definitely saw the point.

"Sorry, buddy," he said to the horse who was already wet. "At least it's not too cold."

He took the shortest route he knew, straight to the ridge. There were a couple of spots that were very rocky and got slick in the rain, but he hoped they'd get through that before it got too bad.

When he reached the stream it still looked fairly normal.

Depending on how much rain this storm dumped, it could be a mess before it was over, and he hoped Mom stayed safe. But she knew this land they loved better than any of them, so she'd be okay.

He rode up the other side and made the swing toward the ridge. He didn't dare guess at where he'd lost his mental focus, he had to start at the spot where he knew the drone had begun following the limestone wall. He had to go slower than he wanted to so he could look in all directions. And the rain wasn't helping any, but at least there hadn't been any lightning nearby. Yet. He'd heard a rumble a minute ago, but it was still well distant and muted. Not that Trey's head hadn't come up sharply.

"I know, boy. It's still okay," he murmured to the horse. *For a while longer.*

If the storm built and the lightning got closer, he wasn't sure what he'd do.

He guided Trey onward along the ridge. It was an exertion for the horse to walk sideways on the hillside, but Trey was the most sure-footed horse on the ranch, except for maybe Latte, their beginner's ride.

He went on, getting wetter. And on, worrying about Trey not just getting even wetter but slipping now and then as the footing got worse. And on, finding nothing, not a trace of Britt, nor any debris from the downed drone.

He stifled a groan when he saw they'd reached the fence line. Unless the drone had gone off course, it could have indeed crossed over the boundary. It could have gone down on Roth property. He could only hope it hadn't taken a Roth down with it.

I should just quit. Give up on the damn things. It's an impossible goal anyway. There's no way to make a packable drone that's both long range and silent.

He'd never entertained the thought before, but it haunted him now as they neared the fence. If they'd been on level ground he would have just jumped Trey over the fence, but here on this slope he couldn't risk it. He needed the horse with him, so he dug in his saddle bag, down past the first aid kit Mom had made sure they all had—and the basic knowledge to go with it, always a need in ranch life—and pulled up the small pair of wire cutters. He dismounted and made quick work of the fence; they'd repair it later.

He remounted and sent Trey forward again, and the willing horse went through the gap without even a sideways look. It was almost as if he sensed now this was Not Normal, that there was something serious going on that didn't deserve one of his snorting observations that Cody was being stupid.

And in the end, it was Trey who headed Cody in the right direction. When the big bay stopped in his tracks, his ears swiveling to the left in the moment before his head turned that way, Cody didn't protest but looked himself. He didn't see anything, but Trey's ears were unmovingly aimed down slope. He knew better than to ignore a signal like that. The horse had heard something, and it wasn't something fleeting, it was something that was holding his attention. But not scaring him. So harmless? Or familiar?

He slid the Ruger Mini Ranch out of the rifle sheath. Every Rafferty had used this starter rifle at some point, and he'd just never felt the need to go beyond it. Perhaps because Dad had fine-tuned the accuracy to where it wasn't an issue. Or because recoil annoyed him if he needed to make a second shot. Spoiled by shooter video games, Chance had told him laughingly.

He slipped the reins over and down, and if a horse could roll his eyes at the downpour, Trey did.

"Quick as I can," he promised the animal, who snorted as if emphasizing that idea.

He headed toward where the horse had been looking. He had to scramble sideways a couple of times to keep his feet on the rain-slick rocks that had eroded off the ridge and tumbled down to give the hill a coating of sliding pebbles. He went down on his left knee once, swore under his breath at the sharp pain, but got up. Looked around. Saw nothing.

He sucked in a breath and yelled out her name. Her first name, for one of the few times in his life.

"Britt!"

He wondered how far the human ear could hear in a downpour like this. Which end of the range would the rain drown out the most? For that matter, how far would a voice carry in this? What—

Stop it. No time for a rabbit hole now.

He went a little farther down. Stopped, and yelled her name again.

And got an answer.

Chapter Nineteen

THE FIRST TIME she'd heard it, Britt was half convinced she'd imagined it. The pain was pretty intense and her mind could be playing tricks on her. Funny, she'd always thought that if pain like this went on long enough, you'd get used to it, or the nerves would get tired of being in an uproar and it would ease up, or at least seem like it. But between her wrist and her leg, the signals never seemed to relent. She could barely think at all. All she knew was there'd been a sharp sound, that damned boulder had started down the slope, and Ghost had gone insane.

And then she heard it again. Her name. Somebody really was calling her name. Through the noise of the storm she couldn't tell who it was, didn't care. All she cared about was that she had help. She wasn't going to be trapped for hours out here, pinned by this damned boulder, soaked and shivering. Hours she would have probably spent telling herself that eventually somebody would notice she hadn't come home, that a search would start, that she wasn't going to die out here.

She sent a fervent "thank you" to whoever was in charge

of cowgirl heaven and called out in answer. "Over here!"

It was another moment of that time blurred by pain before it occurred to her more than one call might be appropriate. Or at least some more information.

"By the rock slide!"

They would know what that meant, whoever it was. Dad, or one of the hands, would immediately put together the fact of the slide with the fact that she couldn't move and realize she was trapped. She didn't think one person could get this boulder off of her, but at least they could go for help. She hadn't even been able to make a call; if there was a deader cell spot in these hills than this, she didn't know where it was.

She heard the scramble of boots on the wet rocks. A tall, agile form in jeans, a slicker, and a cowboy hat came around the boulder that was crushing her ankle.

"Damn," she heard him say.

And then he lifted his head as he looked from the boulder to her face. And beneath the brim of the hat she saw who it was. And almost echoed his fervent oath.

Cody.

Cody the damned Coder. Didn't it just figure? Sitting there in the pouring rain, her right foot pinned with the boulder atop her ankle and with her aching left wrist cradled in her lap, all she could think was that her luck was truly down the suckhole of life today.

Some distant part of her mind registered that she'd never

seen him in a cowboy hat before. She had a very brief moment to be annoyed that it looked good on him before another roll of pain overtook her.

He knelt beside her, setting something down beside him as he did. "How bad?"

"Bad enough," she said through gritted teeth. "Wrist is hurt. And the obvious." She looked toward the boulder about two feet across that had her right ankle and foot trapped. She didn't know how much of the pain was from the pressure and weight of the big rock, and how much might be from actual damage. Either way she wasn't liking it much.

He moved to look. He leaned down to peer closely at where she was pinned. Put a tentative hand on the boulder, although she could have told him he wasn't going to be able to move it, even with his muscles. He looked from a different angle, then another. She was about to ask him what the heck he was doing when he looked back at her. She saw an expression on his face she'd never seen before, and through the pain it took her a moment to realize this was probably what he looked like when he was at his beloved computer, his eyes a little distant as he worked out something in his head.

All of Last Stand knew he was smart. It was impossible not to with his history of clever tricks. But she'd never seen it in action up close like this.

And then, as if he'd made a decision, he moved. And she

was startled when she saw him lean over to pick up what he'd set down before.

"Going to put me out of my misery?" she grated out as he lifted the small rifle.

This time when he looked at her he wasn't lost in thought or some complicated process, he was there, vividly, behind those annoyingly pretty green eyes.

"That wouldn't be a fair fight," he said softly.

Even through the pain she knew what he meant. They had always fought fair, except for the one time they'd both brought others into it. And that one time had ended that idea forever, apparently for both of them, because neither of them had ever done it again.

He lifted the rifle and fired two rounds into the air in rapid succession. She frowned, which made her aware again of the scrape on her cheek, then belatedly realized it was a signal. And even more belatedly thought to ask, worried even through the pain, "Ghost?"

"She made it home safe. That's how we knew."

She relaxed slightly. He turned his head and let out a piercing whistle, the kind she'd never been able to replicate even though her father had tried to teach her. Then he turned back to her.

"Anything else hurt?"

"That's not enough?" she muttered.

"You hit your head," he said, indicating her stinging cheek.

"Minor," she said. "Just scraped my cheek."

"Can you move your other foot? And arm?"

She frowned. "Yes, I—" She broke off when she realized he was making sure she hadn't damaged her spine. "I'm fine, otherwise. I caught myself with that hand—" she nodded toward her aching wrist "—so I was slowed down when I hit. The rock rolled down after. I think Ghost dislodged it when she took off."

She waited for him to make some comment about the mare, because he always did.

He didn't. In fact, he looked almost pained. But all he said was, "Truce, for now, Roth."

She didn't see that she had much choice. She was hurting, and however much it aggravated her, she needed his help. "Truce," she agreed.

A moment later she saw a dark shape loom up through the rain. His horse, who was holding his head up high to keep the trailing reins free; he'd obviously been ground-tied.

And yet he'd come at the whistle.

"That's some horse," she said, appreciating the distraction. "Ground-tied, but he still came."

Cody gave the big bay an affectionate glance. "He is. Keller taught him to ground-tie and come to the whistle, but it took Mom to teach him the latter superseded the former."

She was a bit foggy so had to work it out, but it made her smile despite the pain. "I imagine Maggie could teach him to dance if she was of a mind to."

"She taught me, and when it comes to dancing, I've got two left feet. And one of them's on backward."

If she'd been hurting a little less she might have laughed at that. Which startled her. Who was this charmer?

He got up and went to the horse. She noticed he patted the animal's nose as he went by toward the saddlebags, and she thought she heard him say, "Thanks, buddy." The horse nickered softly. She remembered the bath. It was obvious this pair had a tight relationship. She wondered what it must be like, to be such a perfect match, and not a daily battle such as she had with Ghost. But at least the darn horse was safely home. And she'd sounded the alert in the process.

She gave a tentative tug on her pinned foot, and instantly regretted it. She smothered the yelp that wanted to escape down into a gasp. Cody's head snapped around just as he was pulling something out of the saddlebag.

She shook her head. *Just me being stupid.* But she didn't say it.

He came back, and she saw it was a first aid kit. There was something different about him now, as there had been since that moment when she'd thought he was working something out in his head. His every action since then had been cool, decisive. As if he had indeed worked out a plan and now all that was left to do was follow it.

Again he knelt beside her, digging into the kit. "Wrist first. You may need to move, and it'll be easier if it's not hurting so much."

"Not sure that'll happen unless you've got a big bottle of horse-strength tramadol handy." It came out through gritted teeth as another wave of pain rippled up from her wrist by the simple act of moving her arm.

"We'll get it immobilized first, then go from there."

How the heck was he going to do that? That would take a splint, and there wasn't much around her that would serve. What plants there were were of the scrub variety, and probably so wet right now they wouldn't be stiff enough anyway. They—

"—your phone?"

"What?" Damn, she was foggy. And cold. Another shiver went through her. The rain seemed to be easing up, but she was soaked to the skin, and what dirt there was under her had long ago turned to mud.

"Where's your phone?" he repeated.

She had no idea what her phone had to do with anything, given there was no kind of signal out here, but far be it from her to question her rescuer. Even if it was her most hated Last Stander.

"In my jacket pocket—ahh!" She winced as this time her ankle and foot protested her movement.

"Just hold still and let me get it."

He pulled the phone out, and she noticed then he had a roll of elastic wrap in his other hand. Amazement stabbed through the pain as he straightened out her hand and proceeded to use the phone itself as a splint, wrapping the stretchy bandage tightly around both phone and wrist. And it worked; not only could she not bend it, the pain even eased a little.

"Major points," she conceded, and was taken aback at the smile that got her.

But then he went back to his horse, untied a latigo and lifted down the rope it was holding. He came back but stopped at the boulder that had her pinned.

"Whoa," she said. "Shouldn't we wait for help? That's too big for one man to move."

"But not one horse," he said, not even looking at her as he, oddly, seemed to measure the boulder with a length of the rope, and then again, and again.

"Yes, but—"

"They probably heard those shots, but maybe not. And even if they did, they won't be sure who found you, and therefore where you are. They'll only know that when everybody else makes contact or shows up back at your house. You want to wait that long?"

No, she didn't. Wasn't sure she could. She'd always thought herself fairly tough, but this was coming perilously close to turning her into a whiny wimp. And in front of the last person on earth she'd want that to happen. Although she had to admit, if someone came by and told her this was a Cody imposter, she was out of it enough—and he was acting different enough—that she might just believe it.

She snapped back out of the fog when he leaned back

over the boulder and she realized what he was doing. He'd rigged up a net of sorts with the rope, somehow knotting it so that it formed a very loose mesh. And she realized not only what he was going to do, but that it might actually work. This must have been what he was working out, when he'd gotten that almost spaced-out look on his face.

He slipped the hand-tied net around the boulder so that it would be pulled sideways. That puzzled her until she realized that if he'd pulled it back, not only would it drag across her foot, but if for some reason it slipped, it would be heading right for her, and with momentum. Enough to smash her completely. The shiver that went through her then wasn't from the cold of being soaking wet.

He walked back to his horse. Wrapped the rope around the saddle horn, then patted the horse solidly on the neck.

"It's just a heavy calf, Trey ol' buddy. You just do what you always do and we'll be good."

He came back, which also puzzled her, because she thought he would have stayed with the horse to guide him to pull back. Then he knelt down behind her and she realized he was there to pull her clear just in case things went haywire and the boulder slid free.

In other words, Cody the nerd, the geek, the extreme tech-head, was doing everything an experienced ranch hand would do. Cody the Coder was also a cowboy.

"Ready?" he asked.

"Yeah," she muttered. Then, more firmly, "Yes. Do it."

He shifted until he had a knee either side of her hips. A disconcertingly intimate position, or at least it would be if not for the circumstances. Of course, if not for the circumstances, it wouldn't be happening.

"Trey! Back!"

The horse immediately began to move. In the same moment she felt Cody's hands slip under her shoulders, firmly but not pulling. Not yet. But the contact accomplished something unexpected. It distracted her, for the moment at least, from the pain. Or maybe the boulder had already moved. She looked that way, and indeed saw that it had shifted slightly. That was a relief, somehow, that it was actually the boulder shifting that was easing things a little, because the idea that it was Cody touching her, holding her in essence, was more than a little unsettling.

"Back," he called out to the horse again, who was still, slowly, backing up in an arrow-straight line.

She felt the pressure ease a little more, until she thought she might actually be able to move that leg. If she pushed off with her free leg, she could—

"Hold on another second," Cody said, as if he'd read her mind. And he was so close she felt the tickle of his breath in her ear, and a shiver went through her. The cold, of course. That's all it was.

Trey backed up farther. And the boulder slipped a little more to the side.

Trey backed. Another two steps.

"Now," he said.

She pushed. Cody pulled.

They both fell backward, her on top of him.

She was free.

Her ankle screamed, telling her exactly how much of her pain had not been the pressure of the boulder. The world began to spin around her. And then it went gray and started to fade out.

Chapter Twenty

THE RIDICULOUSNESS OF him ending up lying here in the mud with Britt Roth spread out over him was not lost on Cody. There were, he knew, a whole lot of guys who would love to be in this position with her. With fewer clothes on, no doubt, but still.

Then he realized she'd gone limp and he was slammed back to the reality of the situation.

"Roth?"

She didn't answer. He swore. He carefully maneuvered himself to where he was sitting up. She was still draped over him, but so slumped it had his pulse kicking up with fear. "Britt? Come on, it's okay now. You're clear, and we need to get you home."

She groaned, and he never thought the sound of someone in pain would be so welcome.

"Trey, hold!" he called out, and the horse obediently stopped. The boulder was still in his makeshift net, and he could see how strong the pull was by the way the big bay was bracing himself against it.

He turned back to her. "Britt?" He was cradling her in

his arms now, wishing more than anything those bright blue eyes would open and she'd say something snappy and pointed.

And then her eyes did open. She blinked a couple of times, then focused. "Cody."

"You all right?" He grimaced. Of course she wasn't. "Besides the obvious, I mean?"

"I…think so. I just…that last bit…really hurt." She was almost panting, as if trying to catch her breath.

His jaw tightened. "Maybe we should have waited. I could have gone for help, and—"

She drew in a long, deep breath this time. "And left me trapped here, lunch for the next pack of coyotes who came along? No, thanks."

She sounded much steadier now. His jaw muscles let up a little. This was the Britt he knew. Strong. Tough. Cowgirl tough. Or wowgirl.

"I feel sorry for any coyote stupid enough to take you on," he said.

"Never stopped you."

He started to grin at that one, but it died immediately, because she'd moved a little as she said it, and had winced fiercely. "Let's just get you out of here. If we can make it down to the bottom of the slope we should get a cell signal, and we can call for help."

"See to your horse," she said, and he knew then she was back to herself. For the horse would ever and always come first with her.

He got up, carefully disentangling them, and went over to Trey. Who was patiently holding a lot of rock. He'd already decided he wasn't going to bother trying to save the rope. Time was more important now, she needed medical attention. So he pulled out the knife his father had taught him to always carry and, glancing to be sure it was fully clear, cut the rope.

The boulder rolled, picking up speed as it headed down the slope. It bounced, again and again, then finally stopped a little more than halfway down, when it got caught in a hollow in a limestone shelf. Where it would likely stay until it or the shelf eroded away.

He led Trey over to where she was sitting up again, cradling her wrist—or maybe her phone—and looking down toward the boulder.

"Sorry about the rope."

"It's replaceable."

Trey lowered his head to snuffle at her. "Thanks, boy," she said, reaching up with her uninjured hand to pat his muzzle. For some reason that made Cody feel…strange, and his next words came out nearly brusque.

"You've got two choices. I carry you, or he does."

Her eyes widened in obvious surprise. "You? I can ride."

He wasn't stupid enough to contradict her on that. He merely said, "It wouldn't be easy with that ankle."

"But—"

"Look, let me carry you to the bottom of the slope. It's not that far. Then we'll figure it out from there, depending on if we get a cell signal or not."

She glanced at her wrist, where her phone was serving as a makeshift splint. He could see she didn't like the idea. But he could also see when she realized it was the most logical solution. She probably could ride, because it was ingrained in her bones. But even if he didn't know how badly her ankle was hurt, he knew swinging it over a horse would not be pleasant. Nor would riding with it hanging down when it should be elevated.

And clearly, so did she. Because with a sigh she gave in.

He tossed the reins back over Trey's head, out of the horse's way. "Trey, on me."

Britt looked up at the horse, startled, then looked back at him. "He'll follow you?"

"He will." It had been Chance who had managed that one, even using the military-style command.

"'Some horse' wasn't nearly complimentary enough."

He had to bite back what normally would have been an automatic reply, that compared to Ghost any normal horse would seem a miracle of training and tractability. Truce, he reminded himself.

Besides, that would be an insult to Trey, who truly was a miracle of training and tractability.

He scooped her up, gently avoiding any quick movement that would jostle her leg, and carefully putting her right side against him so she could put her uninjured arm around his neck for support. She did it, though obviously reluctantly. It must truly grate on her to have to take help from him.

He was a little surprised at her weight until he reminded himself all five-foot-eight or so of her was solid muscle. He shifted his arms a little, to be sure everything was in balance.

It was an intimate position. Not as much as lying on the ground with her draped over him, but still intimate. Maybe that's why his gut was churning. He didn't like this. This was Roth, the enemy.

But she was hurt. Which meant everything was on hold. Just as she had declared a truce when his father had been killed, he'd declared one now. So, a truce it would be. He started downhill.

They'd gone a few feet before she spoke again. "Not even going to ask what happened?"

His brow furrowed. *No. Because I know.* But he wasn't ready to have that discussion with her. Not yet. Not when he still didn't know where the drone had come down, and when it was taking a great deal of concentration to get down the wet, rocky slope without losing his footing and making everything worse.

"You were on Ghost," he said, as if that explained everything. Which, in a way, it did. Most ranch horses would have handled what had happened, either rain or drone, without going berserk. Not that that made him any less culpable if it had been the drone. If it was, it had been the perfect storm of crazy horse, an equipment malfunction…and his inattention.

That's two out of three for you, Rafferty, which pretty much makes it your fault no matter how you twist it.

He heard Trey following behind them, the occasional strike of a horseshoe on stone. Then he heard a quiet sound from her, somewhere between a sigh and a moan of pain. He tried to go easier, slower.

"Mom says she's not worth it. Ghost, I mean."

Again, he had to bite back what would have been his normal response, a caustic *Your mom's smarter than you, then.*

Instead, as neutrally as he could, he said, "She'll be even more convinced of that now."

"I know." Another one of those sounds. "But she's my ticket. She's the foundation of everything." She let out a harsh laugh. "Or she was."

He frowned. She already knew the horse had made it back to the barn safely, so what—It hit him then. She wasn't doubting the horse would be okay. She was wondering if she would be. And that rattled him. This couldn't be that serious, could it? Bad enough to end her prize winning, her rodeoing, her long-term plans? Enough to crush even her fierce spirit?

The thought that she might be that badly hurt, that she might not heal enough, might never return to the hellcat who lived next door, full of sass and sarcasm, shook him in a way he never, ever would have expected.

And not just because he felt—in two out of three ways—responsible. But because he couldn't picture a beaten Roth.

"She still will be," he said firmly. "You'll recover. You'll compete, and win, win again, and someday you'll be the breeder to come to for anybody who seriously wants to win themselves."

She shifted in his arms slightly, and he could tell she was looking at him. But he didn't dare not keep his eyes on the rocky slope.

"I hope you're right," she said, an undertone in her voice he'd never heard before.

But then, he'd never heard Britt Roth say she hoped he was right before, either.

Chapter Twenty-One

IT WAS THE strangest feeling. Britt closed her eyes, trying to analyze it. Kept trying to assign another word to it. But only one fit.

Safe.

She felt safe. She was in Cody Rafferty's arms, she was hurting in several places, one particularly badly—she had to admit he'd been right, riding with that foot and ankle dangling would have been hideous—but she still felt safe.

It made no sense to her. The pain had to be messing with her head. Or maybe she was just comparing it to Ghost. With that horse she had to be constantly on alert, aware and ready for the sideways jump at any moment.

Now she could just...relax.

Because she was safe. Cody would never drop her.

Cody the Coder.

God, her world had gone insane.

She'd let her head loll until it rested against his arm. The taut, strong muscle was warm beneath her undamaged cheek. An image floated up, of him coming out of his geeky lair, shirtless and with his jeans half-zipped, baring the arms that were holding her so carefully now, that broad chest that supported them, and the ridged abdomen she was braced against.

Was this Cody, the one she'd half-seriously thought must be an imposter, the real Cody? The Cody she never saw, but others did?

She wrestled with that for a while, glad of anything that would take her mind even a little bit off the throb of her ankle and the duller pain of her wrist. Duller, because he'd been ingenious enough to use what was at hand for a splint.

"Okay?" he asked. "I mean, I know you're not, but—"

"I'm not worse," she said, a little surprised that there'd been a touch of embarrassment in his voice.

"Good enough," he said, and kept going. She could feel, in the shifting tension in his muscles, how hard he was working to be a human shock absorber for her. To make this descent as easy as possible, for her. He really had meant that declaration of truce. But then, she knew he wouldn't kid about that. Because the only other time they'd declared a truce was when his whole life had been blown apart.

Selfishly, she hoped this wasn't the same kind of event for her. That the split second when she had looked toward the sound rather than staying focused on the easily panicked horse beneath her hadn't cost her everything.

At least Ghost wasn't hurt. Although she was starting to have second thoughts about her being the foundation mare for her future plans. If she passed on her incredible athletic skill in the arena, great. But if she also passed on that incredible craziness outside it, not so great. How many people would think the constant risk of injuries like this would be worth the wins?

Right now, even she wasn't sure she thought it was.

"Want to stop for a bit?"

She shifted her gaze at his words. "What?"

"You looked like you were feeling worse."

"Oh. No, I…" She sighed. "I was just questioning my entire life plan," she said sourly. "Or rather, basing it on a crazy horse."

"I wouldn't argue that." His tone was so neutral she knew he'd worked at it.

"I didn't think you would," she said, trying for an even tone herself.

"But," he said, "that's not a decision to make now, when you're hurting. You can't think straight when you're in pain like this."

He was being so calm. So gentle. "You don't have to be so nice. I'm not dying, you know."

"This time," he retorted, but still in that un-sharp voice.

And it was hard to argue when she knew he was right. This could have easily been much worse. If she had hit her head, she could easily be dead. Or to her mind worse, incapacitated. Physically, mentally, or both.

When he came to a halt a few minutes later, and she realized they'd reached the bottom, she felt an odd jab of…something. It was over, that intimate trek down the rocky slope. When she realized what she was feeling was disappointment, she wanted to move her hand or her foot to sharpen up the dull throb, as a distraction.

Well, that's twisted enough.

His horse came up beside them, still calm, and came to a halt. He really was amazingly well trained.

"Do you think you can stand on the one foot while I get my phone?" Cody asked. "Or would you be better down on the ground?"

"I can," she said, then, figuring honesty was not just the best but the only policy right now, added, "if I've got something to hang on to."

"Trey, hold." The big bay nickered in response and planted his hooves. Cody took the two steps over to the horse and set her down with a gentle care that she couldn't miss, close enough that she could grasp the saddle with her good hand.

"He won't move," he assured her.

"What if a snake slithered by?"

"He'd warn us first."

"This," she said in awe, "is a miracle horse."

"Yep. When my mom says it's a miracle I'm still alive, he's what she means."

To her amazement, despite the pain, she nearly laughed. And he grinned at her. That grin her friends talked about, the one that flashed a dimple in his right cheek and made him look…look…

Too darn good, that's what it made him look.

He was already working on his phone. "Signal comes and goes," he muttered. "It'd probably drop a call, but a text should get through."

"Who are you texting?" She couldn't see from this angle, but it looked as if he was changing between apps. He never paused in his tapping and swiping.

"Everybody. I wanted a map fix first. Ry's the closest, he was covering the west hills."

"Your brother's out here?"

He sent the text and then looked at her. "All of them are. And Mom, and Lucas."

"Oh."

"You sound surprised."

"I just didn't think. Or couldn't," she said, hearkening back to what he'd said earlier. She hesitated, then added, "I am surprised that you rode out. I would have figured you'd send another one of your…"

"Toys?" he asked, using the word she usually did.

She waited for the old enmity to flare up then. Thought she almost would have welcomed it. It would have made all this seem less serious. Would have let her convince herself she wasn't hurt as badly as she was afraid she was. That he wasn't jabbing at her, that he'd declared that truce, was scaring her now.

A memory had come to her of that car accident back in

high school, when the star of the baseball team had been pinned, much as she had been, and his ankle had been crushed. He had never been the same, had limped from then on. It had been the end of his dreams of a pro career. He'd finally moved away, saying he wanted a fresh start somewhere where they didn't know what the possibilities had been.

She hadn't understood then, why he'd want to leave his family and friends. She hoped she wasn't going to learn firsthand now.

Cody looked about to say something else, and also as if it were something he didn't want to say. But then he shook his head and muttered, "Later."

She realized she was leaning hard against the sturdy horse, who was standing statue-still. She reached out with her good hand and patted his shoulder. "You are amazing, you sweet boy," she crooned.

Cody's phone signaled. He pulled it out and looked at the screen. "They got the text. Your dad is heading back to the house to get a vehicle. So, we just wait here."

"And be glad the rain passed," she said, turning to look at him. But without her good hand on the saddle horn she'd overbalanced, and instinctively put her foot down to catch herself. She nearly passed out completely this time. And she couldn't stop the cry of pain that escaped.

When it eased and she was able to focus again, she realized she was back where she'd been. In his arms, held against him firmly.

"Easy," he was saying, his voice soothing. "It'll be all right, Britt. Just hang on."

Hang on. To him? She could do that.

She could easily do that.

She wanted to do that.

Clearly the pain had driven her out of her mind.

Chapter Twenty-Two

CODY HAD NO name, no words for what he was feeling once things were out of his hands.

Ry had arrived a few moments after she'd taken that bad step. They'd settled her on the ground, then Ry had remounted his black, Flyer, and headed down to make sure her father found them. The SUV arrived and they had her loaded up, dried off, and under blankets. A few minutes after they got her back to the house, the paramedics had arrived and taken over.

Cody knew Spencer McBride was good, really good, and the way he took over to immobilize her foot and ankle—and grinned at the makeshift phone-splint—would normally have made Cody smile. But watching Roth go pale at every movement, watching her fight against crying out, watching the cold sweat break out on her skin when Spencer had had to brace her ankle, had made him feel faintly nauseous himself.

And then her mother came over and gave him a huge hug.

"Thank you, Cody, for finding her."

"Don't thank me," he said, sounding harsh even to himself. "It was—"

Before he could finish declaring this was all his fault in the first place, Keller and Lucas and Mom arrived.

"I called Chance and let him know," Mom said. "How is she?"

Cody opened his mouth to tell her how badly he thought her ankle was messed up, but realized Mrs. Roth was still standing beside him and stopped himself. She didn't need to hear his fears on top of her own. He was no doctor; let them give her the real situation.

"Spencer said he thinks her wrist is only sprained, that they won't know for sure about her ankle without X-rays, and that they'll probably keep her overnight at least, to make sure nothing hidden shows up," Mrs. Roth said. Then, with another glance at Cody added warmly, "But he said it was good that she was found so soon. She could have made her ankle worse by struggling to free herself, and then trying to get home."

"If I know her," Keller said, "she'll be worried more about losing ground than anything. Both physically and on the circuit."

Mrs. Roth smiled at that. Keller always seemed to have the knack of saying the right thing, just like Mom did. He probably learned it from her, back when he'd had to grow up way too fast.

"Oh, she's going to hate having a cast on her ankle. If she

has to have one on her wrist as well, she'll be unbearable," Mrs. Roth said knowingly, although there was no denying the love that echoed in her voice.

Cast.

Something sparked in Cody's memory, something he'd been reading about a while back. He turned it over and around in his mind, wondering. He knew the technology worked. The question was, was it already available here in Last Stand? If not, if he could get that done in a hurry, it might help ease the guilt he was feeling.

Of course maybe Jameson Hospital already had something like it in place, although maybe not, it was fairly cutting edge. He'd have to check with them, and if they did have it fine, if not he'd jump on it. Then he'd—

His mother tugged gently at his arm, snapping him back to the moment. He tuned back in just as she was saying, "—keep an eye on things here. You just see to Brittany."

It was weird, how strange it was to hear her full name. He knew she hated it when anyone used it. He'd even admitted he could relate; when he'd been younger he'd hated that "ends in y" thing that made it sound like a cutesy nickname.

He belatedly realized Mom had just volunteered them to keep an eye on the Roth place until things settled down. Their hands were loyal and hard-working, so Rafferty help probably wouldn't be needed, but it was like Mom to reassure them. It wasn't until they were mounting up to return home that he realized she had something specific in mind.

"Now you can adapt that drone and use it to keep an eye on things for them." He nearly groaned aloud. She looked at him sharply. "Forgotten your brother's warning already?"

That is taking this silly hostility between you and Britt too far.

No, it wasn't likely he'd forget those words, or the usually unruffled Keller's icy tone. He glanced up ahead, where Keller and Ry were already on their way. Then he looked back at her. He was going to have to tell her, and the Roths. And that made him feel more than a little apprehensive.

"No. It's not that."

"Something you'd like to tell me? Or need to?"

That was Mom, perceptive as hell, and at the most inconvenient times. "When we get home," he muttered, hoping she'd let it go until then.

"All right," she said after a minute. "You've earned that much, after rescuing Britt."

Rescuing. Right. Was it still rescuing when you had quite possibly caused the disaster in the first place?

He spent more time than usual when he got back to the barn and tended to Trey. Stalling, maybe. But not really, because the horse deserved it. He unsaddled him and traded the bridle for a halter, then, figuring the horse had had enough of being wet just as he had, he skipped the bath, cleaned the mud and dirt off of his coat and out of his hooves, then went to a long, hard rubdown.

"You earned it, buddy," he said to the big bay as he worked. "You did it all, and perfectly."

"It certainly sounds like he did just that."

Mom's voice came from behind him; she'd done her own routine with her Seven and put him back in his stall. Now, with Quinta sitting at her feet, he told her the basics of what had happened after he'd found Roth, focusing on the horse's part in it.

"Oh," she said as she walked around to the horse's head, stroked his muzzle, and crooned to him, "you are just the best ever, aren't you?"

Trey's head bobbed, as if nodding, and she laughed.

She waited until he was done and had Trey back in his stall. Care for the animals always came first. It was what she believed and what she'd taught them all their lives.

But when he slid the latch on the stall door home and turned around to see her standing there, waiting, he knew this was it.

"I think…it might have been my fault," he said.

"The drone that crashed."

He should have known she'd figure it out. She was the smartest woman he'd ever known, when it came to figuring people out.

"I wasn't harassing her, Mom, I swear I wasn't." He let out a compressed breath. "I know how it sounds, but honestly, I just…lost track for a minute or two. At the wrong time. In the wrong place. It hit the ridge. Too close to her. I think. I found her before I found it, so I don't know for sure where it was. But it could have been over the line." His jaw tightened. "It was just a combo of things. A perfect storm."

"You, the precisionist, lost track?"

"I was…thinking."

"About what?" she asked. As if there was something that could make up for what had happened.

He grimaced, lowering his gaze to his muddy boots. "Roth," he admitted. "About what you told me, her big plans, for the future. I never knew she…thought like that."

"You thought she was still that little girl who always annoyed you?"

"I guess," he admitted, feeling more the fool than ever.

"Well, that fits. She apparently thought the same about you. Rob said she was stunned to find out about the business you've built with those drones, about the weather station, and that you wrote the ranch software the Roths use."

"Yeah, well," he muttered, studying his boots again. They were going to take a lot of cleaning, and before he ever set foot in the house, or she'd be on him about that, too.

And after a moment, sounding a bit exasperated, she said, "I swear, you two. Sometimes I wonder." He didn't know what to say to that, so said nothing. He was fairly sure he didn't want to know what she wondered. "And then sometimes," she added in an entirely different tone, "I'm certain."

His brow furrowed, and he looked at her. He couldn't read her this time, had no idea what that had been supposed to mean. "About what?"

"Never mind. Let's think about how we can help."

His mind snapped back to his earlier thought. "I have an idea, but I need to do some research. And it might take some equipment. I need to call the hospital, talk to the orthopedics people."

His mother smiled knowingly. "You do that. But think about something more immediate and practical, too. When she gets home, what's going to drive her the craziest?"

Besides not being able to get back at me? He thought for another moment. "I guess...not being able to ride, or maybe even see to her horses for a while."

"Exactly," Mom said as if she was proud he'd seen that. "So, what can you do to help with that problem?"

He sighed. "Do it for her."

"That, too, and I'm glad you thought of it. But I also meant something a little more in your area of expertise, like you did for us in the barn."

"The cameras," he said with sudden realization. "Of course. I should have thought of that. Thanks, Mom." He leaned in and kissed her cheek before whirling to take off for the house.

"Boots!" she called after him.

"Yeah, yeah."

And with a grin and a lighter heart, he looked back at the

woman who had accomplished the miracle of holding a shattered family together. She was smiling back at him, and he knew it would be all right. If Mom approved, it would somehow be all right.

Chapter Twenty-Three

"THIS IS SO sweet of you, Cody."

He turned to look at Mrs. Roth. She was smiling at him, as she had been all day. She'd even brought him a sandwich for lunch when he'd been mounting the last camera in the barn that housed their horses. She was so grateful for his help, while he was spending the entire time thinking it wasn't enough. How did he make up for what he'd let happen?

He dropped down from the ladder and stood in front of her. There was no one else around at the moment, unlike the rest of the day when various hands and Mr. Roth had been coming and going. And call him a coward, but he didn't want to have this talk in front of a bunch of people he didn't know—or Britt's father. Nor did he want to dwell on why he was having trouble hanging on to that faintly derisive "Roth" moniker when he thought of her.

Something about carrying her down that rocky slope, knowing she was badly hurting and why, had knocked it right out of him.

Not to mention how it had felt in other ways.

"Don't be so nice," he said to the woman in front of him.

She gave him a puzzled look. "After all you've done? Setting up these cameras, and helping with the horses while Brittany is out of commission? Why even that silly Ghost of hers, the cause of all this, behaves better for you."

He drew in a deep breath. He'd never have a better opening than this. "Ghost wasn't the only cause of all this."

She waited, silently, her gaze fastened on him. It must be a mom thing, waiting you out until you broke. He didn't even try to resist but explained what he thought had happened with the drone.

"I haven't been back up there and found it yet," he finished, "but it was close to where she was, and even if she didn't see it, I'm sure it made noise when it hit, and the timing is…well, it happened exactly when it would have had to, to be the cause."

"I see."

He felt a bit of relief that it was out, that he'd confessed, but the tension started to build again as she just looked at him. He waited, expecting her to order him off their ranch at the least, slap him at the worst. When she didn't say anything, he asked quietly, "Do you want me to leave?"

She tilted her head slightly, and he felt like some germ-sized creature under a microscope. Another mom skill: making you feel as if they saw every tiny, hidden aspect of you.

Finally, she spoke.

"Tell me something, Cody. Would that horse of yours have spooked at the sound of something hitting a rock?"

"Trey? No. He barely spooks at rattlesnakes."

"Hmm. You know, I was out riding last fire season when one of your drones went by, checking for smoke. My horse tossed his head and snorted, but that was it. And remember when you had that drone lead us to Ghost's dam, when she was down and trapped? None of the horses we rode then spooked at it."

"That's different. Those are ranch horses, they're used to all manner of things. Ghost is…a specialist."

To his surprise, she laughed. "Now there's a word for it. Brittany would like that."

"I don't think she'd like anything I have to say. Now more than ever."

"You are two of the hardest-headed people I know," she said. "Sometimes I wonder…"

This echoing of his own mother's words made him wonder if he and Britt had been a topic of conversation between the two women. Then he nearly laughed at himself; of course they had been. What did two mothers who were friends always talk about, eventually? Their kids, of course.

And then sometimes I'm certain.

About what? The simple fact that his mother had avoided answering that question made him nervous. He'd learned over the years that it was usually the things she kept her own counsel on that were the most significant in the end.

"Does she know?" she asked.

"I...no."

"Are you going to tell her?"

He blinked. "Aren't you?"

Mrs. Roth shook her head. "This is between you two. Now I have to get back to the hospital." She turned to go, then looked back. "When she gets home, you two need to face this...whatever it is between you."

Cody watched her go, brow furrowed. Whatever it is? It was loathing. Wasn't that clear? Hadn't it been for every one of his twenty-eight years? And hers?

Some people just didn't...mix.

"Everything is fine at the ranch. Stop worrying."

Britt fidgeted, surreptitiously testing the limits of movement, trying to calculate what she could do before the pain got to be too much. The doctor's lecture about doing too much too soon and setting back her recovery had been stern and uncompromising, and she had the feeling her mother had perhaps said something about her exceptionally stubborn daughter. And since she'd already ruined his weekend with this Sunday callout, she kept quiet and just nodded obediently.

"The doctor said you're doing very well."

Britt didn't look up at her mother, afraid she would frown. She didn't consider practically incapacitated doing very well. The only bright spots she could see were that the doctor had said her wrist was only sprained, and the ankle was a clean break of just one bone and wouldn't require surgery; the boulder had done more soft tissue damage than anything, hence the swelling.

And at least the injuries weren't both on the same side, so she'd be able to use a crutch to get around. Eventually, she mentally added, remembering again the warning not to rush things.

As if her thought had summoned him, the man appeared in the doorway to her room. She was surprised, since he'd seen her early this morning before signing for her release. In the brusque, cut-to-the-chase manner she actually appreciated, he didn't waste time with niceties, but handed her something that looked like a brochure he'd printed out off the internet.

"This is what I was talking about," he said.

She remembered, among the myriad instructions she'd been given, mostly about what not to do, that he had said someone had called him about a new technology he wanted her to consider. She'd thought he meant some therapy or something, but what she was looking at was quite different. It looked like some piece of Hollywood costuming for a science fiction film.

"It's from a company in Fort Worth, a 3D-printed cast,"

he said. "The technology is relatively new, but it has many advantages for stable fractures like yours. It eliminates any additional recasting during the healing process, since it's adjustable and removable. It can be fastened to be immovable, like a cast, or be removable more like a splint, to allow swelling to subside. Plus it's lighter, easier to keep clean, healthier for the skin, allows for more activities, like taking a shower. And—" he grinned at her, so startling from the usually dead-serious man "—easier to scratch an itch."

Britt had a sudden image of her father, who had broken an arm when she'd been about ten, griping about that constantly, and finally grabbing one of her mother's knitting needles and jamming it down inside the cast to reach the maddening itch.

"I didn't know there even was such a thing," she said.

"How does it work?" her mother asked.

"It requires a 3D scan of the affected body part, which takes less than a minute. You wear a temporary splint or cast while that is sent to the company, and they print it out."

Her mother shook her head in amazement. "That they can print something like that from a computer still amazes me."

"I haven't used one on a patient yet because I didn't have the proper scanning equipment, but I had planned to as soon as possible. Once I established contact with the company who produces them." He smiled yet again, this time at Britt. "But now, thanks to your friend, I don't have to do any of that. Everything's in place and we can fit you as soon as the swelling is down, the end of next week if you're careful. They've even promised a very rapid turnaround. Handy that you know someone who went to school with one of the primary technicians of the company."

Her brow furrowed. Her friend? "What?"

"He's the one who called me about it and then made all the arrangements. In fact, he's actually loaning us the scanning equipment required. Now that's a good friend, Britt."

A good friend? Or a good enemy?

Because she knew who it was. Who it had to be. Cody. Who else could it be?

And suddenly she was back to yesterday, in his strong arms, allowing it, even savoring it.

He'd found her. Saved her. Held her. Carried her.

And now this. He'd thought of this, arranged it, made it happen.

For her.

And she didn't know what she was supposed to think about that. Or feel about it.

Right now she wasn't certain of anything when it came to Cody Rafferty. And that was a place she had never thought she'd be.

Chapter Twenty-Four

BRITT STARED AT the screen on her laptop, at the image divided into four squares. She couldn't overstate the comfort it gave her, to be able to see her horses when she couldn't get to them, even if she did have to credit that comfort to Cody. At least this way if anything happened she'd know, and could send help, even if she couldn't go herself. Which grated on her even more than the pain that occasionally radiated out either from her ankle or her wrist when she forgot and moved wrong. Like she'd done a moment ago, when she'd tried to shift in the bed to get the screen closer.

The painkiller the doctor had prescribed for her was part of the problem, and she'd told him she'd rather tolerate a little pain than be so groggy she couldn't think. But he'd insisted it was to fight the inflammation as well, and if she wanted that down enough to get that new cast, she'd do what he said.

But when she could think, she kept going back to everything Cody had done. Rescued her, set up her doctor with the company in Fort Worth, and these observation cameras.

One showed the corridor inside the barn, one showed the runs outside each stall, one showed Nugget's stall, and the last one showed Ghost's stall, where the gray was dozing as if she hadn't a care—or a scare—in the world.

She's behaving remarkably well for him, Brittany.

Her mother's words hadn't been meant to sting, she knew, but they still did. She didn't like the idea that Ghost would behave better for someone else. Especially a man.

Especially that man.

But worse had been her father's observation this morning, when he'd brought her in her breakfast, a service that she hated had to be done for her. It had been grating enough to be relegated to a wheelchair, even temporarily, but then to move back into her childhood bedroom because she had to be taken care of? But if this new wonder cast thing was going to work, she had to stay off the foot.

"If I'd known all it would take was a man who's pissed at her to make that horse behave, I would have taken care of that long ago," her father had said very dryly, but there had been a touch of either appreciation or admiration in his tone.

"So he thinks he's a cowboy now?" she'd snapped.

She'd gotten one of those looks she hated from him, because it made her feel like she'd disappointed him, this man she so adored. "I think," he'd said after a moment, "that he's like all the Raffertys. A cowboy at the core. He just spends more time on other, more profitable things because he's got the brain for it."

"I'm sorry, Dad," she'd apologized. "I'm just...cranky."

"With good reason, being laid up like this," he'd said, such sympathy in his voice she knew she was forgiven. "But hopefully things will improve once you get that newfangled plastic cast thing on Friday. But you're still not going to be walking around on it," he'd warned.

"I know, I know." What she didn't know was if she could deal with six weeks of this. The aches, the limitations, the fussing.

"Even the most independent and stubborn of us need to accept help now and then," her father had said. "And I know that from personal experience."

They'd ended the conversation reminiscing about the times he'd been in a similar boat, and ended up laughing at it all, something she'd sorely needed.

But she still didn't like the idea that Ghost was behaving better for Cody.

THE GRAY HORSE danced sideways, away from her stall. Cody took one long stride at the same time, staying right where he'd been relative to the horse.

"I'm on you like glue, lady," he muttered. "So you can keep trying but I'm not going anywhere. And you're going in there."

The horse snorted and head-butted him. With Trey that

would be a sign of affection. With this beast, he was fairly sure it was an attempt to knock him on his ass.

"You ever hear of the law of diminishing returns, horse? One of these days even your brilliance on the barrels might not be enough to put up with your attitude."

The horse snorted, loudly, but was looking past him. He realized that in the same moment he heard a voice from behind him.

"And that day may be coming sooner than she thinks."

He spun around to see Britt approaching, in the wheelchair they'd sent her home from the hospital in, with her mother behind it, pushing.

"Should you be up?" he asked.

The minute he said it he expected a snappy retort, something along the lines of *Who made you the boss of me?* That it didn't come told him how rattled she still must be.

"I just wanted to thank you," she said, her tone a bit formal. "For the cameras. It's a huge relief to be able to see them."

"I...good. You're welcome."

He still hadn't told her. And obviously, neither had her mother. He'd thought he'd wait until she was feeling a little better. Maybe after she had the 3D cast on.

Ghost snorted and bobbed her head toward Britt.

Fine time to show you care, horse.

"I think right now this is about the right distance between you and her," he said.

"I won't argue that," Britt said, sounding weary.

A thank you, and now no argument? She must still be in pain. He winced inwardly and turned to deal with the horse. He moved quickly and strongly, shoving his shoulder hard against Ghost's withers. Surprised, the horse backed away from him. And right into her stall. Before she could decide to rebel against the indignity, he had the door shut and latched.

"Nicely done," her mother said with a smile. Before he could respond her cell phone chimed. She pulled it out and looked. "It's Maggie—we're supposed to go to the festival planning meeting together." She looked back at Cody. "And if I haven't said, your video is magnificent. Thank you for doing it."

He shifted his feet uncomfortably, wondering how she could thank him for something he'd done with the same kind of device that had landed her daughter where she was now.

"Thanks," he said, sounding almost as uncomfortable as he felt.

"Will you see Brittany back to the main house so I can get going? This is her first time out and she shouldn't push it."

"Of course," he said automatically, before he thought of what that would actually entail. Not that he could have said no if he had thought. But when she'd gone and he was left alone with the woman in the wheelchair, he almost wished he could have.

"You'd better get back inside and rest. Get that ankle elevated."

"Yes," she admitted.

She started to turn the chair, or try to, but it was painful to watch. He took a long stride toward her. "Just let me. Like your mom asked," he added, in case she was thinking of fighting him.

Silently, she gave up. There was no conversation on the way back to the house. They stopped in front of the two steps of the front porch.

"It'll be easier if I just carry you inside," he said before he thought, before the memories rose up to nearly swamp him. It took him a moment to add, "Then I'll come back for the chair."

She didn't argue.

He'd seen Britt Roth happy. He'd seen her triumphant. He'd seen—and heard—her sarcastic. And more than anything he'd seen her angry, usually at him. He'd never in his life seen her look defeated. Even if she lost at a rodeo, she was immediately looking forward to a victory in the next run.

But she was looking it now.

"How am I going to get through six to *eight* weeks of this? Maybe even more?" she whispered.

He knew how badly she was feeling by the simple fact that she'd let him hear that. She probably was barely aware he was even there. But he answered her anyway, because something in the way she looked was digging at him.

"It won't stay this bad that whole time. It'll get better as you go. And once your wrist is better, you can use the crutches." She looked briefly startled, and he knew he'd been right that she hadn't really meant for him to hear that. She wouldn't like to betray what she'd see as weakness.

"And how long will it take to get back into competition shape after it's healed?" she asked, her voice tight.

"Stubborn as you are? I'd say about three days."

Her eyes widened. For a moment he thought she was going to fire back at him with some typical Roth salvo. But then something crazy happened.

She laughed. She actually laughed.

Cody felt something warm and honeyed break loose inside him. He didn't know what it was, or what it meant.

But he did know he wasn't sure he liked the fact that he liked it.

Chapter Twenty-Five

"THAT REALLY WAS a nice trick, with Ghost," Britt said, because she felt she owed it to him. He had indeed carried her inside, with the same care as he'd carried her down that slippery slope. He'd gently lowered her into the power recliner her father had ceded to her for the duration.

She expected him to say something about a horse you had to trick not being worth the trouble, but he didn't. Instead he said, "You're worried about her losing ground while you're recovering."

It wasn't a question. He'd said it as if he knew it was true. It was, of course, but she hadn't expected him to see it. "Yes," she admitted.

"And yourself, too."

She couldn't deny she was worried, a lot, about her own condition, about getting weak, about the injured joints not regaining enough strength and stability fast enough, or maybe even not working right. And she didn't like how this tiny excursion out to the barn had exhausted her. But she really hadn't expected him to understand any of that.

She knew her surprise must have shown on her face, but he didn't call her on it. Instead, he said quietly, "I could work with her while you're down," he said. "At least keep her in shape."

Cody riding Ghost? That had the potential for him to end up in worse shape than she was. And she was stunned he'd offered. "You sure you want to tackle that?"

"I know, I'm not up to dealing with her on the same level you are," he said with a wry half smile.

She stared up at him silently for a long moment. Too long. But she was trying to understand the urge that had come over her. And she couldn't seem to stop herself from saying, "And I couldn't deal with your tech stuff."

For a moment he just stared back at her. It was awkward, this kind of peace and understanding between them, because it was unfamiliar.

"It's going to be okay," he said suddenly. "You'll get back on the circuit, both of you, and it'll go just like you planned."

She drew back slightly. Now encouragement? From Cody the Coder? "Not quite like I planned," she said. "I'll be getting a late start at this rate, by the time I get us both back in shape. It could be three months of downtime, if it takes the maximum time to heal and then get through rehab."

"So you get a late start," he said. "Make it a big deal. If it's going to be three months, start back up like you started the first time, at the Independence Day Rodeo here in Last

Stand. Let people think that's why you're starting late. You wanted it to be there. Home crowd'll be good, too. They'll cheer so much Ghost will fly."

He smiled, a full one this time. And that dimple flashed again. Damn, it wasn't fair. She hated him. Why did he have to look so good?

And be so nice. And strong. Don't forget those.

She stopped herself before she went on and on with a list of attributes that she would admire a great deal, in anyone else.

"I…that's a good idea," she admitted. "As long as it doesn't get out I got thrown just out riding. That'll have sponsors wondering if I'm as good as they thought."

His smile, that great, dimpled smile, vanished. He looked as if she'd tossed—as she once had—a glass of ice water at him. And she had no idea why.

"Wondering that yourself?" she asked, her tone sour.

"No." His voice matched his suddenly unreadable expression. Then he looked away, turning his head to stare out the front window of the house before saying roughly, "I know how good you are."

For a moment he just stood there. And she just sat there—as if she had any other choice—amid the clutter that had accumulated around this chair she was limited to at the moment, trying to figure out what had changed. After a few silent moments passed, moments in which she grew more and more aware of the various aches and pains she was feeling, she let out a sigh.

"For somebody supposedly so good, I should have known better, heading up there when it was raining like that. I'm not surprised those rocks went."

His head snapped back around. He stared at her, and for a moment she was almost certain he was about to blurt out something. And she got the feeling it was something he didn't want to say.

But before he could there was a distinctive scratch at the door.

"That must be Dodger," she said.

"You want him in?" Cody asked, sounding relieved, which made her think she'd been right about him not wanting to say whatever it had been.

"Yes, he'll be good company. Your brother even trained him to fetch some things, so he'll be handy, too, given I'm about as mobile as this house right now."

When she mentioned Chance, his expression changed again, this time becoming thoughtful. Funny, she'd always thought him so obsessed with his tech toys she'd never credited him much with ordinary, human thoughts. But he only turned and went to the door, letting in the big German shepherd, who paused to sniff at him but then kept coming until he was beside the chair.

"Yep, I'm stealing Dad's chair," she said to him as he looked up at her. "Don't bite me." Cody, still by the door he'd just closed again, looked at her sharply. "Joke, Rafferty.

Chance would never have let us have him if he'd been that touchy still."

Again that thoughtful look. "I know."

When he didn't say anything else, she felt compelled to tell him, "I'm fine. You can go now."

"No, I can't."

She blinked. "Why?"

"I promised your mom I'd stay until she got back or your dad got home."

Since Dad was in Waco helping a friend with a new bull, that wouldn't be soon, and when Mom and Maggie got to talking…well, that might not be soon either.

"You don't have to do that."

"Yes, I do. I promised. Otherwise one of them would have canceled and stayed home."

That rang true. And part of her was glad he'd made that promise, so neither of her parents had had to duck a commitment. But that didn't mean she wanted Cody the Coder hanging out with her.

"I'm just going to read," she said.

"Until you need something Dodger can't fetch, or need to get up."

A brief vision of him helping her to the bathroom flashed through her mind, and heat rose to her cheeks. "I'll be fine," she said stiffly, even knowing that trying to do that on her own, the first day after the accident, could easily end in disaster.

"Yes. And I'll stay out of your way. I brought work," he said, gesturing with a thumb at a laptop she hadn't noticed before, over on the bar that was this side of the kitchen counter.

She gave in because she had no choice. She spent a while contemplating the fact that she was stuck in the living room of the house she grew up in, with the last person she wanted to be with sitting a short distance away, stuck as much as she was, no doubt with the last person he'd ever wanted to be with.

That thought made her cringe inwardly, and she wasn't sure why. Didn't want to think about why. And it drove her to ask abruptly, "Why drones?"

His head came up from the laptop sharply, as if she'd startled him. "What?"

"Why, out of all the tech stuff you could be—" she almost said obsessed "—involved with, why drones? I mean I get that they're handy for some things, useful even, but how did they become your main thing?"

He studied her for a moment, as if he were assessing whether she was actually interested, or just filling a silence. She wasn't quite sure herself. He'd been, after all, quite involved in whatever he'd been looking at, so the silence hadn't been uncomfortable.

At least not for him.

Maybe she was simply losing her mind. She'd write it off to maybe having hit her head harder than she'd thought, except they'd done tests and a scan at the hospital and she didn't have even a slight concussion.

She had just decided he wasn't going to answer her at all—and perhaps rightfully so—when he spoke.

"I'm working toward a silent drone with more range. There's one, the KHA K1000, that was able to make an amazing twenty-six-hour flight because onboard sensors allowed it to ride thermals just like a bird. Problem is, it has a sixteen-foot wingspan. Not exactly portable."

She hesitated, then said, "So that's the what. Still wondering about why."

For a moment she thought he really wasn't going to answer this time. And when he did, it was in a voice she'd never heard from him before. Low, quiet, with a note almost of pain. By the time he finished the first sentence, she understood why.

"My father was killed when his platoon's position was given away by the sound of a surveillance drone's motor. It was just loud enough the enemy knew which way to look. Then they blasted away an entire hill, killing them all."

She stared at him. She had never heard this, never known this part of the tragic story. Of course her parents wouldn't go into that kind of detail, given her age at the time; she'd been a child.

So had he.

"I never knew that," she said, only aware when it came out that she was barely managing a whisper. "No wonder you…"

Her voice faded away as for the first time in her life she understood. Why he was so obsessed. And when he turned back to his laptop without another word, she wondered why he'd told her. Why he hadn't just blown her off, saying it was none of her business. As the Cody of old would have done.

Something had changed. Something major. She didn't know what, and she didn't know why.

But most of all, she didn't know why she liked it.

And it held. The next day he showed up early in the morning. And the next day, and the day after that. He did her chores, the things she would normally have done, and more. He worked her horses, even Ghost, although she suspected from the dirt on the shoulder of his jacket that she'd tossed him at least once. He didn't say anything about it, and she was torn about asking. Because the horse needed the work, and he was the only one willing to take that on. Her father or a couple of the hands had been willing to work her on the lunge line, but nobody on the Roth ranch wanted to try to ride the spooky grullo.

But Cody was. Yet another fact that was shifting her perception of him. And on another level, of herself; she should have known a boy raised on the Rafferty ranch, mostly by Maggie Rafferty, would be both tough and more than competent. And so he rode the horse no one else but her even dared mount.

Yet, strangely, she didn't want him to get hurt doing it. There had been a time when she probably would have gloated over it, but not now.

And she didn't know why.

Maybe it was just this new and unpleasant experience with serious pain. The doctor had insisted she keep up with the meds, but she hated how groggy they made her and wanted off them as soon as possible. So maybe that was why she didn't like thinking about anybody, even Cody, in that kind of pain.

He spent time in the house every day too, as if to keep tabs on her. And if her parents had to go somewhere—funny, she hadn't realized they had so much planned for this week, requiring them both to be gone—he stayed with her. And they even talked, civilly. More than civilly, they talked almost like friends.

He asked about her plans in a way that surprised her; she hadn't realized he was so aware of the rodeo circuit, from when his brother Keller had been competing. She found out more things she'd never known, which she mentally filed away next to the revelation he'd made about his drones. Somehow that in particular had changed her entire way of thinking about the pesky things.

And that third afternoon, when he was hunched over the laptop again—after fulfilling her embarrassing vision by helping her to the bathroom, in a rather businesslike way that actually made it much less uncomfortable than she'd feared—she brought it up again. "Even if you succeed, it won't bring him back," she said quietly.

He didn't even look up. "But it might save someone else."

So. Cody the Coder saw beyond himself and his own pain. But then, hadn't he proved that this week? By showing up every day to help out? She'd known the other Raffertys would help out if needed, because that's the kind of friends, neighbors, and people they were. She'd just never expected the mainstay of that effort to be this Rafferty.

"Maybe you should be working on better batteries, then."

He did look up then. "Smarter people than me are doing that."

She was surprised he admitted there were smarter people than him, when it came to that kind of thing. But then a lot of things had surprised her this week. And it was only half over.

Then, abruptly, he said, "I want to see that 3D cast procedure, so I'm going along on Friday." That didn't surprise her. And she could hardly say no, given he'd had the idea in the first place, and arranged it all. Then he added, "Unless you don't want me to."

She stared at him. Since when did he give a hoot about what she wanted or didn't want?

Since this happened. That's obvious.

But why? Of all the whys she'd been batting around in

her mind these past few days, that was still the biggest. The one she didn't understand, didn't have a clue about.

Why he was doing all of this.

Chapter Twenty-Six

CODY REINED TREY in at the front of the small, sturdy cabin. He noticed the stakes and twine strung out on the west side, where Chance was planning the expansion. With Ariel now living there full time, his brother had decided they needed more space. Ariel insisted she was content with the way things were, but Chance wanted the best for the woman who had changed his life, and every one of the Raffertys would pitch in to see he got it.

He dismounted and threw the reins over the hitching rail just as Chance came around the corner of the building. Cody saw his brother glance at Trey.

"Somebody tell you to cowboy up?" his brother asked, telling him he'd noticed the shift from driving to riding lately.

"Nah," he said. "Just appreciating what a great horse Trey is."

Chance nodded. "Heard about your rescue from Mom. How's Britt doing?"

"Hurting," he said with a smothered wince. Then, because he wasn't quite ready yet, he asked, "You guys still leaving today?" He knew they planned to head for San Antonio, to pick up another dog from the base there.

Chance nodded. "As soon as Ariel gets back. We're scheduled for the meetup tomorrow morning. Then a couple of days of assessing the dog, and we'll head back early Sunday morning. Hopefully with two instead of one."

Cody knew they took Tri with them on these trips, both to show him off as the amazing success he was, and because the animal seemed to understand the purpose, and was great at calming the nervous newcomers.

"Lucas going to see to the Lab?"

Chance nodded. "With instructions not to take him out of the run, just to see he's fed and has water. That's still one edgy dog."

Cody nodded. "You're doing a great thing here, bro."

Chance gave him a rather considering look. "With a lot of help from people who agree with that sentiment. Including Britt."

Cody drew back sharply. "What?"

"You didn't know? She's made a couple of sizeable donations, since she started making real money on the circuit."

Cody shifted his gaze back to the hills, afraid of what might be showing in his face. He'd never known that. Yet another thing to add to the list.

"Where is Ariel?" Cody asked, afraid to even say Britt's name.

"Out walking with Tri. Things kind of…hit her this

morning. They needed some alone time."

Cody studied his brother for a moment. He knew what kind of things he meant. Ariel's husband, Tri's former handler, had paid the ultimate price for serving his country, just as their father had.

"You're okay with that?" he asked.

Chance returned the steady gaze, only his was much more powerful, Cody was certain. You didn't go where he'd gone and do what he'd done and not come back with that different look. "You know as well as anyone grief doesn't come and go to order. He was a great guy and she loved him. I accept that."

"She loves you," Cody said, almost urgently.

"And I cherish that," Chance said with a smile, a soft, gentle sort of smile they'd all been afraid they would never see from him again when he'd first come home. And that made Cody search for something else to say, other than what he'd come here for, because he didn't want to wreck his brother's mood.

"So how's the planning for Keller's wedding coming?" Ariel had been an event planner back in California and had delightedly taken on this project for the family who had so completely welcomed her.

Chance rolled his eyes. "She's amazing, but damn, that's a lot of work. Not that Keller and Sydney don't deserve it—he deserves everything all of us can give—but it makes eloping sound pretty darn good."

Cody's brow rose. "Something you want to tell me, bro?"

"No." But a smile played around Chance's mouth when he added, "Not yet."

Soon, bro. You deserve all the happy you can find.

Chance just looked at him for a moment, with those gray-blue eyes that had seen so much, most of which he kept to himself. Today was apparently going to be an exception, however.

"You didn't ride all the way out here just to check on all that. What's up?"

"I…needed to ask you something."

Chance's expression didn't change. All he said was, "It's a little early for a beer, but at least sit down."

They did, on the front steps of the cabin his brother had adopted as his home and refurbished. Shoulder to shoulder, looking out toward the rolling hills of this land that was in their blood, made it easier.

"Mom told me once you blamed yourself for what happened to Ariel's husband."

He felt Chance go still beside him. It was a moment before he spoke. "I did."

"Why?"

It was a measure of how far he'd come, how far loving Ariel had brought him, that he answered at all, let alone easily. "I couldn't talk the brass out of the mission I knew was suicidal. It was Ariel who showed me you can't convince people who don't have the capacity to listen."

Cody was glad, beyond glad, that she'd been able to do that. But the admission didn't really help him. Not in the way he had been hoping it would. Silence drew out between them, until Chance gave him—and there was no doubting that was what it was—an order.

"Out with it."

"What?" Cody said, stalling.

"Why you feel responsible for what happened to Britt."

He should have known Chance would guess. "Because I am," he said flatly. And he told him what had happened.

"But you're not sure where it went down?"

"I haven't had time to go look for it." *Because I've been trying to ease the guilt by working my ass off over there.*

"So it might not have been over the fence line at all."

"Maybe. But even if it wasn't—"

"You're going to take the blame anyway. Sounds familiar."

He knew Chance was referring back to what he'd just told him. "But that's different. That really wasn't your fault. If that drone was over the line, this is mine."

"Correct me if I'm wrong," Chance said, a bit of drawl creeping into his voice, "but isn't there a borderline psychotic horse involved here somewhere?"

"The one that dumped me in the dirt yesterday?" he asked, his tone dry.

"I rest my case."

"But Britt is twice the rider I am. Maybe more."

"No maybe about it, bro," Chance said with a grin. "Your expertise lies in other areas."

"But that proves the point, doesn't it?"

This brother who had been through hells Cody would never know studied him for a moment. Then, quietly, he asked, "Does she blame you?"

"No." His tone must have given him away because Chance merely waited, one brow raised. He let out a disgusted breath. "She doesn't know. She thinks the rockslide spooked said psychotic horse."

"Maybe she's right."

"I saw it hit the ridge. I know it must have made noise."

"Which she thinks was the rocks breaking loose with the rain?" Chance asked. Cody nodded. "Are you going to tell her?"

"I have to, don't I?"

His brother went silent for a while, then, Chance-like, he distilled it down to the essence. "Only if you want to live with yourself."

She missed him.

How utterly, totally insane was that?

Her mother was in the kitchen, making another ton of her favorite cookies so she'd always have something within reach. Her father was at the kitchen bar with pencil and paper, working on some ideas for her place, to make things easier once she was cleared to be on her own.

And here she was, trapped in this damned chair, moping because Cody hadn't come over yet today.

Cody. Cody Rafferty. She was missing Cody Rafferty.

Yes, insane. That was the only answer.

"How's it coming, dear?" Britt looked up to see her mother leaning over her father's shoulder to look at the paper he had on the bar.

"I think this placement will work. I'll need Cody to look at it, of course, he's the expert."

"What will work?" she asked, her curiosity sparked even as she silently admitted she didn't like that all it took was the mention of his name.

"A sort of intercom, between your place and here," her father answered, still looking at the page. "For when you're allowed to go back there."

Allowed? Her independent spirit bristled. "I have a phone," she pointed out.

"Yes, but this is voice-activated, so you don't have to be able to physically get to it." Her father looked at her then. "In case you fell, or something else went wrong."

"Great," she muttered, thinking of the commercials about the old lady who'd fallen and couldn't get up.

"Think of it like one of those smart-home things," he said. "And it's only temporary."

"And besides," her mother said, "it will relieve your poor

old mom and dad of a lot of stress and worry. I think it's wonderful that Cody thought of that and came up with the idea."

"This was his idea?"

"Yes," Mom answered. "He knew you'd want to get back to your own place as soon as you could, and that when you did, we'd still be worried."

The memory was there instantly. Yesterday, he was sitting where Dad was now, when she'd sighed and said how tired she already was of doing nothing but sitting, and that things she needed to do were piling up at her place.

"Probably why your folks want you here," he'd said. "Nothing to lure you into trying to do too much too soon," he'd said.

"I can get around a little on my own now. I could start cleaning their house."

"No, you couldn't." He'd said it flatly. As if it were a given. That had sparked the old irritation, the instant antagonism she had always felt around him.

"Why not?" she'd demanded.

"Because I wouldn't let you." In that same cool tone.

"Excuse me?" she'd said coldly. "Who appointed you my babysitter?"

He had hesitated then, which was odd when they were almost back to normal. A normal that should make her feel relieved, because the way things had shifted between them made her twitchy in a weird sort of way. And before he could answer, her mother had returned from her shopping trip to town, with the makings of these cookies she loved and would eat too many of. She was going to have to be careful, or she'd have ten pounds to lose before this was over.

"—will be careful, won't you?"

She tuned back in at the sound of her mother's worried voice. "I don't have much choice," she said, nodding toward her immobilized foot and ankle and holding up her equally immobilized wrist.

"We could cancel," Mom said. "The Langleys would understand. They know you're hurt."

"It's their anniversary dinner, you have to go. I'll be fine," Britt insisted.

"Of course she'll be fine," Dad said firmly. "Cody'll be here."

Britt blinked. He was coming over tonight? Was that why he hadn't been here today? "He will?" Gads, she sounded as inane as she felt.

"He promised he'd be here before we left. I've got snacks ready. You two can have a nice movie night," Mom said, as if she were a child she was leaving in the hands of a babysitter.

And that thought had her back wondering what Cody had almost said when she'd asked him who appointed him her babysitter.

"Oh, I'm sure we'll have a great time, given his likely taste in movies," she said sourly. She wanted to tell them to forget it, to tell him not to come. But then her mother's words came back to her. *It will relieve your poor old mom and dad of a lot of stress and worry.* And she bit back the words.

"I'm sure you can find common ground somewhere," her father said blithely. "I mean, you haven't killed each other yet, and it's been five days."

"Only because I can't get to my shotgun," she muttered.

But she realized, with no small amount of surprise, that her heart wasn't even in the joke. Because the Cody who had been in essence taking care of her for a lot of those five days bore little resemblance to her nemesis, Cody the Coder.

Well, except in looks.

Britt smothered a groan and let her head loll back on the cushion of the recliner.

Her body hadn't been the only thing tossed into complete chaos up in those rocks.

Chapter Twenty-Seven

CODY WATCHED KELLER and Sydney walk out toward the barn, holding hands. The sight gave him that odd feeling of satisfaction and wistfulness again.

It's the damned air around here lately. It's infectious.

That had to be it. There was freaking love everywhere. That was what had him so…wound up. It had to be. Didn't it?

As he watched his eldest brother, the one who had gone from boy to man in the space of one visit from the military chaplain to tell them life as they'd known it was over, he thought of the conversation they'd had when he first got back from Chance's place.

"You didn't like Sydney at first," he'd said.

Keller had raised his brows at him. "As I recall, you were the ringleader on that front."

"I know I was. And I know I didn't like her being here for all the wrong reasons. But you took some convincing, too."

"I had to look out for Lucas. Be sure she was the best thing for him."

"And she turned out to be the best thing for both of you."

Keller had smiled. "That she did."

"When did it change? How did you know?"

Keller had stared at him for a long, silent moment that had Cody feeling uncomfortable. Because it was as if he was looking at him with Dad's eyes, those eyes that had seen so much, down to the heart of his children.

"I knew when it became too much to fight off any longer," he finally said. "That's when I saw who she really was, not who my worry about Lucas was telling me she might be." He'd paused, then added in a voice full of such understanding it made Cody edgy, "But I didn't have a lifetime of battling with her to give up."

A lifetime of battling with her. Only one person fit that description.

I swear, you two. Sometimes I wonder. And then sometimes I'm certain.

What had his mother really been saying? Or rather, not saying?

He gave a sharp shake of his head, turned on his boot heel—he'd gone to his not so often worn cowboy boots since he'd been working over at the Roths so much—and headed back to his lair. Where, because he had to move, he started pacing the main room. For one of the few times in his life not even looking at the monitors, which were all still asleep anyway. He'd been in no mood for gaming, business dealings were beyond him just now, and he hadn't had a drone up since Sunday, when it had happened.

This was insane. He was only spending all this time with her because she was injured. And because it was his fault. Nothing else.

He spun around and headed the opposite direction.

Isn't there a borderline psychotic horse involved here somewhere?

Yes, Ghost was exactly that. He knew that firsthand now; the damned mare spooked at a fluttering piece of hay she'd just stirred up herself. But did that really change anything?

Are you going to tell her?

I have to, don't I?

Only if you want to live with yourself.

So he had to tell her. And soon. She was being so nice. When he told her the truth, that would end. But the longer he waited, the worse it would be; he knew her temper too well. She'd blow up at the idea she'd been nice to him when in truth it was all his fault.

But he had to. Chance was right about that. Tomorrow, he thought. After she got the new cast and was able to do more for herself, then he'd tell her. And endure the blast, because he deserved it. Then he could go back to his side of the line and she to hers, and life would return to normal.

Maybe.

He was still pacing the floor, back and forth, when a twinge from the knee he'd bruised up on that slope reminded him that he'd promised to be there when the Roths had to leave for a friend's twenty-fifth anniversary party. A glance at the time told him he had about two minutes to get his ass over there. It would take him ten to drive out and around, so it looked like Trey was going to get another run.

He was late enough that he didn't saddle up but leapt astride bareback. Trey perked up at that, probably because he knew by now that meant they were in a hurry and he was always up for a good run. And it was a good run, highlighted by a leap over the border fence that Cody nearly regretted tackling bareback, but Trey was a rock and landed perfectly, giving him the chance to save it.

He turned the horse loose in the corral next to the house, which Mr. Roth had told him he was free to use. The big bay hadn't really worked up a sweat; for him that had been short burst. He made it to their door just over a minute late, which for him wasn't bad at all.

They were already on their way out to their car, Mrs. Roth blithely saying they knew he'd keep his word. They confirmed the times for the cast appointment tomorrow. She thanked him prettily for "looking out for our girl" before they drove off.

Britt acted almost glad to see him. The smile she gave him when he stepped into the living room startled him, and he was smiling back before he realized. And he was surprised again when the movie she picked was a classic action flick he'd always liked because they got the tech involved right. She even asked him about that, between handfuls of popcorn, and he managed to answer without going off into the weeds like he too often did on the subject.

"This popcorn is really good," he said after his next mouthful. "What's on it?"

"Mom's secret seasoning formula," she said with a wide smile. "She won't tell me what all's in it, she just keeps a little jar in the cupboard. I think she wants to be sure I come over now and then to get it, now that she finally surrendered her meat loaf recipe."

"Moms," he said with a grin.

"They do have their ways," she said, grinning back. And that grin, coming from her, made his stomach do a strange little flip. Or something.

Then her expression changed, and she sighed. "She says I can have the recipe when I give her a grandkid."

He blinked. "What?"

"She wants them."

"Oh." He grimaced. "So does mine."

"Lucky you, you've got three brothers ahead of you to produce them, and Keller pretty much already has with Lucas."

"Does take some pressure off," he admitted.

She hesitated visibly, then asked, "Have you ever been close? With anybody?"

He didn't know what to say. Was she asking out of some genuine interest, or was it just brought on by the pressure she'd mentioned? Probably the latter. Which somehow made it easier to answer.

"Could have been. Once. But we didn't have…enough time." She just looked at him, waiting. Quietly, not prodding, not poking. Who was this Roth, anyway? And finally, he wasn't sure why, it came pouring out. "It was a girl I met at a convention in Dallas, a few years ago. We…really connected." He smiled sadly. "I was head over heels, and she said she was too. Only one problem."

"What?"

He took in a deep breath and said it. "She was dying."

Her eyes widened. "What?"

"She was totally honest about it, that we would only have that long weekend."

Her brow furrowed. "Cody…are you sure that was true?" He'd have been angry at the implication if she hadn't sounded genuinely concerned. Instead, he reached for his phone as she went on. "I've known women who…use things like that as an excuse, like if they're married or—"

She stopped when he held out his phone with the image called up. She looked at it, and he saw color hit her cheeks. "I'm sorry. I didn't mean—"

"It's all right. I know people play games. She wasn't one of them."

He took back the phone, still showing the image of the obituary dated less than six months after that con.

"Why do you…keep that, like that?"

"To remind me to not waste time. Dad's is there, too."

She looked at him as if she were experiencing a tangle of emotions. "Did you love her?"

"I think I would have. If we'd had that time."

"Why on earth would your mom push you, then? She has to know it…would hurt."

He bit his lip, but he was in too deep to stop now. "She doesn't know. None of them do." She simply stared at him. "I've never…told anyone about her."

And he had no idea why he'd told her now.

Chapter Twenty-Eight

BRITT FELT AS if her entire life had condensed down to being between the proverbial rock and a hard place. What had happened in fact had somehow turned her life into a simile so corny she tried not to think about it. The actual rock had done its damage. But somehow her life, at least this morning, had degenerated into the cliché, as she bounced from the one to the other, trying not to think about either. The metaphorical rock, the knowledge she should not put too much hope into this new cast she was getting today, not think it was going to put her completely back on her feet and functional, and the hard place, her totally unexpected, ridiculous, and bewildering reaction to Cody the Coder.

She could barely even think about him that way anymore. As her lifelong enemy, the boy next door she hated with a passion. Because every time she tried to, a different Cody snuck into her mind. The Cody who had rescued her, who had carried her, who had taken care of her.

The Cody of last night. The one she had actually enjoyed sitting here watching that old movie with. Eating popcorn, making jokes. The one she'd actually told about her mother's pressure for her to settle down.

The Cody who had told her something he'd never told anyone, about the girl he'd fallen for and lost, the girl who had stolen his heart and then died so young.

She recoiled from that thought, because she didn't like the way it made her feel, a weird combination of wondering why he'd had so much loss and pain in his life when she, the same age nearly down to the minute, had in essence had so little. She'd lost animals in her life, and had been horribly saddened by it, but her parents and even grandparents were alive and well. And she'd never fallen in love, not like he'd described, so she'd never had that to lose.

But pulling back from it had her wondering why he'd told her. Her, of all people, when he'd never told the people he was closest to, his family. The Raffertys were a tightly knit bunch, all of them finding a way to stay together and yet having their separate lives. Even when his older brothers had found their obvious soul mates, they'd managed to keep it all together there on the ranch that had been in their family for generations, since before the Revolution.

When she found herself starting to wonder how Cody would adapt when his time came, her recoil became a physical thing. She tried to ignore her gut-level reaction as they got ready to head back to the hospital for the 3D-cast scan.

Which Cody would be there for. She'd known that, she just hadn't quite put together that he'd actually be riding with them. They'd started a second movie last night, but she hadn't made it to the end; the darn pain meds still made her too sleepy. That had to stop, and soon. When her parents had returned, fairly late, all he'd said as he left was "See you tomorrow," and she hadn't thought much beyond that before she'd conked out completely.

As if his assurance about tomorrow was all she had needed to sleep peacefully.

A tapping on the bathroom door snapped her out of the crazy ruminations she'd slipped into. Again.

"Honey? Are you ready?"

"I'll be out in a minute," she said as she wrestled with the knitted cover for the toes of her injured leg, which her mother had said she'd need this morning.

"Your dad's out warming up the car, but Cody's here and he can help if you need it."

"Great," she muttered, listening to Mom's footsteps fade away.

Memories of the last time he'd helped her out of the bathroom made her cheeks heat. She'd lost her balance when she'd accidentally leaned too far to keep from putting weight on the injured ankle and had ended up careening into him. He'd caught her, held her until she was steady, and…longer. It was probably only a few seconds. But it had felt both longer and far too short.

The temporal version of a rock and a hard place? And stop putting hard anything and him in the same thought!

She maneuvered her way out of the bathroom now and down the hall. She hated being so limited, and by the time she got to the living room her jaw was tight, not so much from pain as from frustration.

"You okay? I can carry you out there if it's bad this morning."

He sounded so sincere, so genuinely worried that she couldn't doubt him. And she had, through her aggravation, remembered the thought she'd had up at the ridge, about this being a Cody imposter who'd come to rescue her. Except she knew for certain now it wasn't. The Cody he'd been since was probably closer to the real Cody than she had ever seen.

Or wanted to see. Because how on earth could you stay angry with this guy?

As it turned out the scan was the quickest, least uncomfortable part of the process, because the original casts had to be removed, which wasn't fun given the ankle fracture was obviously still unhealed, although the new set of X-rays showed the process was beginning. But the doctor was even more enthused than he had been before, once he saw the swelling had gone away nearly completely.

For Britt the best news at the moment was her wrist. He'd said she could go with only the new splint and take it off for exercises the first week.

"Then I think you'll be using crutches by the end of next week. I was hoping for this, since you're young and fit, and you've obviously followed instructions and taken it easy," he said, sounding excited.

Britt half-expected Cody to make some crack about how much she'd complained about following those instructions, but he didn't. So, she did. "Except on the complaining, that I did full strength."

Dr. Reed smiled, and her mother brushed it off, but Cody let out an audible chuckle.

He talked of how once this was done not only could it be adjusted as needed, avoiding the whole plaster replacement procedure, she wouldn't have to worry about replacing the cast because of skin irritation or getting it wet. Then he and Cody got off into a discussion she could only follow half of, and Cody actually ended up overseeing the scan itself, since the tech was brand new to the staff.

"We're looking into getting our own scanning equipment," the doctor said as the brief process ran through.

"Keep this one until you do," Cody told him. "Somebody else might need it."

"You sure? This is expensive equipment."

Cody nodded. "It's already got the proprietary software that sends the scan to the manufacturer installed, and that takes a while to get and set up, so this way you're ready to go."

Expensive equipment. And Cody had just loaned it out. For her sake. And now was extending that loan just in case somebody else needed it. And another aspect of the guy she'd never seen before slipped into place. And each additional piece was one more bit of proof that she'd been not only stubborn, but willfully blind to who he really was.

When they were done Dr. Reed, who had stayed for the whole process because it was new to him, began to apply the temporary splint to her wrist, and the splint-boot combination to her injured ankle, a thing that looked like it was going to weigh a ton, it was so bulky.

"You need to be more careful than ever, so you don't swell up again and make the new cast not fit properly," he ordered sternly.

"Oh, great," she muttered.

"You're not fully into the reparative stage yet, although the inflammation has greatly subsided. I recommend very little movement until we get that cast on. The wheelchair, but only with help. Pushing it yourself would likely aggravate your wrist in that temporary splint."

"Then she just won't," Mom said briskly. "She'll just stay still or be moved by someone else."

Her gaze shifted from the doctor to her mother. "Wheelchair? Still?" She'd actually harbored the faint hope she'd be walking out of here on crutches.

"Or I could just carry you everywhere," Cody said blandly, as if he were suggesting nothing more complicated than opening a door. As if he sensed the sudden intensity in the room, Dr. Reed muttered something about paperwork and left them to it.

Britt didn't dare look at him, because the memory of the times he'd already carried her had erupted in her brain, and she was afraid if she did look at him her confused, unwanted, but overwhelming feelings about it would show. She tried to focus on the idea of being confined to a wheelchair for days longer. She tried to imagine two more long days of maneuvering through her mother's clutter of furniture and couldn't. Her own taste ran to more sparse furnishings, with space to move…

She suddenly realized she might be able to gain something out of this. "My place," she said abruptly.

"What?" her mother asked.

"I'll do it in my place."

"But honey—"

"It only makes sense. Less furniture, more open space."

"She has a point," Dad said from where he'd been quietly observing from the far side of the room. "One of us will have to stay with her, but it would probably be easier."

"You don't need to stay with me," she protested; either of her parents fussing over her would drive her mad. "Isn't that what that fancy new intercom system is for?"

"And, Ms. Stubborn, just how long would you last before deciding you could do this one little thing by yourself without bothering anybody, and if you survived that one more little thing, then a bigger thing?"

Her head snapped around and she stared at Cody. Opened her mouth to let out a sharp retort. But in the instant before she did the truth of what he'd said hit her and she shut it again. How the heck had he learned her so well?

As if he'd heard the thought, he added quietly, "Just like I would do. Like I did, when I was ten and broke my arm trying to ride Buckshot."

She gaped at him, remembering the spirited, feisty buckskin stallion. "Your dad's stud? You really tried to ride him?"

He shrugged. "Never claimed I was sane."

Again she bit back the retort she would have normally let fly. Because her brain had done the math. He'd turned ten just months after his father had been killed. She just looked at him, her gaze locked with his.

"Well, that's settled then," her mother said briskly, startling Britt out of the moment. Or however long it had been that they'd simply been staring at each other.

And then a nurse came in with the dreaded wheelchair. He was a good-looking young man, someone Britt might have flirted with once, but she was in no mood now. He helped her into the chair with gentle efficiency. And it had zero effect on her heart rate.

Unlike every time Cody touched her.

She almost wished she'd hit her head in the fall. At least it might explain this insanity.

Chapter Twenty-Nine

"Thanks, Mark," Cody said into the phone.

"No prob, buddy. It'll be good to see you. So who is this reckless woman? Someone special?"

Cody wasn't sure he had an answer to that anymore. "A neighbor," he said, figuring that was safe enough, given the woman in question was in the seat behind him. But even as he said it, he was aware his reflexive answer would have been: "*Just* a neighbor." And a week ago, it probably would have been: "The pain-in-the-ass girl next door."

And he didn't know how to deal with the change. Didn't even know how to categorize it. Was it a change in her? In him? A change in his perception of her? Or a change in their relation—

He broke off his own thought, veering away from even using the word *relationship* in conjunction with Britt Roth. This was just…forced closeness, that was all. And all it was going to take to end it was telling her the truth. Once she knew this was his fault, he knew exactly what she'd do. There would be no holding back, as he suspected there had frequently been on her side just as there had been on his this last week.

"I'll be there in time for lunch. I'll even spring for someplace nice," he said to Mark, knowing that unless there had been a huge change since their college days, Mark Pruitt was still a notorious cheapskate. But Cody was more than willing to buy an expensive lunch after he offered to put in a weekend at work.

"I'll hold you to that," Mark answered with a laugh. "See you Monday."

When he'd hung up, he glanced at Mr. Roth, behind the wheel of the SUV. "Mark will head in in the morning and start on it. I'll pick it up Monday afternoon, and bring it back to the doctor's office. That'll cut a couple of days off the process."

"Your friend's going to work on this on the weekend?" Britt's mother asked from her seat behind her husband, beside her daughter.

"Yeah. He's a good guy."

Britt said nothing. Cody didn't look at her, since she was sitting directly behind him and it would have been blatantly obvious.

"That is so incredibly sweet of you, Cody!" Mrs. Roth exclaimed. He shrugged. "Now, don't deny it, you've been wonderful."

"It's what he does, Mom," Britt said quietly. "He does something…wonderful and then shrugs it off as if it were nothing."

Cody went still. He stared unseeingly at the dash of the car, feeling not for the first time as if he'd slipped into some parallel universe where he and the woman behind him hadn't grown up hating each other. Where they hadn't constantly played tricks on each other as kids. Where they now didn't snipe at each other constantly. Where they maybe even liked each other.

Where maybe it was more than like.

"How very Rafferty of him," Mrs. Roth said.

"That Maggie's a hell of a woman," Mr. Roth said approvingly. "Raising you four boys to turn out like y'all did."

"She is that," Cody said, his voice sounding a little tight because his throat was constricted.

When they got back to the Roth place, her mother promptly excused herself to go fix lunch for them all and instructed her husband to come gather up Britt's things that had migrated to the main house. "Since you agree she should go back to her place," she said with a sniff as she strode off.

Cody looked at Britt in time to see her eye roll. And he couldn't help grinning at her and saying, as he had before, "Moms."

And again she grinned back and repeated, "They do have their ways."

Which lightened the mood a bit, a good thing since they'd left Cody to unload the wheelchair and get Britt into it. She wanted to do it herself, but the doctor's caution about doing as little as possible while only the temporaries were in place had clearly registered, and she let him pretty much lift her out of the car and into the chair. And he made himself focus on doing it as gently as possible, trying not to add to the storehouse of memories he seemed to be building, of how it felt to touch her, hold her.

"Thank you for calling your friend," she said once she was settled and they were headed toward her place. It wasn't the smoothest of rides, over the hundred yards or so of open ground between the main house and her smaller place. He heard a smothered grunt of pain as they started out, but she didn't complain.

"He's a good guy," he said again, "and the company won't mind. I helped them with the computer program, back when they were getting started."

"So you're calling in a marker, for me?"

He shrugged. Realized she couldn't see him. Remembered what she'd said in the car. But before he could think of anything to say she spoke, sounding amused. "You just shrugged, didn't you?"

He saw no point in denying it. "Yep."

She laughed. But it faded, and she said with a sigh, "It's going to be a long weekend, if I can't move."

"It's a long process," he said. "You're not even fully in the reparative stage. Then there's the remodeling stage."

She leaned back, trying to look at him. "Remodeling? You make it sound like flipping a house."

"That's what that part of the process is called," he said.

"Process," she muttered.

"Yes. First the body reacts by rushing white blood cells to the damage, to prevent infection. But some of those white blood cells aren't good for the body, so they don't hang around long, and other things take over that fight. But the inflammation keeps going, because it's part of the repair process, and the pain keeps you from moving it and doing more damage."

"I noticed," she said dryly.

He hadn't heard another sound of pain from her, figured his attempt at distraction was working, and since they were only about halfway there, he kept going. "Then the growth hormones kick in, and that draws fibroblasts and epithelial cells. And you start building new capillaries to increase the blood flow."

"Wait…new blood vessels?"

"Yep. But they don't stick around, after the healing's done and they're not needed anymore."

"How do you know all this?"

Because since you got hurt, I've spent most of my spare time researching it. "I read a lot of stuff," was all he said.

"So it's not just the bone 'knitting' itself back together, like I always heard?"

"More like stitching. Those fibroblasts build a sort of framework to support the new bone. Like a matrix."

"So now I'm a sci-fi movie?"

"Kind of cool, huh? Well, aside from the pain, I mean."

"Little trouble setting that aside just now," she admitted, and it sounded like her jaw was clenched.

He stopped wheeling the chair. "We can slow down. Less bounce."

She seemed to study the distance to her door, another thirty yards or so. "I'd rather just get there."

"But you're hurting." He stepped around to the front of the chair. "I'll just carry you the rest of the way."

"You don't have to—"

"Pain slows the process," he said. "Your body needs to focus now."

"Another medical pronouncement?"

Maybe not medical. Maybe something much more elemental.

But he didn't give her much chance to argue. And when he bent down, she put her uninjured arm around his neck as if it were the most natural thing in the world. And it felt right to him. Just as lifting her into his arms, slowly, with gentle care, felt right. As if seeing to her, taking care of her, was exactly where he was supposed to be right now. And for once he didn't stop to analyze it, didn't try to understand, didn't slip into trying to figure out what it all meant, he just went with it.

With her cradled against him he started walking, slowly, taking care not to jostle her, working to cushion every step as he had up on the ridge. Her head came down to rest on his chest, and the feeling grew, the rightness of it, that feeling of being where he was supposed to be, doing what he was supposed to do.

"Thank you." The whisper was so soft, so quiet, he wasn't even sure it was aimed at him. "And don't shrug, please."

That answered that. And made him smile. "I wouldn't. It might hurt."

She moved her head slightly, and then he was looking into those bright blue eyes. "This is much better than the chair."

He swallowed tightly at all the ways that could be interpreted. "Good," was all he managed to get out.

And in those few minutes, as he walked toward the place he'd never set foot inside before, that feeling of rightness became almost overwhelming. Yet at the same time it was as if the world had compressed down to just the two of them, as if nothing else mattered, as if nothing outside them even existed in this moment.

He didn't know what it meant. Didn't know anything beyond the feel of her in his arms.

And right now he, who always wanted to know everything about whatever he was doing, didn't care.

Chapter Thirty

Britt smothered a sigh as he—to her disappointment—put her down ever so gently on the couch. "So you can lie down without having to move somewhere else," he explained, although she hadn't asked. And she could see that being necessary; the traveling, the moving, the careful removal and replacement of the casts, had all jangled the nerves in the injured areas, and the painkillers the doctor had given her in the office had been—at her request—mild enough that they'd only taken the edge off.

Cody straightened, and she saw him look around.

"A bit bare, after their house, isn't it?" she said, a little awkwardly.

"Maybe," he said, scanning the great room into the kitchen. "But I like it. It feels open, efficient, clean." His gaze shot back to her and he said quickly, "Not saying your folks' house isn't clean, just—"

She laughed. "I know what you meant. Not clean in the sense of too much stuff."

"Exactly," he said, sounding relieved.

"Is your…what does your mom call it? Your lair? Is it

like my parents' house, or like this?"

He started to shrug, then visibly stopped himself. "A little of both. I've got a lot of gear in there, but it's all organized and used."

"What about where you live?"

He gave her a crooked smile she found…charming. A word that kept popping into her head, despite her shock at it being in conjunction with Cody. "Some would say that is where I live. And they'd probably be right."

"You know what I mean," she said, unable to explain even to herself this sudden curiosity about the details of how he lived.

And suddenly he wasn't smiling. His eyes, those vivid light green eyes that were exactly like his father's, went somehow intense. As did his voice. "You trying to ask about my bedroom, Roth?"

Suddenly there it was, right there in the room, whatever had been so unexpectedly, shockingly brewing between them. And his words, his voice, that he'd slipped back into calling her Roth, all seemed to underline it. Something had changed, and a voice in the back of her mind was screaming something along the lines of "monumental."

That he had gone there first surprised her though. She was supposed to be the bold one, the reckless one, as her parents had often lamented. Yet Cody had been the one with the nerve to face this.

Well, she couldn't let him back her down. Wouldn't.

Start as you mean to go on, her father always said. And before the question of did she want this to go on could form in her mind, she'd already spoken.

"What if I am?" It sounded almost defiant. Which for some reason she didn't understand, made him smile. A different sort of a smile than the charming one of a moment ago. A smile that seemed to heat her up in the same way that shocking question had.

"It's a king-sized bed, if that's what you're wondering," he said, in a voice that matched that smile.

And bold, reckless Britt Roth blushed at the images that brought on. She tried for her usual snappy retort. "Assume much, Rafferty?"

"I don't assume anything. I have to have proof before I act."

And that sounded almost like a warning. Was he talking about…them? What kicked to life between them whenever they touched? Because it had to happen to both of them, to be this strong. Didn't it?

This was crazy. It was all crazy.

And then, in a perfectly ordinary voice, and as if she had every right to ask, he went on. "The rest of my place is more like this. Kitchen's small, but efficient and orderly. But in the bedroom, I admit, I stack things. Books, my tablet, tech diagrams, on the nightstand. And I tend to toss things when I'm done with them." He shrugged then. "Tunnel vision, my mom calls it. That sometimes I get so focused on something in my head I look past what's right in front of me. And—" the charming smile was back "—I have a serious caramel addiction. The basic ones, the little squares. And those wrappers tend to…float."

The thought of Cody the Coder with a caramel habit nearly made her laugh. It did make her smile, widely. And going from that high-intensity, heart-racing tension to this silliness left her nearly breathless.

Then he moved, leaning down, toward her, and stole the rest of her breath away. Closer, closer, his gaze fixed on her mouth.

He was going to kiss her.

God help her, she *wanted* him to kiss her. She was sitting here with her wrist in a splint and her ankle in a horrendously thick and heavy boot, and all she could think about was that he was going to kiss her, and she wanted it, more than she even wanted to be free of those restraints. So much that the dull ache of her ankle faded into the background, and she lifted her head to meet him.

He jerked back. She had split second to feel hurt that he'd recoiled. Then she heard her front door swing open and realized he must have heard steps on the porch. Cody straightened abruptly as her mother breezed into the room, carrying several refrigerator containers of food.

"This should hold you for a few days, honey," she said, heading for the kitchen as if she'd noticed nothing, although Britt knew she had to have seen Cody bent over her. Maybe she thought he'd just set her down.

"Brought in the chair," came her father's voice as he entered through the door her mother hadn't closed, indeed carrying the now folded-up wheelchair with him. He set it down inside the door, looked from her to Cody. "I was afraid that might be a little rough rolling out there."

"It was," Cody answered, and Britt wondered if she was imagining the slight edge in his voice. And if she wasn't, was it because they'd been…interrupted?

"Thanks, Cody, for getting her in with less pain, then," her father said. "Along with everything else you've done."

Her father bent to unfold the wheelchair back into functional shape. Britt glanced at her mother, busily rearranging her fridge to fit in what she'd brought.

"At least a knock on the door would have been nice," she muttered.

"They're worried about you," he said, very quietly. She looked back at him just as he added, in a wry tone, "It would have been nice, though, yes."

She steeled her nerve. "Nicer if they'd come five minutes later," she said.

His brows rose. Was he going to pretend those moments had never happened? That it had been something other than it clearly had been?

"Five minutes?" His whisper was hoarse now. "Not sure that would be long enough."

Her breath jammed up in her throat, and for a moment she felt almost light-headed. She could no longer blame the craziness of this—that it was Cody having this effect on her—on her injuries, or meds, or anything else. Part of her wanted to run, at least emotionally, from all of it.

But Britt Roth didn't run.

She opened her mouth to speak, but when she heard her mother's footsteps approaching, she stifled the words into a murmured, "Later."

"Definitely," Cody said in the moment before he turned to help her father, who had gotten the wheelchair caught on the edge of the area rug in front of the couch.

Dad parked the loathed thing at right angles to her seat and set the brakes, as the nurse had instructed, but looked at her doubtfully. "Are you going to be able to get into it like he said, with your wrist?"

"I've got one good arm, and the good leg's on the other side, so I should be able to maneuver…"

Her voice faded away as her father took a seat in the chair opposite her, as if he were settling in for the rest of the day. She glanced at Cody, and thought she saw a muscle in his jaw jump. Looked at her mother who, oddly, was also looking at Cody. Then she turned her head to meet Britt's gaze. A very slight, almost knowing smile curved her mother's mouth.

And then, briskly, she was moving. "Come along, Rob. Brittany is fine now, she needs to settle in. Cody will stay a while, won't you, Cody?"

"Yes, ma'am," Cody said, very politely. And respectfully; he was a Texas boy, after all, and raised by Maggie Rafferty to boot.

Her father, looking a little puzzled, nevertheless stood up and followed his wife, who glanced back and said cheerfully, "We'll check in on you later. Maybe we'll even knock next time."

Britt stared at the closing door. A moment later she heard Cody say, sounding bemused, "Do you think she knows—"

"Yes, I do," Britt said, her mouth twisting wryly as she heard her parents' steps on the porch. "And I have a suspicion she's been...expecting it."

"It?"

She looked at him then. Took a deep breath. Felt nerves jangle through her, like in the moment before starting a barrel run. What if she was wrong? What if he didn't feel what she felt when they were close, didn't feel the sparks when they touched?

Five minutes? Not sure that would be long enough...

His tense whisper echoed in her head, swamping her doubts. He felt it, all right. And was probably as bewildered by it as she was. How could they go from a lifetime of thinking each other their worst enemy to...this? It couldn't be simply because she'd gotten hurt, because it had started before that, this easing of tension between them. To be honest, for her it had started when she'd been forced to realize how much she didn't know about him, and what he did.

"She said once that someday I was going to grow up and

see what was right in front of me…" Her voice faded away as she voiced her mother's words. She stared at him, remembering what he'd just said, about what his mother had said to him about not seeing what was right in front of him. "I thought she meant it…metaphorically," she said ruefully.

"And I thought my mother meant it literally, about my clothes on the floor."

Britt was hit with an image of Cody stripping off his shirt and jeans, in such a hurry he just left them there. And tried to fight down her reaction to it, which was that she very much wanted to be the reason he was in a hurry to get naked.

And wondering, if it weren't for her pitiful condition just now, if he would do it.

"My mother's pretty darn smart, especially about people," he said, his tone so neutral she knew it was intentional.

"So's mine," she replied, although she didn't quite manage the same level tone.

"So maybe we should take them seriously."

"Maybe we should."

This time when he leaned over her, she knew there'd be no stopping.

And when she felt his lips on hers, felt the leap of her heart, felt her body's response, blanking all else including any lingering pain from her mind, stopping was the very last thing she wanted.

Chapter Thirty-One

CODY SUPPOSED, IN the quirkiest part of his quirky brain, he could maybe have imagined what it would be like to kiss Britt Roth. If he'd ever been inclined, which he hadn't. Twenty-eight years of her next door, from hospital to home, and he'd ever and forever thought of her as the enemy.

But somehow it had changed, and here he was. And the moment he felt her soft mouth, that mouth had had so often poured out sharp retorts or sarcastic observations, under his the only thought his mind could hang on to was that this was the most amazing, most incredible thing he'd ever felt. He could almost hear his own heartbeat as it slammed into high gear and began to race.

She felt impossible. She tasted even better. And when she opened for him, luring him in, he went without a second thought, probing, savoring. He had to order himself to remember that she was hurt, that anything more than this was out of the question. It slowed him down, but not much.

It was awkward, him standing while she sat, but he didn't care. He was cautious because of her injuries, but that was his only grip on reality. He deepened the kiss, leaning in further. He heard her make a small sound, urgent, as if she wanted more as much as he did. He felt her free arm slip around his neck, holding him close, as if she wanted to be sure he didn't stop. And finally, with exquisite care, he sat down beside her. Never breaking contact, because he never wanted this to end.

And she was responding as if she was just as hungry for this as he was. That left him reeling a little. The taste, the feel, his pulse hammering, and somewhere, underneath it all, the utter impossibility that this was Roth. This delicious taste, this incredible heat, this surging response, was Roth.

No. It was Britt.

He wasn't sure he could ever think of her only as Roth again.

Only because he had to breathe did he finally pull away. That when he did she was as breathless as he was reassuring somehow. She was staring up at him, those royal-blue eyes wide, as if she were as stunned as he.

"Wow," she finally said, and the note of wonder in her voice sent a shiver down his spine.

"Yeah." He couldn't look away from her, from those eyes. He didn't know how much time passed in silence, with them just staring at each other. *Gives a whole new meaning to shock and awe.*

"You don't suppose…"

Her voice faded away. It had held an uncertainty he never would have associated with the ever-confident, fearless Britt Roth. And when she lowered her eyes, as if suddenly too shy to hold his gaze, he reached out and with a gentle finger lifted her chin. Those wide blue eyes met his again.

"Suppose what?"

She took a deep breath. Then, her voice a bit wobbly, she said it. "That...all the years we spent fighting each other...were we really fighting this?"

He liked so many things about what she'd said, including the breathy way she'd said it but mainly that she was referring to the fighting in past tense, that he couldn't answer for a moment.

"Is life really that crazy?" she asked when he didn't speak.

"Maybe..." He had to swallow before finishing it. "Maybe fate is."

"Fate..." She smiled, a little smile, as if she liked that idea.

"Then again," he said as he focused again on her mouth, "maybe we need more...testing."

The smile widened. "Maybe. We shouldn't just throw away twenty-eight years of animosity until we're absolutely sure."

He was sure. It was totally insane, that one kiss had shifted not just his world now but his entire history, but it had. It had, and he could no more deny it than he could deny the effect she had on him. His brain was having to work pretty damned hard to convince his body the next logical—and essential—step wasn't going to happen. That it couldn't, she was hurt, it was off the table. The bed. Hell, the floor, because he was pretty sure that was as far as they would have made it had things been different.

But things were what they were, and there was only one choice. And despite the frustration, it was easy to make.

He leaned in and kissed her again.

BRITT LEANED BACK into the couch cushions, wishing she were as boneless as she felt, because then they wouldn't have had to stop. But the dull ache from her ankle and the remaining stiffness of her wrist—the latter almost more noticeable just now, no doubt because it was so hard to keep her hand still when she wanted nothing more than to touch him—were still there. Odd how she hadn't noticed them at all until they stopped kissing.

He hadn't left her; he was sprawled beside her on the couch, and she noticed blissfully that his breathing was taking as long to slow down as her own.

"You're a heck of a painkiller," she said when she could.

He turned his head, and she got the full blast of those incredible light green eyes. And the corners of his mouth—God, that mouth—were twitching when he said, "As opposed to just a pain?"

She couldn't help it, she grinned. It seemed so silly now,

all those years of antipathy. She was convinced she was right—it was all because of this. And she didn't even care how crazy it might seem, this turnaround that had been as fast as Ghost rounding a barrel.

Ghost. The silly, spooky horse who'd landed her in this situation, wanting more than anything to pursue this beyond kisses but unable to. Then again, if not for Ghost shying violently at the noise of that rockslide, none of this would have happened. She tried to imagine that, being back in that place where Cody was the bane of her existence.

She couldn't.

"I'm sure you can still be a pain," she finally said, the grin still in place. "Just not to me anymore."

"I'll remind you of that when I tell you to stop trying to do too much."

"Maybe I'll just let you do it all."

"Do that," he said, and an undertone had come into his voice that made her body rev up all over again.

"I think I should be more worried than I am about being the focus of the brilliant Cody Rafferty."

He let out a rueful chuckle. "Brilliant? Maybe. But also too often oblivious."

She considered that, studied the face that she knew so well, even as she knew she was only beginning to plumb the depths of the mind behind it.

"Maybe it's the focus that makes you brilliant that also makes you oblivious sometimes. It's like me in the arena: the rest of the world sort of falls away. All that matters, or even exists, is that moment, that run."

Those green eyes widened slightly. "It's exactly like that."

She was still thinking about that look of surprise in his eyes, wondering what else they might have in common at an elemental level—besides both being impossibly stubborn, which they had laughingly admitted early on—as they ate the dinner of her mom's luscious beef stew, one of the big containers she'd brought over. Cody had been hesitant, saying the food was meant to make her life easier, not his, but she'd pointed out his presence was accomplishing that, and the food made his continued presence possible.

She meant that in more than one way, of course. Not just that it was helpful for her to have a big, strong man around to lift and fetch and carry for her. Which it was, but anyone could do that.

Only Cody could do it and have her admiring the way he moved, doing even the simplest things. Which he did without question or hesitation, and often anticipating what she wanted or needed before she ever had to say a word. More of that focus, she supposed.

The next two days were the most amazing of her life, even more than her big rodeo wins. She'd thought those would forever be the highlights of her life, but no more. They ate well, thanks to Mom, who had limited herself to checking in on the intercom—Cody's intercom—every couple of hours. And not, Britt noticed, asking if Cody was staying overnight. Which he did, after tucking her into bed with exquisite care, and gruffly telling her to hurry up and heal. She took that as a wish to join her, which she fervently seconded. She would have loved it if he'd lain down with her here, but he'd insisted she didn't need the jostling of another person in bed with her.

"Not to mention I don't have much faith in my own willpower right now," he'd added, making her heart take a little leap. Then he went back out to crash on the couch. Funny, she'd never asked him to stay, and he'd never asked if he could, it was just assumed he would.

By both of them.

When he wasn't checking on Ghost for her—and tactfully not mentioning what a pain the fractious horse could be—he was here with her. They watched movies, one of his favorite old westerns, and her favorite about tornado chasers. She snoozed on the couch while he worked in the big chair close by, looking up from his laptop screen now and then to check on her. Which she only knew from when she would rouse a little and find him watching her.

And they talked. About any and everything. And sharing remembered pain, of which he had so much more. She coaxed it out of him, the pain of his father's death, and the girl from the convention. It came out haltingly, but it came out, and she didn't think she was imagining the lessening of pressure in him when it did. And after all he'd done for her, she finally felt as if she'd given a little back.

Although she knew down deep it wasn't just that she owed him for all his help. It was more than that, much more. Impossible as it was, that fall up by the ridge was nothing compared to the other tumble she'd taken, the tumble that had feelings about Cody making a U-turn.

And she couldn't shake the feeling there was something else eating at him. It wasn't just that several times he had started to speak as if he were going to tell her something, then stopped and insisted it was nothing. That worried her, but there was time, she told herself.

Time. What a funny thing it was. She'd never felt like this in her life. It was dizzying, the speed of the change, but she could no longer deny it. No matter how crazy it was that Cody the Coder would end up the one who stirred her, body, heart, and soul. She had no idea how this would work, only that it would.

It had to.

Especially after, when he'd come in to check on her late Saturday night, she'd managed to convince him to lie down with her, telling him she truly did feel better. He'd been reluctant and had told her with rueful but obvious honesty exactly why that would be difficult, but when she'd practically begged he'd done it anyway. And she'd slept better than she had since it had happened, with his arms wrapped around her. She'd known he was as aroused as she was, he was so close to her, but as she'd also known, he did nothing about it. Because he knew that right now, it was both unwise and impossible.

Just you wait, Cody Rafferty. We're going to burn this place down one night soon.

Sunday morning she woke early and alone, hearing sounds from out in the kitchen. She sat up, very aware of her aloneness here. She looked at the wheelchair beside the bed. Thought of the tremendous effort it would take, moving an inch at a time to edge herself out of bed and into it by herself. It would be very tricky, balancing on her one good leg and with only one hand to take the pressure of bracing herself on the arm of the chair. Even if they were—thankfully—on opposite sides. And if she misjudged or fell, she could set everything back to square one.

The solution was obviously out in the kitchen. It went against her grain to call for help—it was against her grain to *need* help—but…Cody. That it was Cody made all the difference. Without pausing to analyze the craziness of that, she opened her mouth to call out his name. Then stopped abruptly. What if it wasn't Cody out there? What if it was Mom, or Dad even, and Cody had gone home? He hadn't said anything about leaving, but if someone else was here, he might feel like he should. And it would be very like Mom to appear with a bag full of fixings, to prepare her one of her big Sunday breakfasts.

And if it was Mom, she'd fuss and worry. Unlike Cody, who seemed to know to talk about something else, anything else, keeping up a steady stream of conversation about any and everything except what they were doing. As if her limitations weren't the most important thing, in fact were not even important enough to discuss.

She wondered if he'd learned that from the girl at the con, who had died. "If it was you," she whispered into the air, "thank you."

She sat there, indecisively. She raised her hands to push back hair tousled from sleep and falling into her eyes, then stopped her left hand when she remembered she was supposed to move it as little as possible.

Where had all this caution come from? She was Britt Roth, toughest cowgirl around. But she was sitting here like some sort of neurotic worrywart. How had it ended up that she was not wanting to call for help getting up if her own mother was here, but was perfectly comfortable calling the guy who had turned everything upside down?

The guy she had thought she would hate forever. The guy who had been, one way or another, a part of her life since the day she was born.

The guy she wanted to be part of her life from now on.

And pushed by that silent admission, she finally called out his name.

Chapter Thirty-Two

Cody had a pretty good idea what it took her to call for help. And she'd already told him she liked that while he was helping her do what she had to do, he pretty much ignored what they were doing. So that was what he did as he helped her up and into the bathroom.

It wasn't like him to chatter, especially to a woman, but with this woman he didn't seem to have any trouble. Which might be the craziest part of all of this. While he waited just outside the bathroom door, he kept up a stream about what his weather station was saying would be a nice morning turning to a stormy evening, that Mark had texted the cast would be ready to go on time, and telling her, with a laugh at her stubbornness, that no, she could not ride all the way to Fort Worth with him when he went to pick it up.

"I'll be leaving before sunrise. Your folks'll be here to get you ready to go. I'll head straight back to the doc's office, and meet you there with the casts."

Dr. Reed was enthused enough about this new-to-him process, he'd agreed to stay after his regular office hours if necessary, since it was a good nine hours' round trip to Fort

Worth and back, and Cody had promised Mark that lunch on him. Taking into account city traffic and the possibility of delays, even leaving at six a.m. wouldn't get him back here much before five.

As he got her back into the chair when she was done, making sure she had the wrist and ankle elevated, she started to speak. "I don't know how to—"

"If you're going to thank me, don't. You don't owe me a thing." He heard the edge in his own voice as the thing, the thing he hadn't yet told her, jabbed at him yet again. *No, you don't owe me. You should blame me. For all of this.*

Then she gave him that look, that hot, promising look, and said, "I guess we did agree we'd…handle that later."

When you're healed enough that I don't have to tuck you into bed and then leave, when all I want to do is stay.

He didn't know why he'd said it last night. But once the words had escaped, he was glad he had. Because her simple response of, "I'd better hurry up on that healing, then," telling him she felt the same, had been all that had kept him going since.

And he had to admit, kissing her good night was an experience. An incredible, amazing experience he wanted to repeat, repeat, repeat. But the more he kissed her as she lay in her bed, the harder it was for him to leave her there, untouched. Only the sight of the bulky boot immobilizing her ankle and the splint on her wrist stopped him.

When they got out to the kitchen, she looked around in

surprise. "Pancakes?"

"I can't cook much, but I can do that." He gave her a crooked smile. "Mom made sure we all could at least fix essential food, so we wouldn't starve on our own. For me, pancakes are essential."

"Me, too," she said, smiling back at him.

He went back to the kitchen as she edged up to the table in the dining area. But the moment he was no longer looking into those eyes, his brother's words slammed into his mind yet again.

Only if you want to live with yourself.

He had to tell her. But he didn't want to blow this up, this amazing thing that had happened between them. This thing that never would have happened if not for that other thing that was his fault. He was feeling more confused than he could ever remember. Her being hurt was a horrible thing but discovering what had been hiding behind a lifetime of animosity was amazing. Did the one balance out the other?

Not your judgment to make, Rafferty. She's the one in pain.

He would tell her. He'd already made that silent promise to her. He just couldn't bear to blow this up. Yet.

Monday. He'd do it once she had the 3D casts on. He'd get her set with those, back home and safe, and then he'd confess. And after that, it was up to her. He had a feeling he knew what would happen. For all the surprising sweetness he'd found here with her, she was still Britt Roth and she still had a temper that could start fires. But was it fierce enough she would throw this, throw them away? Or was he being stupid to even imagine that a week of harmony between them could end a lifetime of aggravation and animosity?

Stupid was not a word he often thought about himself. But when it was, it was in dealings with people. It was, he'd realized later, why of all his brothers he'd gone to Chance. He'd known that he, with his tendency to withdraw from the world, would best understand. And he had.

He doubted Chance understood why it was so important, though. Nobody in his family would ever believe he was standing here in Britt's kitchen, half lusting after her, half being ground down by fear of what would happen when she found out the truth. He closed his eyes, and his jaw tightened.

"Cody? What's wrong?"

He didn't want to lie and say nothing, adding to his burden of guilt, so he only shrugged. "Just thinking."

"Solving another problem?"

Startled he looked over at her. "Hoping it's not a problem," he said.

She smiled, and his throat tightened. "I've worried about more things than have ever happened."

He managed a smile back and the moment passed.

The pancakes came out well, which surprised him considering how distracted he'd been. And he was glad to see her eating. Although he wasn't sure glad was exactly the feeling he had watching her eating something he had fixed.

Her mother checked in on the intercom shortly after they'd finished, while he was cleaning up. Although Britt told her he was here, he noticed her mother didn't ask nor did Britt volunteer that he'd spent the night. He couldn't blame her—this had happened fast enough to make him dizzy; he could only imagine how her mother would feel. Then again, there had been that look she had given them, and the way she had hustled Britt's dad out of here…

"I need to check my email. Could you get me my laptop off the desk over there?" she asked when they'd gotten her settled on the couch again. "Preferably without telling me it's old and outdated?" she added, her tone unmistakably wry, yet teasingly light, as was the smile she gave him when she said it.

"I try not to offer an opinion unless asked," he said as he went for the device. "If it works for you, then it's good enough." He looked at it as he picked it up and couldn't resist adding, "Even if it is from the Stone Age."

"Smart-ass," Britt said, but she was laughing. And he felt a new round of wonder at the simple fact that they could be like this. That he could be so relaxed around her, that he could simply enjoy being with her.

He opened the laptop for her before he handed it to her, since it was a two-handed job. "You going to be able to type one-handed?"

"I'll manage." She gave him an arch look then. "Unless you're offering to take dictation?"

He laughed. "You want a secretary?"

"You'd make a really cute one."

He swallowed. "Careful, I'll think you're flirting with me."

"I need to work on that, if you only think it."

Cody had a sudden flash of a future spent with a woman who didn't play games, who didn't hide what she felt, who would never leave him wondering where he stood. Who, once she made up her mind, was full speed ahead. That he was even thinking about that future with Britt seemed both astounding and inevitable.

For a moment he couldn't speak, but just looked at her. Then, finally, because he had to know, he asked, "Are you as…boggled as I am by this?"

Again very Britt-like, she didn't dance around it or pretend not to know what he meant. "Yes," she admitted. "It's crazy. But it also feels as if it's always been there, we were just too…stubborn to see it."

Relief flooded him, at this proof he wasn't way out in left field on this. He was still pondering the craziness of it all when he went out to check on the nexus of all this chaos. Ghost greeted him almost like a normal horse. He knew if he took her out to the corral for a run, things would change in a big hurry. Once she realized where they were going she'd decide she no longer needed this boring human leading the way. So, on this Sunday morning he decided to just leave well enough alone.

"She's fine," he told Britt when he came back. "She'll be wound up tighter than a cheap watch next time she's cut loose, but she's fine."

"She is," Britt said dryly, "a pain in the proverbial ass."

"I would not argue that," he said with an eye roll.

It wasn't until he sat down in the chair where he'd taken to doing his own work that she said, unexpectedly, "Trey's a much better horse."

He gave her a startled look. "What?"

"He'll do whatever he's asked, sometimes before you even ask it."

"I would not argue that either. He's saved me too many times to count."

"On the other hand, Ghost does only one thing I ask."

"She does it exceptionally well, however."

She smiled at that. "She does. But at this point I'm wondering exactly how much that's worth."

He took a guess. "Wondering if she'll pass on the…temperament?"

"You don't have to be polite about it. She's way beyond unruly. And yes, that's what I'm thinking about."

"Maybe she just soaked up the wildness of that storm she was born in."

For a moment Britt just stared at him, then she smiled again. He could get used to her smiling at him. "That was almost poetic, Mr. Rafferty."

He felt a little embarrassed but pleased. "Don't let that

get around," he muttered, knowing full well the old Britt—or rather the Roth of their prior existence—probably would have stored that up as ammo to be used at the most inopportune time for him.

They spent a quiet day together. And he loved every minute of it, from the occasional conversations that surprised him with the turns they took, to the simple silences that were often broken when they both looked up from whatever they were doing or reading at the same time and smiled at each other. He'd never felt this at ease with someone before, not even Gwen. The undercurrent of what he hadn't yet told her still tugged at him, but his vow to tell her tomorrow, once the recasting was done and she was back home, had eased that considerably.

He was actually pondering dinner, even though it was only a little after four, and surprised at how he found himself wanting to do it, not because he was hungry but because she might be. He was about to ask her what she wanted when his phone chimed a text notification. It was Chance's tone, unexpected because he'd figured they'd be settling in with the new dog. Unless there was a problem…

He grabbed it up and opened the text.

It wasn't you.

A second later a photo scrolled into view. It took him a moment to deduce what he was seeing. But then a familiar piece registered.

It was the wreckage of the drone. A small crumpled heap half buried in mud. For an instant all he could do was wonder how—and why—Chance had found it; it had to have been a methodical search. But then he realized the real import of the image. The fence line in the background. The fence line between the Raffertys and the Roths.

The fence line the drone was well on the Rafferty side of.

It wasn't you.

It wasn't his fault that Britt got hurt. The drone hadn't buzzed her and then crashed, setting off Ghost. Even if the idiotic horse had spooked at the drone, it was far enough away to be clear it was the horse, not the device that was the key factor.

He let out a sound that was half laugh, half gasp of relief.

"Good news?"

He looked up at Britt's question, wondering if he looked as goofily relieved as he felt.

"Damn good news. It wasn't me."

"What wasn't?"

"The drone, I mean. I thought—"

He broke off suddenly as he realized that, in his relief, he'd just thrown open the door she hadn't even known existed. And the way she was looking at him, so intently, he knew he had no choice. This wasn't going to wait until Monday. But now that he knew the truth, it changed everything. The idea that her injuries were, even indirectly, his fault wouldn't be hanging over them as he'd feared. They could go on, explore this crazy change in their lifelong connection, without that shadow. So with a much lighter heart, he explained. It came out a little jumbled, but his elation at the ending was all that really mattered.

"But Chance found the debris," he finished. "And it wasn't over on your side, it was well onto ours. So if Ghost spooked, it wasn't my fault." He said it again, just because it felt so good. "It wasn't my fault."

Britt was staring at him. "You thought one of your flying contraptions spooked Ghost and…caused all this?" she asked, gesturing with her free hand at her other wrist and in the general direction of her booted ankle.

He nodded. "But it wasn't as close as I'd thought, not nearly as close. So if she heard it at all, it wouldn't have been that loud."

"But you thought it was."

"I thought it could have been. Until now. Thanks to Chance."

"Get out."

Cody blinked. "What?"

"Get out. Now."

She'd said it so coldly he stared at her. "Britt?"

"That's Roth to you. Get the hell out, Coder. Go home and play with your damned toys."

He gave his head a shake, wondering what he'd missed. He'd never seen her this angry, and he'd seen her pretty mad. But he had no idea why. "What's wrong?"

"What's wrong? *What's wrong?*" She was yelling now. "Out! Now! Or I swear I'll call my dad and tell him to bring his shotgun!"

She started to get up, struggling, and he knew she meant it. And would probably hurt herself trying. He got up and took a step toward her, saying "Britt, stop. You'll hurt yourself."

"Stay away from me. Far away," she said through clenched teeth, stopping him in his tracks. "Just. Get. Out."

Nothing else made sense, but he was as certain as he'd been of anything that she meant it. Whatever had set her off, she needed to calm down before she really did hurt herself. So he held up his hands, palms out, and backed up.

"Okay, okay. I don't know what's going on but settle down."

"You blind, oblivious *idiot!*"

He had been called that before. Times when he'd missed something, some people thing, that should have been obvious. Apparently this was one of those times.

So he did the only thing he could think of to do. He left.

And as he went, he spent every step trying to figure out what he'd done or said that had put tears in the redoubtable Britt Roth's eyes.

Chapter Thirty-Three

"DON'T YOU GET it? He was only here, only helping me because he felt guilty!"

"But you said Chance proved it wasn't his fault," her father said, clearly puzzled. Why were men so stupid?

"That doesn't matter, he thought it was and that was the only reason he was helping so much."

Dad blinked. "Of course it matters."

She turned to her mother, who had remained oddly silent since she'd hit them with the depth of Cody's betrayal. Pretending to genuinely care, even be attracted to her, when in fact he'd simply been driven by guilt. She remembered when she'd thought the incredible turnaround in their feelings couldn't be simply because she'd gotten hurt. And it hadn't been. She'd been missing one important fact. The drone, and him feeling guilty about it.

And she felt like an utter fool for falling for it.

"Mom, will you explain to him? I can't deal with another thickheaded male."

"A little respect for your father," her mother answered, her tone so mild Britt went on alert. She listened warily as

Mom looked at Dad and said, "Rob, you might want to leave this to me."

He agreed gratefully, and walked out muttering, "Women," not quite under his breath.

"Mom," she began, recognizing all too well the expression on her mother's face. Angela Roth was a loving mother, but she was no pushover. She chose carefully when to take a stand, and then she stood until she prevailed.

She had that look on her face now.

"Do you really believe Cody went to all this trouble, built and installed this com system, called in a big favor, in fact put his entire life on hold to help us, help you, all because he felt guilty?"

"You didn't see the relief on his face when Chance sent him that picture," Britt said.

"I'm not denying that he'd be relieved. I'm questioning if you really believe that was his sole motivation. Besides, if he did feel guilty, wasn't going out in that storm and finding you, getting you safely home, enough payback?"

"But he only went looking up there because he did think it was his fault, that his stupid drone had caused it."

"And now he knows—and you know—it did not."

"No, I don't. It still could have been what spooked Ghost," she protested. "Just because I didn't hear it doesn't mean she didn't."

"But it was well onto the Rafferty side," her mother said. "And any normal ranch horse would never have spooked the way that mare of yours did. Seems to me if there's anyone at fault here, it's that horse of yours."

"You've just never liked her," Britt said, aware even as she said it how childish it sounded.

"The horse that's injured my daughter more than once? I don't apologize for that." Her gaze narrowed. "Which brings me to another point—what on earth were you doing riding up there with a storm blowing in?"

Britt sighed. There was no denying her mother when she got like this. "I was hoping having to concentrate on the rough ground and the hillside would keep her focused, like she is in the arena."

"I'd say your experiment failed."

"Only because that drone—"

"So that's it for you? Even though it's obvious he was well within his rights—and property line—you blame him? After all he's done, you can't even be as patient with him as you are with that horse?"

She blinked. That was another knack her mother had, putting things in a way she herself had never thought of. She sat in the wheelchair, her gaze turned inward, idly plucking at the arm under her good hand. And then her mother spoke again, and her tone had gone from stern to soft with understanding.

"I know why you're really so upset, honey. And it has nothing to do with what happened up at the ridge."

Her gaze went back to her mother's face. "Oh?"

"You're upset at the idea that guilt was the only reason he stayed with you, because you wanted him to stay with you because he wanted to. Because you've finally woken up, haven't you." It wasn't a question. She stared at her mother, who after a moment went on quietly. "You've finally realized what's behind the years of sniping and antagonism. That there's an entirely different kind of spark between you."

"What are you saying?"

"That there's more than one kind of predestination. And that enemies flipped can become the fiercest kind of love."

"You think...I love him?" She already knew the answer, because deep down inside she'd known it herself, since the first moment she'd found comfort even as she was in nasty pain, simply by feeling his arms holding her safely, by letting her head rest against his broad chest as he carried her down the hill.

"Don't you?"

Britt's eyes began to sting. "Even if I did, that doesn't change that he was only here because—" She had to stop as her throat tightened unbearably.

Her mother sighed. "If I know anything about my beautiful daughter it's that she has to reach her own conclusions. And that once she gets something in her head, she's as hard to deal with as a certain horse I know."

Britt looked up at the woman who had been there for her her entire life, saw her worried expression and suddenly wondered what she would have done, how ruined her life would have been if she'd lost her, say at the age Cody had lost his father.

"I feel like a fool," she admitted, the tears threatening to spill. "I should have known it couldn't really turn around so fast."

"Maybe it didn't turn around. Maybe you just saw it clearly for the first time." Her mother reached out and cupped her cheek. "You were a stubborn child who grew into a stubborn woman, and I understand that, even admire it sometimes, for it gives you the drive that has brought you such success. But honey, don't drive right past what could be the true rest of your life." She was silent for a moment, as if to let that sink in. Then she said, "I'll be back later to help you settle in for the night. You need to rest. Tomorrow will be busy."

Her mother turned and headed for the door. She'd always known when to back off, too, when she'd planted enough that the best thing to do was leave it to grow. But Britt had one more question, one she both wanted and was afraid to ask. It took her until her mother had the door open to decide.

"Mom?" She looked back. "Are you saying…I mean, do you think…do you think he…"

"Loves you, too?" her mother said with a smile. "All I know—all I need to know—is that he looks at you now the same way your father looks at me. Oh, and one more thing you need to remember."

"What?"

The smile widened. "What all of Last Stand knows. Raffertys don't lie."

And then she was gone, leaving Britt amid the biggest tangle of emotions she'd ever experienced. She thought about this last week, about how he'd found her, rescued her. How he'd seen to every possible need, how he'd helped them all, how he had, as Mom had said, put his entire life on hold to do it, to devote himself to taking care of her. How he'd called his friend in to help, how he'd loaned out what had to be hideously expensive equipment to the doctor, for her sake.

After the incident he'd thought was his fault.

If there's anyone at fault here, it's that horse of yours.

But if Ghost had heard the crash—

This time she couldn't even finish the thought. Because she knew her mother had been right. That he had been well within his rights—and the Rafferty property line.

After all he's done, you can't even be as patient with him as you are with that horse?

That had stabbed home hard. Made her feel petty, even vindictive, and she didn't like the feeling. Had sniping at Cody become nothing more than a habit?

…enemies flipped can become the fiercest kind of love.

Was it really possible for a lifetime of animosity to change direction like a champion cutting horse?

She realized she had reached up and was touching her lips. Because the most incontrovertible piece of evidence had been that kiss. There was absolutely no way to deny what that had been: real, fierce, fiery, and overpowering.

Are you as…boggled as I am by this?

As she remembered what he'd said, what struck her now as much as the words was how he'd sounded, absolutely gobsmacked. As if he couldn't believe it, either. As if his head was spinning with the speed of it, just as hers had.

Her own words floated through her mind again. *I should have known it couldn't really turn around so fast.*

And her mother's response. Those words that had been like a key in a lock, just waiting for her to turn. To accept.

Maybe it didn't turn around. Maybe you just saw it clearly for the first time.

Accurate vision for the first time in her life. The truth of it began to sink in. She was seeing clearly, all right. And right now, she was seeing the mess she'd made of things.

Her phone chimed a text.

When she saw it was from Cody, her heart took a tumble.

When she read it, her eyes began to sting with gathering tears all over again.

It's time for your pain meds.

He'd been religious about that, tracking that for her, bringing her the pills and making her take them so the pain stayed down. That relief would end soon, because they could interfere with the bone healing, but for now it made her life easier. And he'd always made sure her wrist was iced regularly, kept elevated, and the same with her ankle.

And now, even after the way she'd thrown him out, he

was still taking care of her.

Raffertys don't lie.

No, they didn't. So the simple thing was to ask straight out, right? Ask a Rafferty a question and you got an honest answer.

She swiped out the words one-handed before she could change her mind. Calling him would have been easier, but she wasn't ready to hear his voice again, not yet.

Were you only here because you felt guilty?

There was a long enough pause that she thought he wasn't going to answer at all. She guessed the fact that Raffertys don't lie didn't necessarily mean they answered every question.

But then, just as she was putting the phone down, it came.

I came because I felt guilty. But that's not why I stayed.

Honesty. The Rafferty trademark.

She stared at the screen until her tears blurred the words.

Chapter Thirty-Four

CODY SAT WITH his head in his hands, rubbing at his eyes. He finally understood.

When he'd first arrived home, he'd gone directly to his own entrance, avoiding the main house altogether. He hadn't wanted to see anyone, but especially his mother. Not when he'd had no freaking idea what had just happened.

He'd paced the floor, barely resisting throwing a couple of things just for the satisfaction of hearing the crash. He'd tried working on updating the app for the fence line program, but that made him think of the drones that used it, and he was right back where he'd been. He'd tried working a bit on the ranch bookkeeping software, where he'd been adding a couple of new functions, but that made him think of how the Roths had been his first enthusiastic users—and promoters—and he was right back where he'd been. He'd tried catching up on email, but the first one he saw was from Mark, confirming their meeting tomorrow for the casts, and he was right back where he'd been.

Then an alarm on his phone had gone off, and for a moment he'd been glad of the distraction, until he saw it was the reminder for Britt's pain meds, and he was right back where he'd been.

And not wanting to hear her furious voice again—although he was doubtful she would answer if he called—he'd texted her the reminder. At least he'd left the pills close to her on the end table, along with a bottle of water, so she should be set, not having to try and get up. He'd just wearily realized he should probably let her parents know he wasn't there to help when her text had come in.

Were you only here because you felt guilty?

He wanted to deny it. But it would be a lie, because it had started out that way. Just like it would have been a lie to simply keep going along with her assumption that it had been the rockslide that had spooked Ghost. Even if it would have been easier, and this blowup would never have happened.

So this would have likely happened even if Chance hadn't texted him at that moment with the proof. Which he needed to thank his brother for, despite the eruption it had caused. He hadn't needed to do that, go out and hunt that thing down when he was trying to get a new dog settled. But he had, because that's what Raffertys did for each other.

He reeled his dodging mind back in and stared at the phone's screen. And finally resorted to the simple, barebones truth.

I came because I felt guilty. But that's not why I stayed.

He tossed the phone down on the table. He was developing a serious headache, the kind he rarely got. And he had a lot of driving to do tomorrow, starting in too few hours from now, so he needed to get some sleep.

Right. That'll go well.

He lay awake for an hour or so. When he finally did sleep it was fitful, restless, and roiled by dreams of things that it now seemed would never happen. He woke twice thinking he needed to get up and check on her and was halfway out of bed before he remembered.

It never occurred to him that what had happened, or Britt's fury, changed anything as far as tomorrow. It had to be done. He'd said he'd do it, and so he would. But he knew the moment the alarm went off and he got up and moving that mere coffee wasn't going to do it. A triple espresso from Java Time might do it, but they wouldn't be open in time so he'd have to find someplace on the way. Then he had a thought and went for a can of Coke from the fridge. The bite of the beverage helped, and he guzzled it to get the caffeine flowing.

By the time he was in his SUV and rolling, he was only ten minutes behind where he'd wanted to be. It was early enough that he should be able to make it up. If he got there at ten, figure a couple of hours with Mark, then headed back straight, he should hit the hospital between five and six. Unless he had to dodge traffic or any accidents.

Or get in one yourself because you're running on five hours of lousy sleep...

As it turned out he made it up and more, thanks to a

warning from the GPS system that there was a tangle on the interstate south of Fort Worth and he bailed off early.

Seeing Mark again was almost enough distraction. The guy was rightfully proud of the company he worked for and what they did and getting the grand tour and seeing the way they worked not only diverted his thoughts, it also gave him a couple of ideas of things he wanted to look into later. They spent a nice lunch both reminiscing and looking forward, and Mark thankfully was consumed enough with that not to ask about the woman the package he'd picked up was for. Because Cody had no idea what he would have said.

I hated her, then loved her, now she hates me.

Sounded like the lyrics to an achingly corny old country song.

On the way back he decided that was exactly what he needed and tuned in a country classics stream. By the time he hit Waco he was getting into it, by Temple he was humming along, and by Round Rock, tapping a finger on the wheel. Then an achingly sweet classic came on, something about a guy trying to convince his love to stay forever, letting him put his loving arms around her, that he wouldn't let her fall. That hit a little too close to home. The memories of carrying Brit came rushing back, and he shut down the music.

After that his only company was his whirring thoughts. But the bottom line never changed: his reluctance to tell her everything out of fear it would destroy the totally unexpected connection they'd discovered had in fact been the thing that did destroy it. He wanted to hope that she might forgive him, might at least understand why he'd delayed, but to do that she'd have to believe he would have told her the truth today. And while their relationship might have changed, he knew Britt was still Britt…or Roth.

When his phone rang and he saw it was his mother, he almost didn't answer. Only the fact that she knew he was on the road and would worry if he didn't, drove him to hit the button on the media screen. Although the first thing she said after his hello made him wish he hadn't.

"What happened?"

He sighed. "I'm guessing you don't mean in Fort Worth."

"Don't play games, Cody. I just talked to Angie."

Great.

"Then you know what happened. Britt threw me out."

"Yes. What I don't know is why."

That threw him for a moment. "She didn't tell you?"

"No. She said that was up to you."

He supposed he should be thankful for Mrs. Roth's tact and discretion. And he would be, if it hadn't meant he now had to admit it all to his mother. "Look, Mom, it's—"

"If you're going to say complicated, don't. This is no time for clichés, Cody."

That Mom mind-reading thing again. Knowing he had little choice, he told her the whole story, making sure she knew Chance had been trying to help.

"Of course he was trying to help," she said dismissively. "So the question is, what are you going to do now?"

"Aren't you going to chew me out for not telling her sooner?" he asked in genuine surprise as he slowed the SUV to make the lane shift to avoid Austin.

"Triple B, twenty-eight years of squabbling and bickering got turned on its head in a day. There's bound to be some confusion and uncertainty."

The simple understanding in her words and the love that rang in her voice made his throat tighten. He should have known she would see his side of it.

"That girl needs to grow a longer fuse, though," Mom said. "You can help her with that."

"What?"

"Just you being you will show her how. The way you go slow, analyze everything, make sure you know all you can before you decide how you feel about something."

"Mom, she doesn't want anything to do with me."

"Does she know why you didn't tell her right off? Did you explain it as you just did to me?"

"I...no. She didn't want to hear it. She just wanted me gone."

"Then, perhaps, when her feelings were hurt, and she's in pain anyway, and worried about her future, both physically and on the circuit, and she reacted out of pure worry and emotion. We women do that, you know," she added, her tone wry.

"I hadn't noticed," he said dryly.

But he had to admit he hadn't thought enough about where Britt had been coming from. He'd been so blindsided by her reaction that he hadn't really thought about all the factors that had probably caused it.

"Now that she's calmed down, had time to think…she's a smart girl, Cody. Too smart not to see what a prize you are. She'll come around." He didn't know what to say to that compliment, and was glad when she asked, "Where are you?"

"Just clearing Austin."

"Always good news," she said tartly. "You'll make the hospital by five thirty?"

"Should." He hesitated, then, "Mom?"

"What?"

"Do you think…is it right? Britt I mean. Britt and me."

"I think it was meant to be. I always have."

"You never said."

"Because I believe my boys needed to find their own way. And—" her voice broke, something so rare it made him almost tear up himself "—now they have. Kyle would be so proud, and happy for all of you."

"Geeze, Mom, make me drive off the road why don't you?" He could barely get the words out.

"Don't," she ordered, back in control. "Just get here. Work it out. It'll be fine."

He took a deep breath. Searched for words. Finally settled on the ones that said it all. "I love you, Mom."

"And I you, Triple B."

For the rest of the drive, he carried her words, and her confidence in him. It would work out. It had to. Because a weekend with Britt, as they'd been, wasn't enough.

He wasn't sure a lifetime would be enough.

Chapter Thirty-Five

BRITT LOOKED AT the new devices that encased her wrist and ankle in amazement. They were so light, airy with the lattice-like structure, yet they held both her wrist and ankle firmly in place. She felt so much less confined it must have shown, because Dr. Reed warned her not to get carried away and do too much, although he admitted this should make her more mobile due to the sheer lack of bulk and weight as anything else.

He'd also given her the good news that the new X-rays of her ankle showed healing had definitely begun, and that her wrist sprain appeared to be healing faster than expected.

"You're in great condition, so that helps. If nothing else happens, you'll be looking at the short end of recovery on that wrist. It should be safe to remove that splint periodically. The ankle needs to stay put, but you can even shower with it. And you'll be using those crutches and doing rehab exercises before long."

That brightened her mood, which took some doing at the moment. Who'd have ever thought a simple shower would be that high on her wish list? Her mother would be delighted, too, she was sure, since she'd been helping her bathe all week.

I'd rather have Cody doing it.

The words ran through her mind, followed by a tumble of her emotions as she realized that would likely never happen. She wasn't sure that fence could be mended.

When it was done and her parents were allowed into the room, her father said she looked like some new superhero in costume. Her mother smiled and said the bright blue color matched her eyes. Which made her look over at Cody—he had silently been there the whole time—who was now across the room listening to the doctor talk animatedly about the new-to-him process.

Had Cody chosen the color? Was that why—because it matched her eyes? Seemed a bit too artistic for the deep-into-the-tech-of-it guy, but then she remembered the incredible bluebonnets video he'd done. There had definitely been an artistic sort of vision there. But that also made her wonder if he'd just gone with the blue because of the flowers, nothing to do with her eyes, although they were a better match to the shade of the plastic.

The guy won't even look at you, and you're sitting here wondering if he was trying to match your eyes? Right now he'd probably like to gouge them out.

Her mother spoke very quietly, but the words were all too familiar, the words that she'd heard her whole life when Mom wanted her to think about something. "Tell me something, dear. Did you ever think about the possibility that after what happened yesterday, Cody might not make that drive to Fort Worth and back for you?"

She blinked. In fact, she'd been so wrapped up in her emotional misery, it hadn't even occurred to her. "No," she admitted.

"You might want to think about why that is."

She didn't have to think about it, really. Because she knew it had never occurred to her because a Rafferty not only didn't lie, a Rafferty never defaulted on a promise, either.

"—to thank your friend for that video consult, which helped immensely," she heard the doctor say.

"He's a good guy," Cody said.

Even listening to his voice sent a shiver through her. He'd been so...cool, ever since he'd arrived. Understandably, of course, after the way she'd screamed at him.

After all he's done, you can't even be as patient with him as you are with that horse?

She didn't think she'd ever felt as awful, as self-loathing as she had when those words had hit home. But she'd had some long, sleepless hours to think about them, to think about what she'd said, what she'd done. She'd always thought of herself as honest, and she was—with everyone but herself, apparently. Because if she'd been more patient, if she hadn't gone off like a land mine, she would have realized some things then, before she'd driven him away. But she had, and there had been a long, painful aftermath that had nothing to do with broken bones and everything to do with coming to terms with herself and what she'd done.

"We've reservations at Valencia's," her mother announced, and Britt saw she was looking at Cody as they walked out of the office. "It's the least we can do, after all you've done, Cody."

"I don't think—"

"Now don't interfere with my chance to thank you," Mom chided him. Cody's jaw tightened, but he gave in.

And so she found herself sitting at a table that had clearly been arranged specifically to accommodate the wheelchair. She was feeling grateful they hadn't ended up in a booth, both because of the thought of trying to get into it, and that she no doubt would have wound up sitting next to Cody if her mother had anything to say about it.

She was thankful as well as happy to see Valencia manager Elena Highwater when she came out to greet them. Sean wasn't far behind her, and Britt felt a little tug inside as Elena's slightly tousled hair and the glow that practically radiated from her registered. That and Sean's quiet smile told her what had probably been going on in her office in the back.

Did I look like that, when Cody kissed me? I felt like that.

They got the Highwater updates, that Shane's wife Lily was glowing, now five months into her pregnancy—Sean grinned as he said his usually imperturbable brother was a wreck—and that Slater and Joey would soon add to the brood.

"I'm waiting for Sage," Mom said as the pair left them to enjoy the delicious queso and salsa appetizers.

Britt tried to picture it. Couldn't. *At least she didn't say me.* And that thought handed her an opening she hadn't planned on but grabbed.

"Sage," she said quietly, looking at Cody, "would handle that a lot better than I'm handling this."

He didn't look at her, but she saw his lips tighten slightly. And her mother obviously saw it for the peace offering it was, because as they were leaving after a delicious meal of carne asada and the best beans this side of anywhere, she announced she needed to stop over at *Good Boy!* for some dog biscuits for Dodger, and instructed Dad that she needed him to accompany her.

"To carry a bag of dog biscuits?" Dad said, bewildered.

"Yes. You won't mind running Britt home, will you, Cody?"

Of course he minds.

But her mother gave him no chance to really get out of it. And Dad seemed to have finally gotten what she was up to and went along.

"I'm sorry," she said when she and the chair were loaded up into his car and he'd gotten into the driver's seat. "About my mother, I mean."

"Seems like she had a plan," he said, not looking at her, nor making a move to start the engine.

"I know you must be tired, after the long drive."

For a moment he just sat there, silent. Then he turned his head and met her gaze. "I'm tired," he said flatly, "because I didn't get much sleep. And what I got sucked."

"I know the feeling. And I know why," she added before he could say anything else that would add to her guilt. And she realized abruptly that she was getting a bit of the same feeling he must have had, when he hadn't told her the truth. Guilt, she realized, was a very powerful force. "I need to tell you—"

He looked away without speaking, and she couldn't finish. Her heart sank as he reached out and started the car, which seemed a clear indication he didn't want to hear what she needed to tell him.

Without looking at her again he maneuvered out of the parking lot and onto Laurel, heading toward the Hickory Creek Spur. But when they got there, he turned away from home, surprising her. He surprised her again when he turned off the road onto a dirt track. She knew where it led, to an overlook with an amazing view of her beloved Hill Country. It was a special place to the residents of Last Stand, a place they left off the tourist maps and information brochures. A place they kept to themselves, a place to find peace, to look out over the hills, to storm-watch, or this time of year to marvel at the seemingly endless carpet of bluebonnets.

When he'd parked and shut the car off, he flicked off the safety belt and turned in the seat to look at her. And spoke as if they'd never moved.

"Tell me what? That you hate me again?"

"No! Tell you I'm sorry. I didn't mean it." At his look she amended her words. "All right, I did at that moment, because…because I was hurt. Not this," she said, lifting her left hand and moving her right knee, "but…my heart. At the thought that you were only staying with me because you felt guilty. That, on top of…everything else…I just lost it."

"You're worried about all your plans falling apart because of this."

"Yes. That I might not be able to compete this year, which would put me way behind, or maybe not compete at all, which could ruin everything, and whether Ghost is too crazy and will pass that on to her get, and—"

She stopped when he held up a hand. Stayed quiet. She hadn't listened before, but she would now. She owed him that, and so much more.

"And I felt guilty because I thought I'd caused your accident. I was ready to dump the drones altogether, I felt so sick about it—"

"No!" she exclaimed again. "You can't do that. You do too much good with them." She was a little surprised at her own vehemence; she hadn't realized she'd arrived at this conclusion. And he looked startled as well, enough so that she added, "And…I know now why you're so dedicated to it. You can't give that up."

He stared at her for a long, silent moment. Then, slowly,

he said, "You know what I was really thinking when Chance sent me that picture?"

Her brow furrowed. "You said…it was that it wasn't your fault. Which it wasn't," she added firmly. "If it's anybody's, it's mine. I never should have ridden Ghost—of all horses—up there with a storm coming in. It was as much my fault, but Ghost's most of all. Outside an arena she's too touchy for anybody's good."

"That's been a long time coming," he said, his mouth twisting wryly.

"I know. Too long." She sucked in a deep breath. "I'm told I have too much patience with that horse and not enough with people. And now I believe it. I blew up at the one person I shouldn't have. The person who did more to help me than anyone. The person who…turned a lifetime around in the space of a weekend."

She got a slight smile then. "My mom said when you turn twenty-eight years of squabbling and bickering on its head in a day, there's bound to be some confusion and uncertainty."

She felt a burst of relief, then surprise. He'd talked to his mother about this? About what had happened, what had grown between them? Did Maggie Rafferty see the same thing her own mother had seen?

What he'd said a moment ago came back to her. "What were you thinking when you got that picture?"

He met her gaze head-on and held it. And when he

spoke, the pure, simple honesty in his voice and words made her throat tighten. "I was deliriously happy. I was glad it wasn't my fault, but not because of the guilt. Because I thought it meant we could go on without that shadow hanging over us."

...all I need to know is that he looks at you now the same way your father looks at me.

"And now?" she asked, her voice sounding as tight as her throat felt. She was afraid of the answer, afraid she'd ruined it, ruined them.

"That depends," he said. And he didn't tell her on what.

The silence went on as she tried to think of how to express what she was feeling. Finally, carefully, she asked, "Did you ever want to…toss a computer out the window when something went wrong?"

"Yes," he admitted, sounding a little wary.

"But you didn't."

"Too expensive," he said dryly.

"You wouldn't toss something that's worth a lot to you because it…malfunctions. You'd work on it until it was right, until you fixed it. Because you're a Rafferty, and Raffertys don't quit."

He studied her for a moment, and she wondered that anything, even a machine, dared malfunction with that steady, brilliant gaze fixed on them. "Are you saying you just…malfunctioned?"

"I'm saying I've got a glitch, and it's not having enough

patience."

"Maybe that horse of yours just uses it all up."

His tone was beyond dry, making her unsure whether or not to be glad he could joke.

"I won't argue that," she said. "But the important thing is, it's never before cost me something I…didn't want to lose, so I didn't really work to fix it."

"Has it now?"

She looked at him, deep into those green eyes so like his father's, and repeated his words. "That depends."

He shifted in the driver's seat, looking out toward where the sun seemed to be plummeting to the horizon. He tapped a finger on the steering wheel. He had that finger-tapping habit, she'd noticed. Probably a sign that that brain of his never stopped working.

She waited, although she didn't want to. She hated the silence that stretched out between them. It felt like a physical thing, like a guitar string she could almost reach out and pluck.

It would probably snap. Her tone, even in her head, was bitter. And only knowing this was part of the patience she needed to learn enabled her to wait it out.

Finally, he spoke. "It probably doesn't help that we know each other's hot buttons so well."

She didn't know how to take that. Was he saying that's why it wouldn't work? Why they wouldn't work? The thought tightened her chest almost unbearably. And she said the first words she thought she could get out, trying for a joking tone.

"I should hope so, after all these years."

His head snapped around, as if she'd startled him. Then, slowly, he said, "It would take a long time to learn the good things to balance out those hot buttons."

Her breath caught, and it was a moment before she could say, "Probably twice as long."

He gave her a considering look then. "You think you could be as patient with me as you are with Ghost?"

Her pulse leapt, but she held back. "If you can be as patient with me as you are with your gadgets."

Slowly, a wonderful smile spread across his face. He truly was beautiful, she thought. She always had thought it, but before it had irritated her. Now it just made her wish she wasn't so sidelined.

Then he leaned across to her and carefully, gently, kissed her. It was long, slow, and impossibly hot and sweet at the same time.

For this, she would learn patience.

For this, she would do anything.

Chapter Thirty-Six

IT HAD BEEN Britt who had promised to learn patience, but this stupid abstinence thing was pounding the lesson home to him as well. Today had been the worst, but it was his own stupid fault.

It hadn't been going into Last Stand for the first day of the Bluebonnet Festival, he'd been okay with that. She'd been practicing diligently with the crutches, building back her wrist's strength, leaving it in the brace the recommended amount of time per day, and it was progressing nicely. The ankle was slower, but she was doing everything right there, too. In short, she was approaching the healing process the way she approached her training and barrel racing, with full concentration and dedication.

The day had started oddly anyway. He'd needed to stop at his place to double-check that the promo video was running properly, now that the festival was actually here. And despite the effort it took, Britt had insisted on coming inside to say hello to Ry, who was taking advantage of Mom's absence to swipe some leftover pizza for lunch, since Kaitlyn was in town taking photos for *The Defender*.

When he'd verified everything was fine and came back out, Britt and Ry were looking at something on a sheet of heavy paper. A sketch of something, maybe his newest project. And Britt was talking quietly but rather intensely to his brother, and Ry had that resistant look on his face that he hadn't seen in a while. Not since he'd been denying he was an artist, insisting he was only a craftsman as if it were something less.

When they heard him, Cody would have sworn both she and Ry gave a little start. Ry quickly rolled up the sketch, as if it were one of the projects he wasn't ready to have seen yet.

But he'd shown it to Britt. And she wasn't talking.

"Sworn to secrecy," she said brightly.

The couple of hours spent in town was both amusing and embarrassing. They'd never quite realized that the Rafferty-Roth feud had been so widely famous, but between the startled glances and the downright shocked stares when people spotted them together, they were learning fast. And once they'd encountered Mr. Diaz from the feed store, they knew anybody who hadn't seen them here together would know before the sun set anyway.

When she'd stopped for a while to sit on one of the benches scattered among the booths and tourists, he sat down beside her.

"How do you feel?"

She gave him an eye roll. "Like we should change our names."

He blinked. "To what?"

"Hatfield and McCoy."

He laughed. As he had often in the past few days. Something else he'd never known about her, that that sarcasm that had stung so often had been born in a quick wit that he could more than appreciate.

"You told me once you remember everything."

He wondered what had brought that on. "Yeah. Most of the time it's handy, sometimes it's a pain."

"So, you can't ever forget all the angry things I've said to you."

"No." He heard the undertone in her voice and shifted on the bench to face her. "I can't forget. But I can forgive, if you can. And I can decide it doesn't matter."

"Seems this was the path we had to follow," she said.

"Why, Ms. Roth, that was almost philosophical," he drawled, echoing her earlier words and tone. She laughed, and the moment of worry had passed.

And then she turned him inside out by holding his gaze and saying simply, "I love you, Cody."

His heart slammed in his chest. She'd never actually said the words before. How like Britt to choose here, in front of half of Last Stand gathered in the park, to do it.

"Back at you," he said, his throat so tight he could barely get it out.

After that, everything seemed anticlimactic. At least until that evening when, after all the exertion, she had longingly expressed the wish for a nice soak in the tub. Which, she'd said with a look at him, she could do, thanks to the new cast, although she still kept it elevated on the edge most of the time.

It wasn't until they were home that he realized that her mother, who usually helped her with that process, was with his mother, at the festival. And would be for the rest of the day and evening. And all day tomorrow, until the celebration's conclusion.

And Britt couldn't get out of that tub on her own.

The visions that tumbled through his head then were vivid, erotic, and more arousing than they should be, given she was injured. It was difficult enough to shut down the urging of his body when he stood at the bathroom door while she showered. Fortunately, by the time she called him in to help her get out and back on her crutches she was wrapped in a big towel.

A bath would be different. She'd be naked, wet, alluring, and just thinking about it had him calculating whether two could fit in that tub.

He watched her work her way inside, hoping it would remind him—and his body—that right now he was an assistant, not a lover.

It almost worked.

As if she'd read his mind, and with a teasing edge in her voice, she said, "Scared, Coder?"

"That," he said, "is not the word for it."

"Can't handle it?"

"I want," he said flatly, "to handle every bit of it. Every bit of you. But it's only been a couple of weeks, and you need to be careful. I'm not sure I could be."

She sighed. "Showers it is, then."

He wasn't sure how he got through the next couple of weeks. Evenings they spent on her couch, the television on but frequently ignored, because kissing was so much nicer. But that same pleasant pastime also made things more difficult, because both of them were going a little crazy with the restrictions her injury put on them.

"Don't stop," she'd murmured one night when he'd finally pulled away after they'd ended up lying down on the couch, him halfway atop her, his body aching to take this to its inevitable conclusion.

"I have to. I'm about to lose it here."

She stroked a hand down his back, ending up cupping his backside. "Feel free."

His jaw tightened. "Not helping, Roth."

She sighed and pulled her hand back. "Not fair, either, is it? Expecting you to be the one in control."

He drew back slightly, distracted. "Careful, you're sounding awfully patient."

"I'm learning." She looked up at him, and then a slow smile curved her mouth, that mouth already plumped and pink from his kisses. "Maybe that's what this should be. This time before we can…do what we want."

"What should it be? Besides frustrating as hell?"

The smile widened. "A time to learn. Each other, I mean. So, when I get the all clear, we don't have to."

"So we don't have to fumble around like the kids we used to be?"

"Exactly."

"You have a lot of trust in my restraint," he said dryly.

"I have a lot of trust in you," she corrected. "Which," she added, "you've earned the hard way. Dealing with the old Britt."

And so they spent the next couple of weeks doing just that, and Cody wouldn't have traded it for anything, despite the fact that he was as edgy as a bobcat in a thunderstorm. Britt was getting more mobile on the crutches, and was hopeful the doc would let her test a little weight on her ankle soon. And when she came out from the latest appointment and he saw her face, he thought she must have gotten good news.

"You're smiling. He said yes?" he asked as he held the door for her to exit the office.

"Yes," she said, and the smile lit up her whole face. "He said yes. With care, of course, and in limited ways, but yes."

"Limited ways? Like what, walk with only one crutch?"

"We weren't talking about walking."

His brow furrowed. "Then what—" It hit him, hard and fast. His eyes widened as he stared at her. "You mean…?"

"Just get us home, will you? Fast."

He did, so fast he knew even Shane Highwater wouldn't be able to get him out of the ticket if he got caught. He didn't care, and Shane wouldn't anyway.

By the time they got into her bedroom—she allowed him to carry her because it was faster, and this further sign of her own eagerness fired him even higher—he was already so hot and ready it was hard not to shake with it.

He had to take care helping her undress but he shed his own clothes in haste. He helped her get situated, still a little startled that she'd flat-out asked Dr. Reed when she could have sex and how, but beyond delighted at the answer. He could deal with the traditional positions, although he'd be looking forward to one day being ridden by the famous Britt Roth.

For a moment he simply looked at her, at the just-enough curve of her hips, the full, rounded breasts, and oh, yes, those long, lean legs. He vowed one day they'd be wrapped around him as he made her scream for more.

And she was looking at him as if he were some work of art to admire. He couldn't even begin to describe how that made him feel.

"Slow," he muttered as he lay down beside her. "It's the first time, we should go slow."

She reached up and cupped his face in her hands. "We've spent three weeks going slow. To hell with slow. Let's run these barrels."

It was so Britt he couldn't stop his own slightly crooked

grin. And he suddenly saw the wisdom in those long evenings spent exploring, so that he knew every part of her already, and she knew every touch, every stroke that drove him mad.

Still, he tried to hold back, to savor, but when she curled her fingers around his fierce erection and urged him on, when he found her slick and eager and ready for him, he was lost. He ordered himself not to forget that he had to be careful of her leg, but that was his last sane thought as he drove into her, hard and deep. She cried out, a shouted "Yes!" that echoed what he would have said if he had the breath. But he didn't, so he kissed her again as fire rippled through him, and reveled in the sweet, tight clasp of her body around him.

As his hips moved he knew he wasn't going to last, this had been building too long. He'd have to make it up to her next time, because—

She cried out his name as those inner muscles clenched, proving she'd been as close to the edge as he had been, and squeezing him into capitulation. He gave up on the next stroke and stayed deep, feeling the pulse of it down to his toes, groaning with a wonder he'd never felt before in his life. It was fierce, fiery, and as everything with Britt seemed to be, over the top.

He collapsed against her, barely remembering not to jostle the leg propped on pillows.

"To hell with slow indeed," he muttered when he could

gather enough breath to talk at all.

"Best run of my life," Britt said.

He raised up on one elbow and looked down at her. And this time he said it first. "I love you, Britt."

The smile she gave him made it all worth it, even the years of taunting and teasing and acrimony.

"Back at you," she said, echoing his words.

And the lifelong feud was officially burned to ash in the heat of that love.

Chapter Thirty-Seven

Last Stand Fourth of July Rodeo

THEY STOOD BESIDE the fence, watching the Creekbend High School rodeo team circle the arena, flags high, excitement crackling all around them. Britt was grinning, remembering the day she'd ridden in this same opening event. There was nothing like Independence Day in Last Stand. She'd never been prouder than the day she'd been chosen to lead the pack, the big American flag hers to hold.

Someone passed close behind them, bumping Ghost. The gray grullo's head came up, but at a word from Cody on one side and a nicker from Trey on the other, she settled. The solid, steady Trey had been an incredibly calming influence on the edgy mare. Just as Cody had been for her.

"I can't believe it," Jen said. Her friend had come down from Dallas to see Britt's return to the circuit; she was the only one outside of Last Stand who knew how seriously Britt had been hurt.

"Believe what?" Britt asked, turning to look at her.

Jen nodded toward Ghost. "How the holy terror behaves for him."

Britt couldn't help the smile that overtook her. "So does this one," she said softly, putting a hand over her heart.

She knew how some would interpret that, taking umbrage at the idea that it took a man to tame the horse—and her—but that didn't bother her. Because she knew it wasn't the man, not in the way they meant. It was her love for him that allowed her to take that extra breath and head off that explosion of temper. Or else he'd been right and now that she didn't have to expend all her patience on Ghost, she had more for everything else.

Or maybe it was simply that she'd found a whole new kind of happy, and it overwhelmed everything else.

She thought of the conversation they'd had this morning, when they'd awakened in his bed.

"You sure you don't mind spending all day at the rodeo?" she'd asked.

He'd given her a sleepy-eyed smile that sent her pulse racing. "As long as Ghost isn't your first ride of the day."

She'd melted in an instant, and proceeded to do exactly that, ride him until she heard that most precious sound, her name ripping out of him as he erupted inside her. And in the panting moments afterward, she marveled anew at how he'd let her take charge, saying with a grin she needed the exercise. Therapy and all. Never mind that she was completely healed.

Besides, he pointed out, he'd done all the work before she'd gotten the cast off.

Who'd have thought sex with Cody the Coder would be the most amazing thing in the world? And it had only gotten better as time passed. So good that it was almost hard to remember that a mere three and half months ago she'd hated him with a passion. Or thought she had; she was fairly sure now that passion had just been this, turned around because they'd both been too stubborn to see.

She was so delighted at being fully mobile again she didn't mind going back and forth, so they usually ended up dividing their nights between her place and his. To her surprise she found she didn't mind his lair and hadn't since she'd walked in and seen the beautiful Milky Way screen saver on the biggest flat screen.

"I feel the urge to burst into song about the stars at night in Texas," she'd said.

"They are big and bright," he'd agreed, and they'd both laughed.

"Girl," Jen whispered into her ear, pulling her out of the reverie, "you are goner than I ever thought you could be."

"I am," Britt agreed.

"Not that I don't get it," her friend added. "He's even prettier than you said."

"You don't know the half of it," Britt answered archly, remembering again this morning.

She glanced at Cody, who had half turned to talk to Kaitlyn, who was here to take photographs of all the action. Rylan, Britt knew, was busy finishing a project back in his studio, something that, to Britt's own amazement, was more important to her than even this return to the rodeo she loved. A project she had proposed, and that the entire Rafferty clan—minus Cody of course—had heartily agreed upon, even if Ry had been a bit nervous. But Britt had persisted, and he'd begun.

"Is he really going with you? On the circuit, I mean?"

"For the first leg, at least." Britt grinned. "I could hardly say no, since he's one of my sponsors."

She didn't care how that sounded to people either, although she guessed some who didn't know them made some assumptions about their relationship and what order it had all happened in. But once Cody had gotten his ranch management software to the point where he felt comfortable selling it more widely, it had seemed obvious that advertising it on the circuit only seemed logical. And of course, there would be the added benefit of having him with her.

But that wouldn't start until next week. Before that, there was tomorrow. Their joint birthday, and the party her mother and his—delighted not just at the cessation of hostilities but at the new connection between their families—were madly planning. And which, oddly, Cody had requested they all attend on horseback.

"—all for it. I've never seen you so happy. Or relaxed." Jen waggled her eyebrows at her. "And judging by his contented look, I can guess why."

Britt couldn't help herself—all she could do was grin

back at her friend. She remembered this morning, and how not so long ago she'd told her father she didn't find anything tempting at that hour. Now she couldn't think of anything more tempting than Cody, naked in her arms and driving into her body.

And an hour later, when she headed down the chute for her first run in far too long, even that felt different. She'd been afraid it would feel less somehow, now that her life was so full of other things. But instead it had become more, as if the foundation this thing she loved was now built on had lifted it even higher.

Ghost ripped around the barrels as if nothing could slow her down, as if the cloverleaf turns were as simple as a straight run. Her own seat was solid, without even a twinge from her ankle. And the roar that went up from the gathered crowd when her blistering time was announced made Ghost prance and her own heart leap.

She was back. And, for so many reasons, better than ever.

CODY KNEW EVERYONE except their parents were puzzled. But the meetings he'd had with the Roths and Mom were about to pay off. It had been a long, detailed process, involving easements and boundaries and paperwork, but it was done.

He and Britt rode side by side, her riding her trusty

Nugget today. They were all there, a party of twelve riders plus three dogs, Mom's Quinta, the Roths' Dodger, and Chance and Ariel's Tri. He knew Britt was immensely curious, but the new Britt, as she called herself, waited patiently. In fact, the only time she wasn't patient anymore was when they were in bed, and he was fine with that. Beyond fine. Way beyond fine.

He saw her notice the stake with cloth flag attached as they rode by. She gave him a questioning look, but he only smiled at her.

Life on the Rafferty ranch had changed so much. Keller and Sydney married in a beautiful ceremony at the Hickory Creek Inn that drew half of Last Stand, and their formal adoption of Lucas was completed. Then Chance and Ariel joined in a smaller, private ceremony—including Tri as well-trained ring bearer—that had included several of both her new and late husband's brothers in arms, there to wish her and Chance well. Ry and Kaitlyn would be next, he figured, although they were going to have to hurry, because he was in a hurry. A hurry to have this locked in, to be attached in ways he'd never imagined he'd want so much.

When they arrived at his goal, he called a halt. Britt looked at him, still obviously curious, but also smiling, because this was her favorite spot, high ground with a view of the hills one way, and an expanse that included both their ranch houses the other.

"Hope y'all remember the way here," he said to all of

them. "So you can find your way to visit us."

Then he looked at Britt as he reached back and pulled the roll of papers out of his saddlebag. He slid off the band holding them and unrolled the big page, showing the computer rendition he'd done of the house she'd once described to him, when he'd managed to get her talking about her dream home.

He handed it to her and finished quietly. "Assuming you won't mind living up here."

She stared at the rendering. Looked at him. Looked back at the property stakes they'd passed. Looked at her parents, then his mom, who were all smiling widely. And he saw the moment when she figured it all out, when she realized the stakes marked out a large area that sat smack across the property line, half on one side, half on the other.

"We can be the permanent bond between the Roths and the Raffertys," he said. "If…" He couldn't seem to go on. It had seemed like a good idea to do it here and now, probably because he hoped the circumstances would get him the answer he wanted. But he couldn't get any words out.

But she could. "If what?"

And suddenly he could do it. Because he saw the answer already glowing in those incredible blue eyes. "If you'll marry me."

The glow flared into fire. "You sure you're ready for that, Coder?"

"Damn sure, Roth." He swallowed tightly. "You told me

once you don't make promises you might not be able to keep."

"Still true. And I know I'll keep this one."

"So will I."

"And a Rafferty always keeps his word."

"Yes."

"Then we're on," she whispered.

And when he leaned over to kiss her, it was to a round of applause from everyone they loved.

"Did you know you can 3D-print jewelry, like they did your cast?" he whispered as he broke the kiss, mindful of their audience. "I'm working on a ring that will symbolize us, but won't get in your way with the horses."

Britt burst out laughing, and this time it was she who leaned in to kiss him. "That is so…so Cody. I love it, and that you thought of it that way."

Cody knew this was the best day of his life. As they rode back—this time to the Rafferty house—he was almost delirious with it. So much that he almost missed Britt exchanging a glance with Ry, who nodded at her. He shrugged it off, figuring he'd find out what that was about later. Right now he was busy holding her hand as they rode, thinking about the house they would build, straddling that line, joining the two ranches.

It wasn't until they were back and inside the house that he realized—that obliviousness again—that something else was up. Because Mom stopped everybody on the front porch, even though it was a bit crowded. Then she went inside, but quickly came back with something in her hands. A piece of heavy paper, with something drawn on it. He flashed back to that moment when he'd seen Ry and Britt in the kitchen, when he thought he'd startled them somehow. They'd been holding something that looked very much like this piece of heavy sketch paper.

"I found this, going through some things I'd put away because it hurt too much to look at…then."

She held it out to him. He was beyond puzzled now, but he took the page and looked. "For Cody" was scrawled at the top, and his breath jammed up in his chest. Because he knew that writing. He hadn't seen it often, and not at all recently, but it was etched into that memory of his permanently.

His father.

"He was planning your painting, Cody," Mom said, so softly.

He stared at the page, wondering in some small part of his mind why his hands weren't shaking, because he sure as hell felt shaky inside.

It was a sketch of, of all things, the ridgeline, the end of it, the exact spot where he'd made the big turn in the bluebonnets video. On the left there was the line of stone, on the right the hills spilling out into the distance, seeming endless to the horizon. And above that part were two words in the same, painfully familiar hand. "The Future."

"He knew," Keller said softly. "He knew, when he got

you that first computer, that you would be the one to lead us into that future."

"And he was right," Chance said, holding up the new phone Cody had finally talked him into.

Ry stayed silent, but he looked almost nervous. Then Mom spoke again, turning his stunned gaze back to her.

"We were going to frame this and give it to you, but—" she looked at Britt with a huge smile "—when she saw this, Britt had a better idea. A much better idea."

Britt? She'd been in on this?

"Come inside," Mom said, and opened the door again.

He took one step inside and stopped dead. On an easel, facing the door, was a painting. The painting. *His* painting. The one his father had never had the chance to paint. It was the sketch he held, rendered in vivid color, the same colors he'd captured in the video, laid over the exact lines depicted in his father's sketch, capturing the same energy and love of this place that was in their souls.

He was no longer the only Rafferty not to have one.

When he could move again, he turned to search out Ry, for he knew whose hand had accomplished this. For a moment the brothers' gazes locked, and Cody guessed his own eyes were as suspiciously bright as Ry's were. He remembered all the years when Ry had denied he was an artist, because he was certain he could never measure up to their father's skill. Only when Kaitlyn had made him see the truth had he dared to even try.

And now he had produced this.

"It's not Dad—" Ry began.

"Shut up," he said, afraid he was going to bawl here in front of them all.

"I never would have even tried it," his brother said after a moment, sounding exactly as Cody had expected, "but Britt hammered me until I had no choice."

He turned to look at her. She wasn't even trying to hide the tears that had obviously come as she watched him react to the surprise she'd arranged. She'd understood how much it would mean to him, how much it had always nagged at him that he was the only son who didn't have this piece of their father. Mom had even offered to give him the one in the living room, but he'd said no. Because it wouldn't have been the same. It wouldn't have been something done especially for him.

But this was.

"We'll put it in the living room, so he'll be with you every day," Britt whispered.

"I love you, Britt." It was all he could think of to say. All that mattered.

"And I love you," she said, stretching up to kiss him.

He was feeling a bit steadier when Lucas suddenly laughed. Everyone looked at him. "I just thought," the boy said, grinning at Britt, "you'll be Brittany Rafferty. That sounds funny."

Cody saw the corners of Britt's mouth twitch as she

looked back at him. "That's it. It's all off."

"Hey, who ever calls you Brittany anyway, except your mom? Besides, the good part cancels that out."

"Well," she said, in that husky tone that turned him inside out, "there is that."

"I didn't mean that part," he said, not even caring that his entire family was here listening. "I meant that you won't even have to change your initials."

That family, his and hers, soon to be one, burst into laughter. He pulled her into his arms and kissed her thoroughly.

And this time they got a Texas-sized cheer.

The Raffertys were complete.

THE END

Want more? Check out Rylan and Kaitlyn's story in *Once a Cowboy*!

Join Tule Publishing's newsletter for more great reads and weekly deals!

If you enjoyed *Cowgirl Tough,*
you'll love the other books in…

The Raffertys of Last Stand series

Book 1: *Nothing But Cowboy*

Book 2: *A Texas Christmas Miracle*

Book 3: *Once a Cowboy*

Book 4: *Cowgirl Tough*

Available now at your favorite online retailer!

More books by Justine Davis

The Texas Justice series

Book 1: *The Lone Star Lawman*

Book 2: *Lone Star Nights*

Book 3: *A Lone Star Christmas*

Book 4: *Lone Star Reunion*

Book 5: *Lone Star Homecoming*

The Whiskey River series

Book 1: *Whiskey River Rescue*

Book 2: *Whiskey River Runaway*

Book 3: *Whiskey River Rockstar*

Available now at your favorite online retailer!

About the Author

USA Today bestselling author of more than 70 books, (she sold her first ten in less than two years) Justine Davis is a five time winner of the coveted RWA RITA Award, including for being inducted into the RWA Hall of Fame. A fifteen time nominee for RT Book Review awards, she has won four times, received three of their lifetime achievement awards, and had four titles on the magazine's 200 Best of all Time list. Her books have appeared on national best seller lists, including USA Today. She has been featured on CNN, taught at several national and international conferences, and at the UCLA writer's program.

After years of working in law enforcement, and more years doing both, Justine now writes full time. She lives near beautiful Puget Sound in Washington State, peacefully coexisting with deer, bears, a pair of bald eagles, a tailless raccoon, and her beloved '67 Corvette roadster. When she's not writing, taking photographs, or driving said roadster (and yes, it goes very fast) she tends to her knitting. Literally.

Thank you for reading

Cowgirl Tough

If you enjoyed this book, you can find more from all our great authors at TulePublishing.com, or from your favorite online retailer.

Made in the USA
Coppell, TX
27 May 2022